THE WOMAN NEXT DOOR

The Woman Next Door

YEWANDE OMOTOSO

Chatto & Windus

LONDON

1 3 5 7 9 10 8 6 4 2

Chatto & Windus, an imprint of Vintage,
20 Vauxhall Bridge Road,
London sw1v 2sa

Chatto & Windus is part of the Penguin Random House
group of companies whose addresses can be found at
global.penguinrandomhouse.com.

Penguin
Random House
UK

First published by Chatto and Windus in 2016

www.vintage-books.co.uk

A CIP catalogue record for this book
is available from the British Library

HB ISBN 9781784740337
TPB ISBN 9781784740344

Typeset in Stempel Garamond by Palimpsest Book Production
Limited, Falkirk, Stirlingshire

Printed and bound by Clays Ltd, St Ives PLC

Penguin Random House is committed to a sustainable future
for our business, our readers and our planet. This book is made
from Forest Stewardship Council® certified paper.

For Emily Doreen Verona Atherley and
Percy Leroy Rice
For Ajibabi Daramola Oladumoye and
Gabriel Omotoso Falibuyan

The wall is the thing which separates them, but it is also their means of communication.

Simone Weil, *Gravity and Grace*

ONE

The habit of walking was something Hortensia took up after Peter fell ill. Not at the beginning of his sickness, but later, when he turned seriously ill, bedridden. It had been a Wednesday. She remembered because Bassey the cook was off on Wednesdays and there were medallions of lamb in Tupperware in the fridge, meant to be warmed in the convection oven, meant to be eaten with roasted root vegetables slathered in olive oil. But she hadn't been hungry. The house felt small, which seemed an impossible thing for a six-bedroomed home. Still, there it was.

'I'm going out,' Hortensia had shouted at the banister. According to the nurses, she wasn't supposed to leave him unattended but Hortensia held the nurses and their opinions in contempt. She didn't see the need to knock on the door and tell him she was leaving, either. She had convinced herself that Peter's hearing, unlike his deteriorating body, was intact. That he was capable of hearing even while buried beneath blankets, hearing through the closed door of what she called the sickbay, hearing down the stairs, hearing as she closed the front door behind her. She'd gone out through the pedestrian gate, looked up and down Katterijn Avenue and turned right towards the Koppie.

The Koppie, a small rise in an otherwise flat landscape, was the obvious place to walk to that first time, and every time since. Being neither fit nor young, it was important to her (especially with her bad leg) that the slope was gradual enough not to be a bother; but still high enough to afford Hortensia a sense of accomplishment each time she climbed it. She was petite and her strides were small. Her walk had grown laboured over the years but in her youth, with her small stature and vigorous movements, she had been regularly confused, from afar, for a child. Her curly black hair cut close to the skull didn't help her appear any more adult. Up close, though, there was nothing childlike about the sharpness of her cheekbones, her dark serious face, her brown eyes.

Once on top of the Koppie, Hortensia liked to trail through the grasses and low bush. She wore her hiking boots and enjoyed the crunch of their soles on the rough ground. All this had been a surprise that first time; enjoyment of nature wasn't generally something Hortensia engaged in. But at the advanced age she was, with over sixty years of a wrecked marriage behind her, this enjoyment was precarious. The slightest thing could upset it.

The top of the Koppie was planted with wild-growing vines and scattered pine trees. A path cut through the long grasses and although it looked maintained, Hortensia couldn't help but think of the Koppie as a forgotten land. Once it became of interest to her she quickly noticed that the kids of the neighbourhood didn't play there, and the adults of Katterijn seemed to flatten the hill with their gaze, discount its presence.

Soon after she started climbing it – to get away from a dying man, to give him room to die faster, to catch fresh air, she couldn't work out which – some old bat from the committee mentioned it; put it on the agenda in fact. Katterijn committee meetings never failed to make much ado of the quotidian, to wrestle the juices from the driest of details, to spend at least an hour apiece on the varied irrelevances experienced by the committee members since the last meeting.

The Koppie was also a surprise because Hortensia had reached the age of eighty-five without having understood the meditative power of walking. How had she missed that? she scolded herself. But now, with Peter almost gone, it seemed right that she discover walking, that she do a lot of it and that she not resist the contemplation it provoked in her, the harking back to the past, the searching. These were all things Hortensia had grown skilled in avoiding. All her life she'd occupied her time with work. In return her company, House of Braithwaite, had enriched her and, in exclusive circles particularly in Denmark, amongst interior designers and fashionably nerdy textile-design students, made her famous.

Before the Koppie, memories were balls of fire sitting in the centre of each earlobe. A headache, her doctor in Nigeria had called it when it first started, but this was no headache. It was resentment, and Hortensia found that if she looked away from the things that were rousing – the memories – she was not happy but nor was she in agony. And then, so many years later, to discover walking. To discover that if she remembered while walking, the memories were bearable. Was it the fact of simultaneously thinking back while moving forward in a wide-open space, unconstricted? Not that the walking made the memories come sweetly. They came with anger and it helped that the Koppie was deserted, so Hortensia could shout and not be disturbed by any other living thing except some squirrels and, judging by the small mounds of sand, a colony of ants.

Katterijn was an enclave of some forty houses within Cape Town's suburb of Constantia. Not all owners lived on the premises; many were European, leased their properties out and boasted of their African summer homes at dinner gatherings. The Estate had its origins as a wine farm. When Hortensia and Peter had moved to South Africa the agency had made a fuss about the great history of Katterijn, which went as far back as the late 1600s. A Dutch man, Van der Biljt (Hortensia found the name unpronounceable), had visited the Cape, a guest of the Dutch East India Company. Corruption was rife in the company, and Van der Biljt was a reluctant part of a team posted by the directors to bring order to the venality. The parcel of land was gifted to him to sweeten the deal, encourage him to settle after the mission was completed, should he so wish. He so did and eventually used the land to produce wine as well as fruits and vegetables. Some said Katterijn was the name of his lover, a slave concubine, but others – more invested in a de-scandalised history for the neighbourhood – insisted Katterijn was his daughter. What about the history of the slaves? Hortensia had asked, because it was in her nature, by then, to make people uncomfortable. The agent did not know anything about the slaves of Katterijn; she directed their attention, instead, to the marvellous view of Table Mountain.

It had been 1994. South Africa shed blood and had elections. The USA hosted the World Cup. Nigeria beat Bulgaria 3–0. Already sick, nothing excited Peter, but soccer still could. And as the players put the ball through the goalposts fair and square, a democratically elected president in Nigeria was arrested; the previous year a perfectly decent election had been annulled. Hortensia and Peter agreed to leave Nigeria. After the perpetual warmth, they were reluctant to return to England's cold climate. South Africa with its new democracy, its long summers and famed medical facilities would ensure the best conditions as Peter got sicker. They'd arrived to their new home and Hortensia had realised that she would be the only black person living in Katterijn as an owner. She'd felt disgust for her surroundings, for the protected white gentry around her and, in her private dark moments, she felt disgust for herself as well.

Despite its beauty, Katterijn turned out to be ugly and, to begin with, Hortensia was unable to fathom why. Not one for uncertainty, she preferred simply not to notice the prettiness at all, then the puzzle of how something apparently good-looking could generate disgust would be avoided altogether. The houses were white and green and the lawns were wide and planted with flowers, bushes and grass that presented a manicured wildness. Gardens made to look like they'd sprung up that way, except they hadn't, they'd been as good as painted into place; branches trained and bent into position. The Katterijners had simply mastered a popular pastime, making a thing appear to be what it is not. But by the time Hortensia had worked all this out she was too tired to move again. And besides, she wondered if such a place wasn't just right for her.

Once a month a Katterijn committee meeting was held. As far as Hortensia understood it, the committee had been started by a woman named Marion Agostino who also happened to be her neighbour, a nasty woman who Hortensia did not like. But then again Hortensia did not like most people. She had stumbled upon the meetings by accident, soon after she arrived in Katterijn. No one had thought to mention that by rights, as an owner, she was entitled to while away time with the other committee members. The information was let slip. At the time Hortensia had felt that the initial omission was not forget-fulness but deliberate, and it was easy enough to assume that the slight was based on skin colour. Armed with the knowledge, Hortensia had taken the short trip to Marion's and pressed the buzzer on her intercom.

'It's Hortensia James from next door.'

She had not been offended by the absence of any show of welcome from her neighbour or the other residents. They had not come to Katterijn to make friends, something both she and Peter had managed without for the bulk of their lives.

'Wait, I'll call my madam,' a disembodied voice said.

Hortensia leaned her shoulder against the wall.

'Hello?' That must be Marion.

'It's Hortensia. From next door.'

'Yes?'

This was the moment when Hortensia understood she would not be invited in. The slight annoyed her briefly, but she waved it away as unimportant.

'I'll be attending the meetings.' It mustn't sound like she was asking permission. 'The committee meetings.'

'Hmm, I hadn't realised you were owners.'

Hortensia still listening at the buzzer like a beggar. 'Yes, well, we are.'

'Oh, well, I was confused. And . . .' Hortensia could almost hear Marion searching for another gear, '. . . is that gentleman your husband?' She wasn't asking so much as scolding.

'Who, Peter? Yes.' Again this hadn't surprised Hortensia. She'd fallen in love with a white man in 1950s London. They had been asked on many occasions to verify their courtship, to affirm that they were attached, to validate their love. Within a year of being together they were practised at it. 'Yes, Peter is my husband.'

'I see.'

In the silence Hortensia supposed Marion was thinking, inching towards her next move, preparing another strike, but instead she heard a sigh and almost missed the details of the upcoming meeting. Marion even threw in a dress code as a parting gift.

'We dress for our meetings, Mrs James. We follow rigorous decorum.' As if she thought dignity was something Hortensia required schooling in.

The meetings seemed to have been created for the purpose of policing the neighbourhood; keeping an eye out 'for elements', the community librarian had explained to Hortensia. Foolishness, she'd thought, and soon been vindicated after attending a few sessions. The meetings were a show of a significance that did not exist. Old women, with their wigs, their painted nails, their lipsticks seeping down whistle lines; scared and old rich white women pretending, in the larger scheme of life, that they were important. Hortensia attended because the women were amusing, nattering on in earnest about matters that didn't matter. She enjoyed to think she was laughing at them. But really it passed the time, took her mind off whatever else there was.

There were times, however, when the meetings moved from amusing to offensive. Once, a black couple moved into Katterijn, renting a duplex not on the Avenue but off one of the minor roads. They had two children. A neighbour, an old man, green at the gills and one-toothed, complained that the children ought not to bother his postbox. The matter was raised in committee. He claimed that the children were assaulting his postbox, messing with it. How did he know this, had he seen it? No, he had smelt it when he climbed down his stoep to collect the mail. He knew the smell of brown children. Could this botheration come to an end? he pleaded. Hortensia had cursed him, walked out of that meeting. And as if the Heavens had heard the man's plea, the botheration came to an end – he died.

Regardless, Hortensia always went back. To mock them, to point out to them that they were hypocrites, to keep herself occupied.

*　　*　　*

Hortensia checked her watch. Give or take, there were usually ten people present, ten of a possible thirty or so owners. Tonight twelve had shown up. It was all women, all over sixty, all white. This was Katterijn. The meetings were usually tedious but this time apparently something important was to happen. 'Crucial' had been the word used by her neighbour Marion.

'Evening,' Hortensia greeted the batty librarian whose name, just then, she couldn't remember.

'Hortensia, good you're here. Today is crucial.'

As if the word had been circulated, sent out in memo by Marion. True, there was an extra breeze of excitement. Hortensia, as always, chose a chair near the door. She did it deliberately to remind whoever might bother to notice that she could leave. Well, they could all leave, but it was particularly important to her for them to know that she could leave first.

'Evening, ladies.' Marion Agostino seemed to press these words out of her nose. Her smile was painted in a red too red for white skin, Hortensia thought, showing her distaste, hoping people would notice. 'Today's meeting is particularly crucial.'

A shiver went round, scented in a bouquet of Yardley, Anaïs Anaïs and talcum powder. Sometimes Hortensia hoped the women were pretending, like she was. She hoped they were there for the same reason, even if secretly. Not for the discussion of fencing left unfixed, bricks from previous works uncollected; nor for hedges to be trimmed or three quotes to be inspected; but for the promise of something non-threatening and happily boring with which to pass the time, get nearer to death, get closer to being done with it all. After so many years of living – too many – Hortensia wanted to die. She had no intention of taking her life but at least there were the Katterijn committee meetings, slowly ticking the hours off her sheet.

'So.'

Hortensia watched Marion lengthen her stubby neck and lace her fingers together atop a manila folder obsequiously named (in elaborate stencil) Katterijn Committee Meeting File. That the same tattered folder had been in use for the twenty years Hortensia had been whittling time away at these meetings proved the kind of nonsense they'd been up to.

'Yes, there is this pressing matter, but I first wish to deal with issues pending from our last meeting . . .'

True to form, Marion was circling the issue, circling. Marion the Vulture. Hortensia looked around the table. They were bickering about a swing in a park, just by the highway that headed back towards the city centre. A group of vagrants had taken possession of it. Clothes were seen drying there, strung along the bars. Offensive smells had been noticed. Someone resolved to take the message to City Council. Then there was the clutch of trees that was blocking someone's view of Table Mountain, but someone else's grandmother had planted them, and so on.

'Okay, so now,' Marion was readying for her big strike of the evening. Her hair was dyed a wan colour to conceal the fact that she'd been living for over eighty years. At one meeting Hortensia had overheard her refer to herself as a woman in her late sixties and almost choked on the tepid rooibos tea she'd been drinking.

'. . . finally, ladies, to the matter at hand. I'm not sure if any of you realise – in fact the only reason I found out is because of my first granddaughter, I'm sure you all recall that she's a law student – well, the point is, a notice has been made of a land claim in Katterijn. The notice was published in the *Government Gazette* by the . . . Land Claims Commission.'

'What's that?' Sarah Clarke asked.

Sarah was the only other person on the committee who got so much as a word in edgeways. She was the resident gossip, now in the unfamiliar position of asking a question, since there was little that Sarah Clarke did not already know.

'It's the . . . Commission . . . it deals with land claims, things like that.'

Hortensia rolled her eyes. Not that she cared but, naturally, she knew all about it and said so, explained that the Commission was set up in the Nineties to restore land to the disenfranchised. While reaching into the hallowed folder, Marion spat a look at her.

Marion pulled out a map of Katterijn, which she unfolded in the centre of the table with a reverence Hortensia had seldom seen shown for paper.

'The Land Claims Commission, Sarah, is one of those things with a self-explanatory name. And now,' she rose to point out the parcels of land, 'a group of some . . .' she rifled papers, more a show of importance than a real search for information, 'some three families . . . well, one big extended family, the Samsodiens.'

Marion rifled some more, until Hortensia had to concede that perhaps she was actually looking for information and, more than that, the woman looked nervous.

'What's the claim, Marion?'

'Just a moment, Hortensia. Just a moment.'

She found what she was looking for. 'The claims process has just this month been reopened, so . . . what I mean is they'd been closed since 1998 and then, for various reasons, on the first of July —'

'Why were they closed?' asked a woman whose name Hortensia could never recall.

'Well, Dolores, they were closed because . . .' She rifled. 'Doesn't say here, but —'

'The Commission was only open to claims from '94 to '98. That was the window-period.' Hortensia was enjoying herself. It wasn't like Marion to give away such easy points but, while she was being generous, it was Hortensia's aim to collect. Their rivalry was infamous enough for the other committee women to hang back and watch the show. It was known that the two women shared hedge and hatred and they pruned both with a vim that belied their ages.

Marion looked crestfallen. She was of course accustomed to doing battle with Hortensia, anywhere from the queue at Woolworths to outside the post office, but these committee meetings were like sacred ground to her, sacrosanct – she never got over the shock each time Hortensia questioned her authority.

'The Commission,' Hortensia continued, ignoring the glare in Marion's eyes, 'came about as a result of the Restitution of Land Rights Act that was passed by the then-new government.' Hortensia relished the use of those words 'new' and 'government', aware of how much they affected the women.

'Alright, alright, Hortensia. If we can just get back to the actual issue that we – gathered here – must deal with. The history lesson can continue *after* the meeting is over. Thank you. The Samsodiens are claiming land. The Vineyard basically. I'm surprised the Von Struikers aren't here, I'll make a call and request they attend the next meeting. It might be their land, but something like this will affect us all. Don't even get me started on what it'll do for property prices.'

Hortensia hated the Von Struikers. Bigots of the highest order, they owned the Katterijn Vineyard, bottled a limited-edition white wine and sometimes a red, neither of which Hortensia found drinkable. Not because of its taste; even if the wines were the best thing ever, she would have found them unacceptable. The thought of drinking anything made by Ludmilla and Jan Von Struiker made her sick.

'They make me sick,' Hortensia had once railed to Peter after a dinner at Sarah Clarke's, where Ludmilla had let slip the year that she and Jannie had arrived in Cape Town to start their 'small venture'. 'It took her a whole minute to realise what was wrong with coming to South Africa in the Sixties.'

Ludmilla pronounced 'v' with an 'f' sound and resembled the largest of the babushka dolls. Once, when Hortensia still deigned to entertain them, she'd offered her cheeks to be kissed in greeting and caught a whiff of foul breath. All these details she piled together as incriminating.

'The claim dates back to the Sixties when the Von Struikers acquired the land. I've made copies here for all present – you can study the details so we can discuss at the next meeting. It's going to be a long haul.'

'How do you mean?' Hortensia felt like a fight.

'Well, we're going to challenge it of course. I certainly won't be allowing this and I doubt Ludmilla and Jan will be, either. I'm sure, if pushed, these people would be hard pressed to substantiate the claims. People looking for easy money, if you ask me.'

'When you say "these people" what you really mean is black people, am I right?'

'You most certainly are not, and I would—'

'Marion, I'm not in the mood for your bigotry today. I distinctly remember asking you to keep your racist conversations for your dinner table.'

'I beg your—'

'Ladies. Please. Let's try and finish the meeting. Marion, I assume that's all for now?' Sarah had her uses. Thick as she was, she made a good buffer. 'Shall we continue at the next meeting? Do we need to type up a formal response to the Commission? Perhaps you want to speak to Ludmilla first then feed back to us.'

'Well, yes, but actually.' Marion was smiling; so soon recovered, Hortensia thought woefully. 'There is one more thing. Specifically with regards to the Jameses' property.'

Hortensia's ears pricked up.

'This is a special case. Well, not *case* as such. It's not a claim but rather a request.' Marion relished the moment and, despite her absent-mindedness just moments before, she appeared to have memorised all the details of this 'special case'; she knew it word-for-word, and the spaces in between – as if she'd written it herself.

'I received a letter from a woman, Beulah Gierdien. She had a grandmother named Annamarie, who was born in 1919, right here,' Marion said and a few of the women looked around the meeting room, half-expecting to still find the afterbirth dangling on the back of a chair or laid out on the plush azure carpet. 'Annamarie's mother was a slave woman on the farm for which No. 10 was the main house.' Marion looked pointedly at Hortensia. 'It states here that No. 12 – that would be my property – is where the adjoining slave quarters were, but that . . . well, that bit is . . . I think they got their facts wrong there. I do intend to challenge that but, anyway, where was I . . .? I must say it's a rather protracted and odd request.' She was enjoying herself. 'There's no money involved, Hortensia, so you can relax.'

'Get on with it, Marion. I need to be getting home soon.'

'Well, it's precisely that home that Beulah Gierdien seems interested in, Hortensia. Or at least one of the trees on the property. She refers to it as a "Silver".'

'The Silver Tree. Yes, I have one of those. What, she wants the tree?'

'It's not quite that simple.'

The librarian, Agatha, coughed. A woman, lips newly Botoxed, poured herself some water but struggled to drink. People stretched in their chairs; someone's yawn cracked and silence settled again.

'Apparently our Silvers – your single Silver Tree and my several – marked the edge of the properties in that day. There were no fences. Anyhow apparently the trunk of your Silver has some carvings on it.' Marion arched an eyebrow. 'You'd need to confirm that, Hortensia, but that's what she's saying were the markers.'

'Markers for what?'

'For where Annamarie's children are buried. For where Annamarie requested, in her last will and testament, that she be buried.' Marion was beaming.

'She wants to bury her grandmother on my property?'

'Correction, she wants to bury her grandmother's ashes on the property. The woman's been dead a while already.'

Through the excited chatter Hortensia snapped her fingers for Marion to hand over the documents. There were several sheets of paper, handwritten in a neat cursive. Hortensia started to scan the pages.

'Perhaps, while you familiarise yourself with that, Hortensia, we can call a break. Ladies.' Marion, her face beatific, rose and the other women followed suit.

'And the reason she wrote to you?'

Marion shrugged. 'She got the contact for the committee via the *Constantiaberg Bulletin*. My guess is she assumed the owners lived overseas and her best bet was to write to the committee.' It was always gratifying when outsiders acknowledged the significance of having a local committee.

Hortensia stayed sitting; she continued reading. The Katterijn Estate had originally been 65 hectares of land that, as the years collected, got parcelled and sold and parcelled and sold. By the 1960s only a small portion was being farmed, and this was the land the Von Struikers now owned.

In the mid-nineteenth century Annamarie's grandfather, Jude, had worked on the original wine farm. He'd also formed the group of slave men used to construct most of the buildings from that era, some of which still stood: the post office, Beulah wrote; the library, which was actually stables. They built the roundabout and planted most of the trees that formed the generous groves within the suburb. Jude was a dark man with paper-white eyes and small feet that his wife, apparently, had teased him about. Hortensia grimaced as she read, just the sort of memory-lane nonsense she found difficult to swallow – people fawning over their individual and collective histories.

Jude and his wife had children as slaves, but grew old in freedom. Their daughter, Cessie, gave birth to Annamarie. Jude and his wife, on being granted their freedom, had been permitted to remain on the land as workers and earn wages. Annamarie's parents had inherited the same agreement and stayed on in Katterijn – raising their family. Annamarie learned how to read. But by 1939 the Land Act of 1913 caught up with the small family and they were forcibly moved off the land. By then Annamarie was twenty years old, a mother herself and a wife. Except her first child had died at birth and, after another child died too, her husband walked off somewhere one night and was found floating in the lake. Father and babies were buried under No. 10's Silver Tree.

Hortensia looked up. Marion was standing by the refreshments table chewing something; their eyes met. Marion offered a smile, which Hortensia ignored and returned to Beulah Gierdien's notes.

After the tragedies Annamarie settled in Lavender Hill and married again. They had a boy, Beulah's father.

Hortensia laid the papers down.

A few of the members were milling around the tarts,

the meeting having gone on for longer than seemed bearable. Someone had prepared flapjacks, scorned at first (for fat content, for too-largeness) but eaten by all. People piled their plates, filled their cups and settled back in their seats.

'So you see, Hortensia, this is not about your favourite topic, the race card. For once we're on the same side.' Marion's smile looked set to burst and set the world alight.

'Not so.'

'Pardon?'

'Not so, Marion. We are not on the same side. You should know this by now. Whatever you say, I disagree with. However you feel, I feel the opposite. At no point in anything are you and I on the same side. I don't side with hypocrites.'

Marion was red. And quiet.

'I am not in agreement with you to push back on the Samsodien claim. Let those who are justly claiming their rights to the land – land owned by hoodlums, I might add – let them claim it.'

'And the Gierdien woman?' Marion managed to let out in a squeak.

'This,' Hortensia indicated the pile of papers in front of her, 'is sentimental claptrap and I won't be taking any notice of it at all. That you thought to waste precious committee-meeting time on something so trivial is, indeed, a puzzle to me.'

Marion's shoulders slumped in defeat. Sarah Clarke slurped her tea. The meeting was adjourned.

TWO

On the drive back home after the meeting, Marion played Hortensia's derision over in her head.

'Well, she can't just brush the whole thing aside,' Marion told the steering wheel. 'Just watch me. See if I let her just brush it.'

It was a cool evening, not too chilly and only just darkening.

'Race this, race that. Everything race – "when you say 'these people'" . . . Cow!' Marion braked in time to spare a cat scuttling across the road in the half-light of dusk.

Over the years the two women had argued about many things, each new encounter tense with enmity. In truth, they couldn't have been more opposite. Hortensia, black and small-boned, Marion, white, large. Marion's husband dead, Hortensia's not yet. Marion and her brood of four, Hortensia with no children.

In the early days, when Hortensia still attempted to socialise, the Clarkes, who lived across from the Jameses, had had a dinner party. Peter pleaded fatigue, Hortensia went out of boredom. It was uneventful, until Sarah mentioned an article she'd seen in the latest *Digest of South African Architecture*. Hortensia hadn't seen it. It was a *Who's Who* of local architects. Sarah looked innocent enough when she said that she'd expected to see Marion listed.

'Well,' Marion was caught off guard. She'd read as far as K (Karol) and then put the magazine away.

'Marion?' Hortensia pressed, the party suddenly looking up.

'I don't remember any women from my generation being included,' Marion said. 'There might not have been many of us but from reading that thing you'd think we didn't exist at all.'

'We hardly do,' someone Hortensia didn't know piped up and the conversation was steered safely away. Then, like a gift, Marion casually commented on Sarah's Mackintoshes and Hortensia ventured to point out, in a loud enough voice to be heard by most in the parlour, that the chairs were fakes; and, without being asked, she took the trouble to explain why. Dinner parties became a place to posture. Marion once held court on the wisdom of pedestrianising Long Street. She showed her sketches (her handbag was never without a notebook and a pencil). In return, Hortensia spoke for several minutes on the error of formalising the informal.

'If you take the cars off Long Street, you'll take away the people. There will be too much space and too little chaos.'

Marion made snide remarks about commercialised plastic-making; fiddling with crayons and thread was her approximation of textile design – any three-year-old can do it. Hortensia mentioned the presence of one of her fabrics – a brocade – used to panel a wall in the new Cape Grace wine bar. A modest article (Hortensia kept the clippings, as she did of all her works that made the news) in the Sunday paper, decor section, on the consolation of beauty in otherwise unsettling times. Trivial, Marion said, but struggled for words when Hortensia took pains to impart her disdain for a six-year degree that teaches you to knock walls together.

'You do realise Architecture can exist without Architects?'

Hortensia referred to the profession as one of the biggest cons and had absolutely no time for the navel-gazing self-importance and total inconsequentiality of architectural academia and their ponderous supposings. She knew a little about it as she had once been the guest of the architecture department at the University of Cape Town. She'd been invited to join a panel of external examiners on a project involving textile fabrication. She'd consented out of hubris but remained unimpressed.

'I visited your alma mater,' she'd told Marion the first chance she got.

'And?'

Apparently Hortensia's dislike was too much for words. She simply grimaced and walked on, leaving Marion in no doubt that her architecture school had just suffered the worst form of insult.

Other times they argued about maids and madams. It started at the grocer's. Hortensia behind Marion in the queue. She observed as her neighbour started to empty her basket.

'How are you, Precious?' Marion asked the woman at the checkout counter.

'Fine,' she responded.

'Truly? Promise?' Marion asked again. 'You usually look happier.'

The woman offered an uncomfortable smile. As Marion unloaded her items onto the counter she seemed to think it necessary to explain to Precious why she had bought them.

'That's for Mr Agostino. Tummy trouble. Oh, this is for my granddaughter. Fussy baby, that one. She likes this type, won't eat any other. This is for Agnes – you know Agnes, my girl at the house. Oh, and I saw that and thought: wouldn't Niknaks like that? Niknaks, that's Agnes's child. We thought of adopting her, but . . . you know . . . How much does all that come to, Precious?'

Hortensia had stared aghast through it all, in the rare position of being tongue-tied. She had a chance to set her tongue free at a gathering. Marion said that Agnes, her housekeeper, was part of the family: that the sixty-five-year-old woman had been pivotal in raising her kids, one boy and three girls, and that Marion in turn had attempted to make her life easier, sent Agnes's kid to a good school, built her a house.

'You want credit for that? That's blood-money. Mixed in with missionary work. You think you did well by her, don't you? Perhaps you'd like a medal?'

Marion was speechless.

'St Marion. Charity-giver. My foot! You can't buy it, Marion. You want to give something, you know what you should have given? You should have given Agnes your own house. And taken hers. Swopped suburbs. That's what you should have done, my friend . . . Or, better, here's a thought: Hero Marion, you should have ended apartheid . . . if you later wanted something to be able to brag about. Oh, and she is not like part of your family, she is employed by you. If she were part of your family, she wouldn't have to clean up every time she visits.'

Hortensia made a hook with her index and middle fingers, to go with the word 'visits'. Marion left the party.

Everything seemed to be about race for Hortensia, but Marion thought life was more complex than that, more wily.

She parked her car. As she climbed her stoep, her cellphone began to ring.

'Darling . . . why do you sound so upset? . . . I'm sorry I missed Innes's birthday . . . No, I didn't forg— . . . No, I didn't just *not come* . . . Marelena, I've had some issues to deal with here . . . The accountant called me, about Dad and his . . . well . . . What do you mean, am I surprised? How was I to know? . . . Your brother isn't even taking my calls, Gaia refuses to give me her number in Perth . . . I sent her an email the other day; don't suppose I'll hear back . . . As for Selena, you'd think Jo'burg was the North Pole, the amount I hear from her . . . I need some help, is what I'm saying . . . Help-help. Money! . . . Zero, is what the accountant said . . . Marelena, would you please listen? . . . Marelena? . . . Yes, gone – all of it, gone . . . All . . . I see . . . Okay, Okay . . . Yes, of course you need to speak to your husband first . . . Well, will you call me? . . . Okay. Bye.'

'Agnes.' Marion put the phone down and arranged a

chair the way she liked it, concealed from view by her row of Silvers. 'Agnes!' She banged against the front door. 'I'm calling you!'

'Ma'am.' The woman appeared.

'Take.' Marion handed over her keys and committee file. 'Put on my desk.'

Of course there were other things to be concerned about, besides Hortensia.

'Oh, Agnes! Tea. Bring tea.'

Max had finished their money. They, Marion and Max, had had lots and lots of money. And just before he'd died he'd gone and finished it. The fool.

'Agnes!'

'Ma'am?'

'Tea. Use the china – the proper stuff. And bring the binoculars. And a biscuit for Alvar.'

Marion tapped her temple, listened to the padded steps retreating across the stoep, back into the house, up the hallway towards the kitchen.

'Don't break anything!' The woman must have Parkinson's or something. Whatever that disease was where your hands shake. Dropped the handmade ceramic antique soup bowl – blue and white. Dropped it. Broken. Irreparable.

All the same, if the accountant was right, she'd eventually have to let Agnes go. Stupid Max. Stupid stupid stupid.

'Come here, Alvar! Come here, boy.'

Alvar was approaching two years old. The dachshund had been a gift to Marion from Marelena and her children. They'd been tactful enough to wait several months after Max had died before presenting Marion with a white wire cage, a yellow ribbon round it. But even so, the notion of a replacement could not be avoided. Her children had been raised never to talk about the obvious, never to mention the thing in the room that gave off a stench. Marion had taught them either to move or bear it, but never to let on. Pointing things out was too unpleasant.

The reality was that within days it became clear that Alvar was going to be a much better companion than Max ever was. Apart from in the arenas of passing on human sperm and earning money to keep a family, Alvar won over Max in all spheres. He had a much better sense of humour, he didn't snore or fart in his sleep, he was always happy to see her and he came when she called. Marion named the dog after Alvar Aalto, her favourite architect. She saw in Alvar the same restraint of design (the mark of genius, surely), tasteful simplicity, an appreciation for natural materials and textures. No one else could quite see how a dog bore the same characteristics as a Master Builder, but they let it go.

Agnes brought the tea. The weight of Alvar was a comfort in Marion's lap. 'Wrong set. The proper one, I said.' Marion took the biscuit. 'And bring another biscuit, Agnes.' Who brings a dog a single biscuit?

Marion had been twenty-six – principal of her own firm but lonely – and there was Max at a dinner organised by business associates. Her friend took her by the elbow to a corner of the dimly lit lounge and said: this is Max Agostino, Italian and rich. And Max had ducked his head down as if embarrassed and shaken her hand. The friend (who was it?) then wandered off, as is the thing to do with such set-ups, and Max said something accommodating. Something like, 'Now you know everything about me, let's talk about you.' And Marion had smiled. It hadn't been everything about him. She, the friend – whoever it was – had left out that he was tall, that the neatly trimmed hairs along his temple, light grey, were the same colour as his eyes. He was well composed, Marion had noted, in his dark grey-suit and silver cufflinks. She teased him about it – that he wore office-wear to parties – and then noted with alarm that she was flirting. She looked at her glass, wondering how much she'd drunk, and Max, noticing it was empty, offered to refresh it.

When she asked, he explained the way he made his money, but the financial world was a puff of smoke to Marion and she enjoyed the fact that Max's work was inaccessible, uncatchable. She made room for this bit of mystery in their relationship and it did the job of keeping him, at least some parts of him, strange to her. When they made love the strangeness was there, that he was someone she couldn't quite get all of.

There were the little surprises. That he wasn't circumcised, that he lowed when he came, that he didn't mind crying in others and frequently did so himself, over simple things like a sad part of a movie or a baby being born. Otherwise Max was predictable, steady. And he loved her.

After a small wedding, they discussed where they wanted to live. Katterijn was Marion's preferred neighbourhood but houses in the area were seldom advertised. In a moment of luck, while talking to an estate agent about another home they had viewed in Bantry Bay, the agent mentioned one in Katterijn that was about to go on the market. The news turned Marion nervous and right until they drove up to the house she carried a secret wish that, although the particulars clearly stated No. 12, the house up for sale was really No. 10. No. 10 Katterijn Avenue was a house she'd designed. Not just any design, her first.

In the time it took the agent to retrieve the keys and open up No. 12 Marion composed herself. The disappointment nestled in her belly, but she marched through the house as if she already owned it. She folded her arms at the entrance of each room, her eyes taking it all in.

'Honey, what do you think?' Max kept asking, but Marion ignored him, dismayed that he knew no better than to discuss impressions in the presence of the agent.

Outside she walked a few metres to the left and then to the right of the wooden trellised gate.

'What about that house?' she asked, taunting herself really.

'No. 10? Oh, it's not for sale.'

Marion nodded, she knew that No. 10 had already changed hands. The first owners, the Norwegians, had made a private sale to a corporate consultancy firm looking for somewhere to house their travelling staff and entertain their top clients.

'Well?' Max asked, his patience thinning.

Marion told the agent to give them some privacy so they could talk. But once the short man was out of range, she paced while Max waited.

She had been top of her class, a position she wrestled from a male student who not only found her presence in the school annoying, but her ambition and fierce competitiveness vulgar. Damon Lewis, principal of DLA, attended her final-year project presentation; he took her aside afterwards and rookie architect Marion had the heady sensation of never having applied for a job, never having sat for an interview. It pained her, though, on the first day of work, to see snot-nosed Harry Cumfred, her long-time adversary from architecture school. Initially they were set to work together, under various project architects, until Cumfred was given his own project – a bakery in the east city had burned down, a heritage job that would win him an award and a nod from Council.

Marion boiled for almost a year until she was finally given the opportunity to design her first house. It was high-profile. DLA's reputation had been built on the quality of their residential work. The new clients were a Norwegian couple, not much English but fluent in French. Marion had taken French in her matriculation exams and aced it – she was given the job, with Cumfred glowering in the background. Marion, however, made one mistake. In her haste to prove herself she put everything she had into the design. She tucked features into the details that in truth she should have saved for her own home. By the time she'd noticed her error, the house was done; DLA could not praise her enough and the clients loved it.

The house was reviewed in one of the journals of the day. And it was during the short interview that the sense of horror began to come over Marion. Something like giving a gift to a friend and only then realising you actually wanted it for yourself, but of course not that, something much much bigger with a lot more at stake. The more congratulations and accolades the house received, the deeper that feeling had sunk.

Marion paced; unable to help herself, she looked across the low wall at the other property. No. 10 was larger than No. 12. It had a grander forecourt, while No. 12's front door was but steps away from the front gate. Next door had subtle character (the best kind) made all the more charming by a small koi pond at the bottom of the sloping back garden. It had an oak, and hung from one of its strong branches was a swing. It was one of the largest houses in the Katterijn Estate. It stood on ground where the great manor house would have stood when the Estate was still an Estate. Max took a call from his business partner about a deal they were closing.

'Alright,' Marion said.

She stopped pacing and walked to the agent, who was leaning against the side of his car smoking a cigarette.

Marion and Max moved into their home within a month. By Christmas Marion was with child. She'd started her own firm with none other than Harry Cumfred. He'd suggested the alliance; we're the best there is, he'd said, and she'd found she couldn't disagree. She worked until the day before the birth and, leaving the child with the nanny, was back at work within a week. Her firm, importantly stationed on Loop Street, flourished, expanding to almost thirty employees including one new partner, two associates, four project architects, an army of draughtspeople and administrative staff. She brought in most of the residential work; Cumfred used his old-boy network for the larger schemes he believed would make them formidable. He teased her about her houses, although her clients were millionaires, the jobs far from paltry. Their families sometimes socialised – Cumfred had married and they'd had twins – but Marion never quite believed in his friendship. She'd gone into business with him because working together was the best way for her to keep an eye on him. She suspected he had done the same.

Marion grew another bump, disappeared for a week or so, but for the most part things stayed the same. She went through periods of ignoring No. 10. And at other times the house consumed her.

By 1969 Marion had two kids, Stefano and Marelena, and one on the way, Selena. The third pregnancy was tougher than the others. She spent many days in bed before and after the birth. When she came to and some weeks had passed, she noticed a removal truck parked outside. The corporates had sold to a Dutch family. Once more No. 10 had slipped out of reach.

It was after Selena was born, with the recommendations of the fatherly family doctor pressing in on him, that Max ventured to suggest Marion stay home; dared ask, his tone sounding so close to insistence. Marion said no – out of the question. For one thing, she had argued, I'm already doing more than my share. It was true that the thing Marion understood the least about her husband took him away more frequently than she'd initially anticipated. And she was surprised to learn she was the kind of woman who actually wanted her husband around on weekends. Maybe not so much because she missed him, but more because she needed him to be there. She found parenting hard and she wanted him to struggle along with her. The trade-off – the money and the immense comfort his job bought them – did not make up for his long absences.

Annoyingly, however, when Max was home, Marion couldn't help noticing the ease with which he loved their children and how they all loved him back. She envied Max his tidy life, his crisp suits and business trips. How much less complicated things were for him. He didn't seem to hear the manipulation in Marelena's cry, the need to be stoic and wait it out. Stefano was wetting the bed; this was brushed aside. Selena's nose was rather large, but Max found that comical. (Although he was slightly put out when he saw Marion leafing through his family albums. She pointed at his great-aunt's nose – aha, she said, triumphant.) But, mostly these details didn't matter for Max. Instead of husband and father, Marion had landed herself a gust of wind. A pleasant one when present, a well-loved one, but insubstantial, itinerant.

And there were other things. The fine lines of life, the careful negotiations. Once, Agnes had asked if she could bring her young toddler with her to work; the crèche she normally left her at was closed for a period and would it be okay? Marion had said no, but Agnes had cried and the baby (was it Stefano or Marelena?) had cried too – they were very attached to Agnes. And Marion had capitulated but then fretted for days. Max was away and she'd phoned him.

'What exactly are you worried about?'

'I just . . . don't you understand? Must I explain everything?'

Despite Marion's quiet resentment, they seldom actually fought.

'I'm not trying to argue. Look, how can I help?'

'I just feel that . . . having another . . . a young child around . . . it would distract her, I'm sure. From her work.'

Marion felt the sting of embarrassment; she couldn't say it out loud – she didn't want her kids to play with the black child. She didn't want them touching. But she couldn't say it because if she said it, then it would really be there and she wouldn't be able to just ignore it, which was infinitely easier and, thus far, largely possible.

'Just tell her no then,' Max said. He was probably sitting on the edge of some hotel bed, his legs crossed. 'Tell her you've realised that it won't be a good thing after all.'

His tone was calm, he plotted out the solution as if he had more where that came from. He wasn't someone with a whole life that he needed to constantly keep in line. His life's borders seemed to police themselves.

Marion fought with herself, in her head. The reason she hadn't wanted Agnes to bring her child to work was because the child would be a distraction – that was the reason. And the reason she suggested Agnes did not wash her clothes in with the family's load was because this seemed sensible, to keep things separate. Why complicate the washing? She explained it as slowly as possible to Agnes, but checked for several weeks after to make sure she was following her instructions. And the reason (it was Marelena who asked) that Agnes had a bruise on her head was because black people were dangerous and the police had thought Agnes was one of those black people. No, Agnes was not dangerous. Yes, most black people were dangerous and they were causing trouble. No, Agnes was not causing trouble. No, it wasn't unfair. It was in fact very fair. Life was fair.

Life may have been fair, but it was getting out of control. Slowly more and more of Marion's energy was taken up in keeping her life in line. The more Max was away, the older the children became, the more porous those borders grew. The kids had questions. Marion was intelligent and perfectly capable, except that the questions the children asked were zigzag. Did a black beach have black sand? If that is a black bench, why did they paint it white? It messed with Marion's mind. She still had the practice, but it became harder and harder (with Cumfred looking on) to be a normal person, with borders intact.

As a young adult she had explained her country to herself in a way her children were refusing to adopt. With all their prodding it became difficult to see only what was comfortable, to keep looking away from what she'd rather not see. It was in this battle that Marion lost all possibility for happiness. And, because it is much easier to fight your husband than the government, Marion waged a quiet war against Max and she used the love of their children as artillery. And she eyed No. 10 and she waited.

In the middle of 1994 No. 10 was sold again. When Marion pieced the story together she learned that the matriarch of the Dutch family had died and taken with her the intent to keep a foothold in Africa. Marion bristled that the Dutch never mentioned to her their intention to sell. She concluded it was out of spite – there had been enough dinner parties at which the news could have been casually thrown out, but instead the transfer happened quietly. Marion woke up one morning to a black woman, with short-cropped greying hair, hardly any breasts and a skinny waist, conducting an orchestra of movers with elaborate hand gestures. Commando, that was the word that came to her mind that cold morning as she watched this woman from behind the French doors that opened onto her north-facing stoep.

It was an insult, a black woman suddenly in a house Marion had dreamed for decades of possessing; no, a house that was rightfully hers, which other people kept taking. In addition she was some kind of minor celebrity. Marion had never heard of Hortensia but Sarah Clarke had referred to her as a design guru. This seemed an impossibility to Marion. She'd pressed Sarah for more details. Apparently a friend of the Dutch had said something about fabric design. She makes cloth? Marion had asked Sarah, too upset to veil her angry curiosity with coolness. A week later with the librarian Marion played it down. New neighbour coming, Marion. A design person like you, what are the chances. Marion had smiled with what she hoped was disinterest. Don't be silly, Agatha, I'm an architect, she sounds more like a haberdasher.

What were the chances, though. Of designing someone else's house as if it was your own, of living next door but never within, of becoming obsessed. And now to once more lose the elusive trophy to someone who drew squiggles and called that design. As for the woman's husband, Marion assumed that was him (a white man, one of the longest white men she had ever seen) he was mostly out of sight that first day but appeared from time to time and trailed behind his wife offering a glass of refreshment, a cordless phone, a plate of fruit. The binoculars had been a gift from the grandchildren, but Marion had never intended to use them to birdwatch. Spying on her neighbours was much more entertaining. Except that morning was cause for upset, not amusement. Amusement would have been watching the Clarkes, who had proven themselves common because they had succumbed to trend and bought three pet pigs; amusement would have been the Von Struikers, whose arguments had reached a display of violence that could only mean they were yet again on the brink of divorce. Rich people and their dramas were amusing. Hortensia James was a thief.

THREE

A careful balance had been messed with. On account of her walking faster than she usually did, Hortensia was out of breath. Imagine Marion thinking she could bother her with this Beulah nonsense. Except that it had annoyed her. She felt heat at her ears and along her limbs, as well as a strong burning sensation where her heart was. She stopped walking and stretched her arm out against the gnarled skin of a pine tree. The trees always made her feel old, made her feel her age. She dropped her head forward and her eyes took in thick spreading roots, fallen leaves, sodden dirt. She'd taken a step and annihilated a string of ants. They had been busy with the soggy shell of a snail. Beulah and her blasted grandmother and her stupid dead children. The anger bubbled up, the indignation, ever at the ready. Beulah and her ancestors with their cloying sentiments were as good a reason as any for that familiar feeling to stir. Hortensia let out a growl and shook her fists.

When she started walking again she looked about, glared at the pine trees. Was it a sign she was not well in the head, that she came to the trees to quarrel? To cuss and spit out the most venomous anger she could find in the pit of her gall bladder. What did the trees care? She could direct the full blast of her hate at them without having to deal with their snivelling.

She took brisk steps, pushing until her lungs insisted she pause. The tree bark had faces. She was certain the trees were looking at her, all fifty-seven of them (she'd counted). Hortensia stopped walking, leaned. Her mind was going; she was angry with trees and her mind was going. She moved on. Her walk had been the first thing to go that really hurt. A dash of grey on her head, a slight dip in breasts small enough for dipping not to matter, an extra line on her neck had never bothered her. Her eyes were good, her teeth were hers. But the loss of her walk was the first sign that time was wicked and had fingers to take things. It wasn't just dates up on a wall, it was a war. Time took away her walk. She awoke one morning with the left leg aching, a throb that would come and go but never permanently leave. So now she lumbered, she limped; many times she sat, but since she'd reached sixty-five she hadn't sauntered. When you're Hortensia James and you have pride but no walk to saunter it with – well, life is difficult.

Hortensia counted the trees. She counted to feel human again, to come down from being a spitting thing to simply being her regular normal pissed-off self. She counted. The trees had been planted in a scattered fashion but since her first visit here, almost two decades ago, she had worked out a way to navigate through them, counting them, as if the numbers were the notation of an angry prayer. Ten. She'd grown accustomed to favouring the right leg, refused to go to the doctor and find out what exactly was wrong with the left. Fifteen. The ground was wet from yesterday's rain, the leaves shiny and green. Hortensia ensured her Pumas made contact with the ants; she didn't just trample the creatures by accident, she sought them out. Her regular normal pissed-off self. She tightened her lips. Twenty-five.

At thirty-five she stopped to catch her breath. She began again but then stopped at the next group of trees, leaned against a trunk, sighed. From where she leaned she could see the tops of most of Katterijn's properties, including hers. Hortensia pushed off from the tree. A nip came and she pulled her zipper higher, dug her hands into the velvety pockets of her tracksuit bottoms and moved along.

She took the long way home, circling all of Katterijn, along a road her neighbours referred to as the Noodle, but she called the Noose. She looked up to try and gauge when the rain would start again. She passed a few neighbours walking their dogs or pushing the grandkids; some younger couples, new to the suburb, holding hands. When was her life ever simple enough for someone she loved to want to hold her hand? As she walked, Hortensia looked through people. If someone waved she looked away. When she turned the last corner even her sore leg appeared to perk up at the thought of the ottoman in the lounge and a hot chocolate. But there, standing outside No. 12, with arms akimbo, was Marion Agostino.

'Hortensia.'

Because of her special hatred for Marion, Hortensia stopped to address her.

'Marion,' she said. Their eyes met for a few seconds and then Hortensia carried on. She limped to her gate, aware Marion was watching her, picking her apart in her mind like carrion. She searched for her key.

'Hortensia.' Marion approached as Hortensia stood and fumbled with the gate lock.

Hortensia closed her eyes, which was the closest she'd come, in the last decade or so, to prayer. There was a time when she actually did pray – Oh God, and so on – but these days she figured she was old. These days she dropped her eyelids for a few seconds and then lifted them, relying on God being all-powerful and getting it. Getting something to the effect of: help me be rid of this woman, make her mute, maybe paralysed from the neck down; make her forget I exist, take her away, dear God, Amen.

'Yes, Marion.' Hortensia gave the gate a slight push and it swung open (Hortensia James's gate did not squeak or squawk or make any other unbecoming noises). She waited for what was coming.

'You can't ignore the Gierdien request.'

'Yes, I can. Goodnight, Marion.'

'Wait . . . I was also . . . We can discuss the matter at the next meeting, but I also . . .' She made her face sweet and Hortensia felt sick. 'I was thinking just now. How is Peter? Good?'

'Peter is dying, Marion. Anything else?'

'Oh dear!'

'Yes, afraid so. Goodbye, then.'

Hortensia had already closed the gate behind her when Marion issued her next shot.

'And how's the leg?'

'Bad.'

Marion, despite being white and dressing only (as far as Hortensia could make out) in khaki pencil-skirts and peach-coloured shirts, despite being fleshier and a fervent dyer to blonde of her grey hair, reminded Hortensia of her mother. Here were two women Hortensia knew who asked only questions with bad-news answers. Marion, for instance, would never ask how House of Braithwaite was doing, because she knew it would be good news. Marion didn't ask how the shoot with *Vintage Magazine* went, when they came to interview her and photograph the interior spaces of her home. Marion never asked what Hortensia's bank account looked like or where she'd put her trophy for Best Christmas Lights from last year's neighbourhood contest.

Hortensia popped the key back into her pocket and climbed the steps. She stopped and, using her good leg, shoved one of her garden pots into position. Her mood was spoiled. Spoiled so that no ottoman or mug of hot chocolate could repair it. She'd have to sleep, wake up into another day.

As for her mother, Hortensia thought, now savouring the bitterness on her tongue, liking the way it curled right there on the very tip – that woman, while she lived, had only one question to ask Hortensia, year after year of her marriage to Peter: when are you bringing me babies?

Hortensia let herself in. The nurses hadn't bothered to turn any of the downstairs lights on. She slammed the door, which saved her having to announce her presence with words, and meant by the time she'd shrugged her jacket off and put on her house-slippers, the women would be stepping down the stairs with their bags and nurse-things. A few words of instruction for the night and they'd be gone, giving her, Hortensia, some peace and allowing Peter to progress towards his death unhindered. So much dignity had been sucked out of death, Hortensia thought, now looking forward to hot chocolate again, her ears attuned to the unmistakable sound of nurse-shoe on stair tread.

'Mrs James, that you?'

They'd become a part of the house. Since he'd stopped talking and all movement was an act of persuasion, the hospital had dispatched two nurses daily. Hortensia had resisted when a night-nurse was suggested. Not the nights too, she'd said. She'd even said please.

'In here.' She preferred not to talk to them but they insisted. In general, people like to talk to old folk.

'Nice walk?' One nurse – their names came in and out, like breathing – stood at the doorway of the coat-room.

Hortensia chose to ignore her question.

'Anything I need to know?' she asked instead, balling her socks into a squat brown basket.

'He's fine, sleeping. Medicated for the night. Nothing to worry about. We'll be back bright and early.'

Hortensia watched the pep in this woman bounce her down the hallway; her colleague joined her and out they went.

Bassey knew to leave the tin of hot chocolate out before he left for the day, as well as her favourite mug, blank of image or text, a chalky sea-urchin white. Hortensia stirred, liking the feel of the grooves on the 1942 miniature silver spoon. She remembered a long-ago friend and his anecdote about his uncle, who was a chef. The man was known for eating a cut tomato and being able to tell whether it had been sliced with his silverware or just some normal run-of-the-mill knife – he could taste it. Hortensia took a sip, flipped the light and headed for the ottoman. Her life was burdened. An expert appreciation for beautiful things, right and proper things, was her only remaining comfort.

When Marion realised she was staring bankruptcy in the face her first thought had been: how do I get out of this? Max had been the one with the loopholes. Look where that got him. But then she'd thought of the painting.

Marion gave Agnes the morning off, ignoring the look of shock on the woman's face. She wanted to search through the house without Agnes watching, being suspicious and asking questions. The first wave of debt collectors would come within the next few weeks, Marion's lawyer had told her. He'd staved them off for as long as he could.

Marion climbed the stairs to the attic, holding onto the banister, not liking the strain in her Achilles heel. They'd want the house. She cracked open the swollen door. Swollen because of the leak – the rains in '98 that weekend they'd gone away and come back to ruined carpets. Cobwebs stuck to her cheeks and she tried and failed to get them all off.

'Heavens!'

Only desperation could have brought her up here. A shaft of light felt palpable, like a witness. Marion saw the gleam from the gilt frame of a small portrait she'd hidden away. Her parents in wedding clothes, posing in the manner of people who are scared but have learned to pretend. When she'd packed up her mother's room (her father had already been dead ten years) she'd been surprised to find the portrait preserved, challenging the reality of their divorce. Why had her mother not got rid of it? And then she, Marion, had discovered her own inability to throw the picture away. As if the photograph, this record of the past, had some magical power.

Marion glanced at the faces, grimaced. This was going to be hard. Best to avoid as much as possible. Gosh, there was the valise full of Max's suits. Marion teetered in the tracks of space left between the many things she'd stored away over the decades. There was only one thing she really needed. She moved towards a wall of boxes, certain she had hidden it behind there. A scratching noise gave her a jolt. She was relieved she'd closed the attic door.

'Alvar! Stay out.'

He scratched some more and then she heard him skitter down the stairs. She'll feed him later.

All the while worrying about being found buried underneath boxes and photographs of frightened people, Marion made a path to the back wall. There it was. Muscles she hadn't known were tense eased up. She'd been careful to bubble-wrap it, but even so she realised she'd been careless to leave it here and felt lucky to find it undamaged. If Max was right, the painting would fetch enough to last her till she finally died. But she'd need to hide it for the next few months, or however long the scavenge would go on for. The hunt. She lifted it and found it light enough to carry. She moved back towards the door, averting her gaze from her parents, her cheeks pinked with shame.

Back downstairs, she sensed the commotion rather than heard it. Out on her stoep Marion watched the ambulance park alongside No. 10. Had the man finally croaked?

Alvar curled in her lap. She watched the activities, half-distracted. She was thinking about the painting. About hiding the painting. A stretcher was carried out of Hortensia's home. On it was a covered body. Marion felt too harassed by bankruptcy and lawyers to enjoy her neighbour's misfortune. The ambulance drove off, Hortensia trailing behind in her car; she'd looked more irritated than worried.

'Ma'am.'

'Oh my goodness, Agnes, you gave me a fright. You're back early.'

'Sorry to scare you.'

Marion noticed Agnes eyeing the dusty bubble-wrapped parcel by her side.

'Well, never mind. Continue with your work.'

Once Agnes was safely occupied in the kitchen, Marion dragged the painting back upstairs and leaned it against the wall in her bedroom. But it looked at her. She wanted it close but out of sight. Underneath the bed. She got onto her knees, pushed aside her bedroom slippers – always ready, to attention. She knew it was stupid to keep the painting around. The whole business could get quite nasty, her lawyer had warned, especially if you're suspected of circumventing the law. As she leaned and slid the painting underneath the bed, her brow creased. She had to hide the painting away somewhere no one would suspect to look for it. When the creditors came with their investigators, prying and questioning and . . . investigating . . . where would be the last place they would think to look? Marion had to restrain herself from calling Hortensia immediately. Despite her excitement about this new solution, she had the presence of mind to know such an action would be inappropriate. She'd have to wait a bit, although time wasn't something she had in abundance. And she'd have to cajole Hortensia, somehow convince her and avoid suspicion – even with a newly dead husband, the woman would be sharp as a needle.

Too excited to feel foolish, Marion carted the painting downstairs, yet again, and set it by the front door. She made herself tea and allowed the taste of the idea to sink in. A perfectly good idea. And of course she won't mention the bankruptcy – Heavens, no. Pretend the alarm is broken or something. Hortensia, can you help me keep this? It's the most valuable thing I own . . . would be terrible if something happened . . . if someone broke in and stole it . . . Won't you . . .?

Yes, they argued but there had been some favours over the years. Precisely three. Peter had asked Max's advice and Max had whispered to him about a particular stock. When the price tripled Peter gave the Agostinos half an impala. He'd killed it himself. Marion was horrified but eventually had to concede the sweet tast of Karoo meat. Before his death Max had offered another financial tip that paid off. How is it her husband could help others make money but lose all of his own? Anyway the point was the Jameses owed the Agostinos. It was time to call in the favours.

The thought seemed to settle Marion, bring a calm she hadn't felt for months, not since Max's financial acrobatics had become apparent to her. The inevitability of bankruptcy had surfaced the way the ghost comes only after the body is dead and buried.

Of course she would now need to swallow her pride

to ask Hortensia for help, but that wound would eventually heal. It would be a small price to pay for a chance not to die a pauper. Marion rehearsed the words she would use and looked through her binoculars across at her neighbour's house – No. 10 Katterijn Avenue. The words were hard to form. Since the first lines she'd scratched on tracing paper over fifty years back, No. 10 was hers.

Corbusier claimed a house was a machine for living in. Marion, to her studio master's amusement, explained her position. Didn't we have enough machines? Did everything have to be likened to cogs and wires in order to make it worthwhile? A house is a person, she'd argued, to the sound of guffaws from the rest of the class. But she'd pressed on and turned in her essay. What was house design if it wasn't the study of armour, of disguises, of appearances? The most intimate form of space-making, the closest architects might ever come to portraiture. Interesting, interesting, the teacher had said, but not substantiated enough. Marion thought him an idiot with a mind as narrow as a pin and did not allow his tepid response to dampen her own enthusiasm. She'd wanted to design houses the way other girls her age wanted babies.

How do you go to someone who has taken your baby and ask them to help you with something delicate? The pleases and thank-yous. Marion tried them in her head; they wouldn't come. Not even slowly. Unless there was some other way to do it . . . She could go to the funeral, for instance, play up a bit. Marion's mind moved through the steps. The phone rang.

'Yes, darling . . . Yes, I wondered . . . I see . . . I wasn't asking for that much money, Marelena. I didn't even mention an amount. I just needed to know that in the event . . . Well, tell your hubby I don't need his money, then. I have an idea anyway, so maybe I won't need your help after all . . . I'll tell you when I've worked it all out . . . What do you mean, why am I being so . . . I realise that, Marelena . . . Yes, you too . . . okay. Bye.'

Marion eyed the painting. Send flowers, go to the funeral, then wait some days; at the right moment, strike. Worth a try.

Back on the porch, Marion drank her tea but it was cold and she could only taste bile. After No. 10 was complete and the Norwegians living in it, nothing had alleviated that sunken feeling in the bottom of Marion's belly. Not a marriage to Max, not one child after another. Not starting her practice. Nothing.

FOUR

'Would you like to see him?' the mortician asked Hortensia.

I've seen him already, Hortensia thought, but she nodded. You were supposed to nod, you were supposed to want to say goodbye one last time in private. The world was funny, encouraging you to speak to dead bodies. Hortensia tried to get comfortable on the low couch with missing studs while the woman – had she called herself Meredith? – made a phone call. 'Are you ready for her?' the woman said into the receiver.

Hortensia tuned her out. The nice thing about being old is that you can literally moderate your hearing, and these days there was little worth listening to. The mortician's office was two chairs, the couch and a wide desk with nothing on it except a pair of hands belonging to . . . Meredith (maybe) and a lamp that made Hortensia wonder if the woman worked nights. All the furniture was low; it looked as if someone had tried to go for minimal and chic, but ended up with cheap instead. Meredith, a large woman, bulged out of the chair, a Raggedy Ann doll sitting for tea with Barbie furniture. Hortensia studied her, unashamed when the woman caught her eye occasionally. The thing about turning off your hearing is you lose all inhibition. Hortensia examined the mottled skin of the woman's arms that poked out from black puffy sleeves. Her chubby wrists. She had a strange birthmark on the tip of her index finger, a dark splodge of ink-black that had the effect of making her look grimy.

'Pardon?' Hortensia said, turning the dial.

'Sorry for the wait. We're almost finished preparing him.' She pushed her chair out and rose. 'Be right back.'

Hortensia shrugged but not enough to be seen. This was another skill of her age: the infinitesimal shrug that let you pour heaps of blame, hopelessness and a sense of being victimised onto the world without having to contend with any resistance. Meredith – or was it Judith? – closed the door behind her, only to open it again a few minutes later.

'Ready?'

The woman's back was wide, and Hortensia felt like a child as she traipsed behind her down the passageway. It was safe, like being in a human slipstream. The mortician's shoulders, and the shock of red curls that fell onto them, reminded Hortensia that she had to ask Malachi the gardener to trim back the ivy by the gate. Probably he hadn't noticed, he was the kind of gardener that didn't notice things. Then there was the continual problem of her concrete pots by the entrance steps. Hortensia had had the pots made, specially cast; she'd had the paint factory use an acid-based dye. Four pots, square-shaped because the entrance porch required corners, strong lines versus baroque curves. On each square pot was a white image, the silhouette of a bird with a delicate elongated beak that might suggest a hummingbird, but only if you looked closely. The birds, when the pots were arranged as they should be, ascended as if heading skywards. Malachi moved the pots around often. For instance, if he was turning their soil or if she'd asked him to plant something bright and pretty. Then he'd return the pots along the right-hand side of the porch, one for each step, but the birds would be jumbled, some facing east, some west, no skywards-effect. The suffering she experienced at the hands of a gardener without an eye for these things.

'I'll leave you for a few minutes. Take your time, Ma'am.'

Hortensia moved closer to the bed. She put her mouth in a line, surprised at herself, at the agreement she was making with her face that this was not the time for tears. She edged forward, took a look. Of course it wasn't him. It never is. And, unable to stop it, the thought came that she too would lie down one day, not ever to get up, and maybe someone (the cleaner or the nurse in charge) would edge forward. Of course it would be the cleaner or the nurse. It wouldn't (couldn't) be anyone who actually knew her. It wouldn't be anyone who would be able to tell that this wasn't her; that, in death, she wasn't herself. And wasn't that somehow a failing – having no known-one there to witness? What could be more fitting than dying and having people who knew you from when you were alive; have them present to look into your casket and confirm that 'It isn't you'; that no, you were quite different in life; that yes, death had taken something, there had been something to take. Hortensia's eyes wandered with her mind, she looked to the corners of the small wooden-panelled room, she looked to the ceiling. Imagine having people witness that, in death, you looked the same. And then her eyes fell to the dead body that was not Peter.

His face was grey-green and small. It had sunken in, as if he'd taken a very big breath, sucked all the air in and hollowed his cheeks, but not got the chance to breathe out again. She felt sorry for him. She reached out and touched his cheekbone. The skin was like wet, but it wasn't. Damp somehow.

His hands were knobbled, in particular his ring-finger. The knuckle swollen, his golden band trapped in place. Hortensia moved her hand to the ring, to the cold of the soft metal. It was now too late. She sucked her tongue to distract herself – what was the point of crying now, whatever was the point? She turned to call the mortician back, tell the plank of a woman that she'd seen him enough. And just then Hortensia remembered that the paint-seller had called that colour, for the pots, 'Magic Teal'. And after the pots had been delivered Hortensia had thought how unlike its name the colour looked. And, without any way of explaining it, she'd felt cheated.

After the viewing at the morgue, the tangle of arrangements started. Hortensia baulked both at the sympathy that spilled out from people and at the assumption that, at her advanced age, she had buried many already, that she understood how things worked. This produced a rather obscene casualness in the mortician, whom Hortensia now reliably recalled was a Ms Judith Mulligan. At their second meeting Judith had asked Hortensia whether she'd notified 'the regulars'. And then later Judith had asked her if Peter had a Facebook page. It was a miserable time, not because her husband had died but because most of the living – people Hortensia had to associate with – appeared to be numbskulls.

Some man telephoned about a tombstone for Peter. Yes, apparently Peter had commissioned his own tombstone. She tried to get rid of the guy but he was resolute. The man had gruff in his voice, the kind of voice you'd think a sculptor, someone who worked with stone, should have. I don't understand why you're calling me, Hortensia said, her already short temper at its shortest that week. But Peter must have prepared Gary – that was his name – for this encounter with his wife. After Gary's protracted explanation, Hortensia relented and agreed to receive him and inspect the work of art before its installation. The stone was to be placed, adjacent to the buried ashes, on a snatch of ground Peter had purchased a year back. Hortensia had joked at the time that it wasn't big enough to fit a car.

Gary arrived in a white truck. He hooted at the gate, which was unnecessary – there was a perfectly working intercom. He had a beard and eyes so squinting you could hardly see them. Hortensia wondered, with a small sneer, if he could see anything, if his work could be any good, but when he unveiled the stone she stopped – Gary, sun-beaten, leather-skinned Gary, had made something beautiful. The base was thick, and a thin slab projected out from it at an angle, all in white marble. Hortensia was surprised at the thinness of the slab. 'Won't it break?' She was careful to sound disinterested. They were standing in the driveway, looking into the back of the truck. He shook his head. 'Reinforced,' he said. The slab was covered, meticulously, in a fine pattern of black dots, like tar bubbles. Hortensia wanted to run her hands over them (she could almost feel them already, the bumps) but she restrained herself. She found that she liked Gary's design and she was worried that he'd notice. 'Alright,' she said and offered directions but he said he didn't need them – he knew already where the plot of land was.

So much else was happening. It didn't help that Hortensia kept forgetting things. The mortician wanted to know the name of the hospital, the doctor who'd signed the death certificate. It was all written down – why was she asking her? 'I don't know, Cathy-something,' Hortensia had said. 'Dr Cathy Marcus or something like that. Oh, there were many doctors, though. Oh, you mean the one who signed? Marcus . . . or something.'

Hortensia also forgot simple things. She forgot to ask Malachi to make a cutting of the bougainvillea for the vase on the bureau in the hallway. She forgot to tell Bassey, who was the only man large enough to fit anything Peter owned, to go through her husband's things, take whatever he wanted. She forgot that Peter would want her to contact Unilever in Ibadan – who would still be there of the old crowd? Let them know about the death. The so-called regulars. She'd even forgotten to tell Zippy, who had phoned from London, all concerned to find out how Peter was doing. Hortensia felt like an idiot telling her sister, three days after it had happened, that her brother-in-law was dead.

'Oh, my darling, poor thing,' Zippy said, but who was Zippy's pity directed at: her or Peter?

'It'll be okay,' Hortensia said.

'Should I come? I should come. Shouldn't I? You sound so normal, why didn't you call me the minute it happened? I'll come.'

Hortensia let her baby sister carry on for a while, then she used all her powers to persuade Zippy that the funeral was nothing, rather come out for a longer time afterwards, when Hortensia would need the support. It sounded right, even though none of it was true. She listened a bit more to admonitions that were simply a younger version of the ones she'd received from their mother, before telling Zippy there were things she had to attend to, and ringing off.

There'd also been a surprise. No death is complete without one. Hortensia placed her teacup down, taking small joy – a sense of the rightness of things – in the crisp clink-sound the bone china made as she set it on the saucer. A breeze blew up onto the patio and she looked out and noticed that the clouds were threatening rain. Hortensia could hear Bassey preparing dinner. Everything was normal, except that her husband was dead and apparently she was no longer the executor of his will. Someone else was, a someone she now had an appointment with the following day. Hortensia curled her lip; it was involuntary. If she were with company she would fight the urge, fight the way the corners of her mouth just naturally wanted to sink to the ground, but since she was alone she let them go. She picked up her cup again and took a sip of Earl Grey, prepared with Chinese Black Congou tea and not the usual Ceylonese. This small detail made the moment bearable.

Within seconds of meeting the young lawyer, Hortensia knew she didn't much like him.

'Come this way,' Hortensia said to him, noticing by the fluster in his eyes that he'd have preferred niceties before business.

'I'm sorry,' he said as he followed into her study.

'Come, sit down. Sit over there.'

While he took a seat and arranged his briefcase, Hortensia pressed the intercom. 'Bassey. Tea, Mr Marx?'

'I'd prefer coffee, Mrs James, if it's not too much trouble.'

'Black?'

'Thank you.'

She finished her instructions to Bassey and sat on her throne. She wouldn't call it that for anyone else to hear, but it's what she always thought when she lowered her posterior onto the leather. Hortensia smiled and Marx, carelessly, thought she wanted to be friends.

'I am sorry for your loss, Mrs James.'

She tightened her lips, fixed her spectacles to her face and gave her let's-get-to-business look.

'Your husband,' he said, 'was . . . well, I wanted to . . . What I'm trying to—'

Hortensia raised a hand. Bassey knocked.

'Come.'

He was a large man with breasts of his own.

'Set it there. Thank you, Bassey. Never mind, we'll pour ourselves.'

She began again after the click of the door.

'I don't want us to waste time. Apart from being old, I have some meetings to attend. I think you realise that my husband did not inform me of his change to his will. I think you understand what things must have been like between husband and wife for such an action not to be shared.' She pushed her reading glasses down her nose, so she could look at the boy through her mud-brown eyes. She knew people found her eyes quite frightening. He didn't disappoint her. 'Now, what do we need to do? You have the paperwork in that briefcase of yours?'

She sat back, happy with the effect of her speech. She waited as Marx spread the papers on the desk.

'Can I pour?' Hortensia asked.

'Thank you.'

'Let's get on with it.'

'I know you weren't expecting me.' He was recovering.

'When did he make the change?'

'Three or four months back. I can trace the exact date if it matters.'

Hortensia shook her head. Peter had had one last surge of good health, lucidity, before falling into his final hole. He must have done it then.

'I don't need his money by the way. The house is in my name. This isn't about that.'

'Yes, Mrs James. I am aware that you are worth a large sum of money.'

'I don't like to put it that way.'

'Mr James spoke a lot about you.'

Despite herself, Hortensia was interested. What might Peter have said? She had no notion. But she didn't ask for Marx to expand and he didn't seem to think there was any more to say on the matter. He placed a file on the table.

'Well, as you now know, he made me the executor of his will.'

'Did he take me off as a beneficiary?'

'Oh no, you're still a beneficiary.' He was fidgeting; raised his cup but put it back down.

'Is something wrong? With your coffee?'

'It's hot.'

'I see.'

He cleared his throat. 'I really don't—'

'Mr Marx, please proceed. I don't have all day.'

'You are still a beneficiary. Just not the primary one.'

Marx kept his head down. He managed a sip of his coffee, it brought colour back to his face.

'So who's the primary one, then? Did he go and leave his money to the hunting club? Idiot, I told him not to be foolish.'

'Well, actually, Mrs James, there's another beneficiary – a person.'

Hortensia waited.

'I'm really sorry for the difficulty of the situation.'

'Mr Marx, I don't know you that well and you obviously don't know me. This, I assure you, is not difficult.'

'Yes, Mrs James. The other beneficiary, you see, is daughter to Mr James, so he informed me, and she goes by the name of Esme.'

He made himself busy, rifled unnecessarily through the papers in front of him.

Hortensia sat back in her chair. She needed a few moments; she held her face. Always hold your face – she usually knew how to. But this time something rippled, she felt the twitch in her right cheek, put her hand there to steady it. There was confusion first, then anger. Betrayal a close third.

'I see.' She smiled at Marx. 'I understand. Well, okay,' she said, more to herself than to the lawyer. 'Well, we didn't really have to meet for this. You could have sent me an email.'

Marx seemed unsure whether to return the smile. He chose not to, went on to explain the details. Hortensia had to get in touch with Esme, in fact meet with her. The will 'expressly' stated that no one was to notify Esme of her inheritance except Hortensia. Peter's trickery.

'Where's the girl?'

'She's an adult, Mrs James. Forty-nine years old, by Mr James's calculations. She lives in England. The minute you contact her, arrangements have been made for a ticket, accommodation, and so on.'

Like a play-date, Hortensia thought.

The rest of the meeting was dotted lines to sign upon and corners of pages to initial. Perhaps because of the intimacy of leaning over paperwork, or the sense of familiarity brought by the sharing of bad or, as he put it, difficult news, Mr Marx, at one point, loosened up enough to comment, 'She'll be one rich woman, that's for sure.'

Hortensia thought this was crude of him. She'd so far been nice to him, which is to say she hadn't been unpleasant. She wished she could take back her courtesies; in fact if she had had a weapon, she would have struck him. Except that the person, in that moment, she really wanted to hurt – to kill – was Peter and it pained her greatly that he was already dead.

Peter hadn't been religious, but he'd had religious affectations Hortensia had never been able to fully decipher. He'd whistle 'Morning Has Broken' and then sing it, but get the words wrong, the song disappearing down his throat. He played golf on Sundays but wanted carols at Christmas. And now he dies and asks for a church.

Hortensia stood at the entrance of the church. A Land Rover crunched over the gravel and parked, irreverently Hortensia thought, beside the empty hearse.

The priest touched her on the shoulder. 'Let me go and prepare,' she said and Hortensia listened to her shuffle up the aisle. The priest, despite having a youthful cherubic face, had a laboured gait and Hortensia found it painful to watch her; she somehow felt guilty, as if it were her fault.

A stooped man and plump woman got out of the parked car and walked towards the entrance. The woman had the kind of fat on her body that had become familiar and would never leave. She looked comfortable. Hortensia studied them from behind her dark glasses and extended a hand when they came within reach.

'Our deepest condolences.'

She nodded because there was nothing to say. Hortensia had never met them before. They stood there for a few awkward seconds and then walked on past her into the empty nave. She imagined they would find somewhere to sit.

Five more people arrived. A woman who said Peter had been her biggest client, a hedge-fund-looking woman, but Hortensia was too pissed off to ask.

'I love Simon's Town,' the spike-heeled woman said, looking back towards the avenue of trees along the road that led to the church.

In place of condolences the woman spoke of her beautiful drive from Hout Bay, and Hortensia felt her mood swing, felt herself become a widow who required pity for the loss of her beloved and resented this woman who offered none.

There came an elderly couple who claimed Peter was the best golfer in their club. The man had also hunted with Peter, when Peter was still hunting, and he told anecdotes of little bokkies being dondered, which made the priest, who had returned to Hortensia's side, give him a pleading look.

A man arrived late, after everyone including Hortensia had already sat down. At the end of the short saccharine service, while everyone else rose, he stayed sitting on the hard wood pew at the back for a few extra moments. Hortensia had been sitting too and when, at the end, she stood and walked past him, something in the way the man was holding his face with his eyes closed made her realise that he was praying.

She walked to the back of the church, where a stretch of snacks looked about to go to waste, and startled to find her neighbour's face staring at her.

'Marion, what are you doing here?'

'I'm sorry about Peter. I wanted to pay my respects.'

She wanted to gloat. Hortensia was calculating how to walk past this nasty woman, perhaps walk to the tea table and bite into a banana muffin. She squeezed her shoulders in, as Marion took a step closer to her.

'I really am sorry.'

Hortensia, from the corner of her eye, noticed the praying-man rise and walk out of the church. She felt bolstered; he'd prayed a prayer, perhaps she could float on the wings of whatever blessings he'd bargained for.

'Marion—'

'I know, I know. We're not friends.' Marion looked around as if expecting a chorus of agreement, but no one was paying them any attention. The cherub was inspecting a long koeksister and the husband-and-wife golfers appeared to be arguing. 'I just thought to come. I just . . . I just thought to come.' She raised her hands, then collapsed them to her sides, an exaggerated shrug.

'Please, Marion. Let me get past.'

Marion, her face glum, shifted aside and Hortensia went in search of a muffin.

After the church, all the mourners (except Marion, Hortensia noted with relief) went to Peter's patch of ground where the tombstone stood waiting. The ashes, collected in a simple wooden box, were placed into a hole. And, even though she could feel the tears gathering in the corners of her eyes, when a wiry man began shovelling the sand, there was also a part of Hortensia that wanted to tell him to stand back so she could spit.

FIVE

At a certain point, after it had started, Hortensia knew. She didn't agonise over whether she was wrong, whether she was misjudging her husband, shouldn't she give him the benefit of the doubt, or anything like that. She simply knew, from a smell, from a frown or a smile that hung out of place.

By that time they'd been in Nigeria for five years. Hortensia had become well studied in Peter's movements around the house on his return from work. She had practically memorised the number of steps it took him to get from the front door to the guest bathroom. The seconds it took to relieve himself. The running tap. And then to his study; the faint smell of a cigarette. Only after that would he seek her out in the living room.

'Have a good day?' he'd ask, pecking her on the cheek.

How long had he been coming home that way? When had she become the sort of wife you needed to have a pee and smoke before you could face her?

The lies followed, the way one thing necessitates another. Important office meetings that ran on till night-time, weekend-long conferences. Hortensia sometimes despaired that her husband was not more creative.

Sometimes he came home and she had already turned

off the bedroom lights, lain down, awake. She counted his steps, tracked how he wound through the house. On the nights when he figured she was asleep, his movements were different; he wasn't pressed to use the toilet, didn't really need to calm his nerves with a cigarette. Instead it was a quick visit to the lounge, a few moments of silence as he reached the carpet. He often, she surmised, stood by the silver tray placed on the teak sideboard, where the housekeeper left the mail. If she strained, if she raised her head off the pillow, Hortensia would hear the tear of paper as he ran the letter-opener through. If it wasn't a letter from his mother, it was otherwise just some rubbish mail from England. Hortensia wondered what her mother-in-law wrote in that slanted cursive with its flourish, indicative of anyone literate born in the early twentieth century. Did she ever tell her son that she missed him? Did she ask after Hortensia, maybe suggest – but never outright – the magic of new life, the glisten it can give a marriage? Would she know, would she guess that things were bad, that her son was bored, or maybe even in love with someone else?

After a few more minutes Hortensia would sense her husband's presence before he actually entered their room. Then the weight of him on the bed. No part of their bodies touched. Once she was certain that Peter was asleep, Hortensia would get up to clean the bathtub.

The bathtub had proved useful. When they'd first moved in she'd thrown doubt at the cast-iron tub, quaint but perpetually stained. The first night after she'd guessed a third person was now present in her marriage, Hortensia had been unable to lie still, next to Peter in their bed.

Her heart pounded as if she was running a marathon. But instead of scrolling through in her mind who it could possibly be, her thoughts alighted on the stains – cumulus and menacing – unchanged all these years after much effort from the housekeeper. Hortensia got up, certain the woman simply hadn't tried hard enough. On her knees in the bathroom she found the action of scrubbing tight and mechanical, she liked the music of her breathing and the scrape of bristles against weathered enamel. Despite no real change in the appearance of the blemishes, Hortensia convinced herself that her scrubbing was working, that the stains were slowly disappearing. It became her project. If he heard her, Peter didn't mention it. The exercise was precisely what she needed to be able to hit the pillow and die into sleep; lying awake beside him had become intolerable.

Some nights if, after the tub, Hortensia was not tired enough, she swabbed at the sink, polished the mirror, mopped the tiles. Their bathroom became the cleanest in the house. And if the physical exhaustion of housework still wasn't good enough, Hortensia would attempt to expend her mind. She'd go into her study and sit at her desk. Some of her most successful designs happened after 1 a.m., as if the condition for good design was darkness, fatigue and morose solitude. If that were so, though, it would have been a new insight for Hortensia. A student at Bailer's Design College, she had always needed to work in daylight – sunlight in fact. A thing she'd realised, on arriving in Brighton fresh from Bridgetown, young and determined, would be in short supply, despite the misleading name of her new town.

The name would explain itself over time, but the weather would remain unimpressive.

The only other non-British student in Hortensia's class was a girl named Kehinde. She was younger than average, sixteen, but full of talent and chutzpah. It was known by the students that Kehinde was from Nigeria but, for the four years of study, she denied it, referred to herself as a Startian, from an unknown unnameable planet. She answered only to the name K, rather than the mispronounced (deliberate or not) versions of her name that her classmates called her. Although Hortensia had not been friends with K, they'd had one honest conversation. Hortensia found herself alone with K one evening in the workshop. A young fashion designer was teaching at Bailer's for a term. He had caused some excitement in Florence, at one of the infamous Giorgini soirées, with what he called 'capes and clutches'. At Bailer's he encouraged the students to see textile design and fashion as one-and-the-same thing. He instructed them in pattern-making. Hortensia enjoyed the sewing machine, she liked the force of the pedal (the power of that) and steadying the needle, with her right hand on the balance wheel. She paused in her concentration.

'Why do you lie?' Hortensia asked.

'About?' Kehinde didn't look up from cutting; she'd marked out the borders of the garment in white chalk.

'Where you're from. Are you ashamed?' It had been boiling in Hortensia for a while now. They were both teased endlessly, Hortensia for being Barbadian, for singing when she spoke, for rounding words in a way that amused her classmates, for being dark; but mostly they spurned her for being a good designer, for the audacity of that.

'I'm not ashamed. I just thought that would be the easiest way.'

'To what?'

'To give them something to muck about with.'

K's strategy had puzzled Hortensia, who'd never even considered bringing a strategy with her to Brighton – perhaps a failure of her otherwise-robust imagination. On confirmation that she'd received the coveted British Council Art Scholarship (her teacher had practically browbeaten her into making an application), she'd celebrated with Zippy, enjoyed the proud gaze of her father, Kwittel, and endured a litany of cautions from her mother, Eda. It was really one cautionary remark repeated in various forms – Be careful. Eda, ever tightly wound to the possibility of coming troubles, predicting Armageddon, emboldened by the Bible, King James Version, whose first testament she had put to memory, with its smiting and endless tribulations. Hortensia had ignored her mother's warnings, but soon, arriving unprepared for battle, regretted this. Regardless, she wrote simple letters home and received simple ones back. Eda's shaky writing dominated the square pages. Hortensia wrote back in black, all-capital letters (she'd discovered a great capacity for penmanship), and told of a beach that wasn't a beach, not the sea baths to which she was accustomed. Despite Eda's repeated 'Are you alrights?', Hortensia left out stories of what she called 'the freeze'. Hard stares from fellow students and lecturers alike; stares from people who looked through you, not at you; stares intent on disappearing you; and stares you fought by making yourself solid. People found it civilised to imitate the sound of a chimpanzee whenever they passed Hortensia or K in the corridors. They were not the first black students to ever attend Bailer's and yet it seemed a riddle had to be solved each time a black person presented at the college. A boy once asked Hortensia how her brother was. I don't have a brother, Hortensia replied. Oh, but you do, here – the golliwog on the Robertson strawberry-jam jar.

In 1950, a year after Hortensia arrived at Bailer's, the rest of the Braithwaites boarded a ship, the *Spig-Noose* docked at Dover and they caught a coach to Waterloo Station. An older cousin of Kwittel's, Leroy, had completed his service with the Carib Regiment; he'd been stationed in Italy, saw no action, but had a heart attack all the same (apparently hereditary); he'd chosen to stay on in England and, with Hortensia already in university, had encouraged Kwittel to bring himself and the rest of his family out. Leroy had offered London as a promise of better, and Kwittel had sold this to his sceptical wife. A few weeks after arriving in London, Kwittel found work as a postman. Hortensia's classmates managed to divine this piece of information about her life. People who thought themselves funny asked her: if the black postman delivers the mail at night, wouldn't it be blackmail? It was one of the few stings that actually hurt. Hortensia's father was not only the closest thing she had to a best friend, but he was also the best person she knew in the entire world.

Kwittel Braithwaite had two furrows that ran on either side of the bridge of his nose. When his daughters, Hortensia and Zephyr, were young they liked to feel those furrows with their small spongy fingers. The grooves had formed over many years of studying, his wife liked to say, a tinge of awe in her voice. The wire spectacles that had been instrumental in creating this feature were the same ones Hortensia tried to describe decades later, to an assistant in the front room of her optician's in Cape Town.

If her relationship with her father was filled with admiration, Hortensia's relationship with her mother was ruled by restraint. The tension came from Eda's need to dominate, and Hortensia's to resist. Hortensia thought of her relationship with her mother as being governed by a repulsive force that sat between them and kept them, at any given time, at least a hundred centimetres apart. If, by some accident, they came any closer or even touched, it was only for seconds and then they glanced apart like two similarly charged black magnets.

They hadn't always been that way. Before the age of twelve, things had been different. But then they had one of their many arguments. It started as something quite regular. Eda was plaiting her daughter's hair and Hortensia was sitting between Eda's thighs, wincing and complaining about the style her mother was fixing. Hortensia, who felt she had a better understanding of what suited her and what didn't, wanted something different and she was telling her mother so. Occasionally she got a knock on her head for twisting and complaining too much. Perhaps that day she had received one too many knocks, because something settled in her, some kind of resolve. When Eda was done and released the child from between her bony tight-lock thighs, Hortensia excused herself to the room she shared with Zippy. When it was time to prepare food and Hortensia was called, there was suddenly a lot of screaming. That evening there was no dinner.

Hortensia had not only undone the plaits her mother had prepared, she'd found a pair of scissors to cut the hair as short as possible. Then, still unsatisfied, she'd sought out her father's blade and managed not to draw even a spot of blood, but achieve a soft, smooth and very close shave. She looked, Eda shouted, like some bug-eyed alien and she threatened to swat the thing back into outer space. Hortensia was saved by her father who, she suspected, would forever lose some of his wife's affection for having shielded her from Eda, for siding with her. That evening war was declared. Hortensia noticed that Eda had become injured with a wound that would never heal. A wound that even after many years, despite Hortensia's own disappointment in her marriage (a sadness she never managed to hide from her mother), would prevent Eda from offering her eldest daughter – her precious person – comfort.

Soon after graduating from the Bailer's Design College, Hortensia travelled from Brighton up to London. It was 1953. She moved in with her mother and Zippy in Holloway.

Defeated by cancer, Hortensia's father had passed away one year before and it felt strange to be living without him. To not see him beneath a lamp, a book in hand. He'd never completed high school, but treasured history and taught himself much of what there was to know about the world. Many evenings were spent instilling the same curiosity in his daughters. Paramount to him was teaching them from where they came; in this way he taught them pride.

Before he died, Kwittel admitted to his wife that he had been sick before they boarded ship. In fact he knew he was dying but thought this rush northwards, via the

Atlantic Ocean, would be good for his family. And when he was dying and Eda mentioned going home, he made it clear to her that he wanted to be buried in England. He was being devious; he knew his remains in London would ensure Eda stayed put, ensure Zippy could finish school and make something of herself. He knew superstitious Eda, itching to go home as she was, would never dare leave his grave to be tended to by strangers.

He died quickly and Eda bore his death as if she'd read of its coming in the clouds. She infected her daughters with her subdued grieving, and none of the three ever fully recovered from the sombre shadow Kwittel's death cast.

The home at Holloway was two rooms. Eda and the other residents of the house all cooked on the landing and shared the bathroom facilities. At night Hortensia sat, missed her father and suffered her mother, who was proud of her daughter but concerned about her marriageability. Zippy was fourteen years old, the sisters were not quite friends, but there was conviviality and genuine warmth between them; a fierce sense of protection from Hortensia and a persistent curiosity from Zippy. She never tired of rifling through Hortensia's drawings.

'I like this one.' Zippy pointed to a sketch of a series of chairs.

'You call the number I give you?' Eda asked, looking up from her ironing. She ran a small laundry and ironing business from home. Her face was worn, her lips always downturned since her husband's death. She also drove trains for London Transport.

'You look tired, Mama.'

'You call?'

'No. Not yet.'

'Well . . . call. The boy waiting.'

Hortensia sighed.

'And this one.' Zippy had a special ability to zone out their mother's nagging, perhaps, Hortensia thought, because the nagging was seldom directed at her. She watched her sister flick through her sketchbook.

'I'm going to start selling my own designs,' Hortensia said, looking at Zippy although the statement was intended for Eda. She'd started getting her documents together for the registration of House of Braithwaite.

'Your own designs?' Eda asked, lifting the iron and taking a moment to glance at her firstborn.

'Yes.'

What Hortensia didn't tell Eda was that she had no need to call 'the boy' Eda was trying to fix her up with. Instead, she and Peter were in the last stages of their courtship. He had asked for her hand in marriage and she'd said yes.

They had been courting in secret for three years. Later, when Peter would tease Hortensia for her love of beautiful things, what he couldn't have known was that he'd been that for her once too – a beautiful thing, perfect and in need of nothing. The year they met, Hortensia's first summer in England, Peter was tutoring in Pure Mathematics and Statistics at Croydon College. Hortensia was on vacation from design school. Mr List, the same enthusiastic teacher that had introduced fashion to Bailer's, had noticed Hortensia's talent and invited her to join him as his assistant.

He ran a summer pattern-making class at Croydon College. Accustomed to being received coolly at Bailer's, the young teacher's interest in her work had surprised Hortensia. She accepted the offer, keen for the extra money. She moved in with her Uncle Leroy. Her mother sent a letter with the details of the family's imminent arrival.

Within days of starting her job at Croydon, Hortensia had observed Peter from afar; he was distinctly tall and difficult to miss. Up close one day in the cafeteria, Hortensia saw that he had freckles on his face, they were dark brown and she found them pleasant. She smiled at him and he stammered a greeting.

Almost on arrival Eda found something to worry about. She didn't like the hours Hortensia was keeping, the journey into Croydon. She said as much to Hortensia who, as usual, didn't pay her any mind. And as if danger follows worry, one night, after staying late in Croydon to enjoy a drink with some of the students, Hortensia began her journey home. She was dressed in high heels, which was unusual despite her short stature. She wobbled in the heels, walked slowly, shivered from the cold (how could this be summer?). One came up on her left and another on her right. A hand pressed against her back meant someone was behind her too. Teddy boys were always spoken of but, up till then, she'd never encountered any. In the early days of their marriage, when there was still laughter, Hortensia would claim she had had all three boys on their backs by the time Peter showed up. He'd respond by saying, 'If on their backs means standing with their fists jabbing the air, then yes.'

They were boys, though, and whether due to Peter's

size or Hortensia's curses (she reined them in with screeches, spitting and raising her left hand, fingers spread, for effect), the hooligans seemed to catch a fright and eventually ran off. Peter asked if he could walk with her and Hortensia told him she'd be fine. It's not you I'm worried about, he said. He grinned and shone all his teeth at her. This wide smile struck her as such a precious thing. She'd never fallen in love before.

SIX

There came a time when Hortensia did wonder who the person was. She played a game, thought up faces, dreamed them. There were moments where she thought very clearly that if for any reason she found the woman and was left alone with her, she would kill her. Then there were days she felt she had to meet, speak and reason with her, find her number in Peter's book. But of course there was no such book. So it seemed natural, one day, to follow him. And it seemed sensible to get a disguise, so he didn't notice that he was being followed. She would later hide the camouflage in the storeroom off the kitchen – a place she knew Peter would never look.

The woman was small and young. She wore strappy heels but still had to raise herself onto the tips of her toes to greet Peter with a drawn-out kiss. Her hair, curls of black, was so shiny Hortensia wondered if it wasn't a wig.

She had a face that Hortensia had never seen before, not even at the Staff Club. She could be a new employee flown in, but the company had very few women engineers. Maybe a secretary?

Peter and the woman began walking and Hortensia walked behind them. Banga market was at its most crowded at midday. It was one of the older markets of Ibadan and, for some reason unknown to Hortensia, was unpopular with the expatriate community. The two ducked down an alley between a row of stalls and Hortensia followed, side-stepping litter and puddles from a short spray of rain. If it wasn't for the clang of the grinders gnawing away at the skinned beans and the incessant call of traders, Hortensia thought she would be able to hear what they were speaking about. She felt brave. It helped that she blended in and they – oyinbos – were conspicuous. She wore scuffed Nikes and a dark-green tracksuit, but none of that mattered because she'd covered the whole thing in a black burkha.

A boy clutching a chicken pushed past Hortensia; he apologised but didn't bother to turn around. They entered the wet-food section of the market. The woman pointed at a tray of cow hooves and Peter laughed at something she'd said.

'Alhaja,' a trader with peppers said to Hortensia. 'Èwo lè fẹ́?'

Hortensia shook her head.

The smells of Banga pervaded everything. Akara balls frying in oil, the air heavy with burnt residue; singed hair off a goat's skin; wet chicken feathers. Nothing interested them, Peter and the woman, except each other and wher-ever it was they were bound for. They didn't stop at any of the stalls, pressing on through the crowds. When the path narrowed, Peter, his spindly frame, walked behind the woman, his hand on the small of her back. Where the path opened up again they walked side by side and held hands. They turned a corner and the heavy base-notes of Banga receded; replaced by the innocuous scent of peeled oranges. The woman stopped to admire a tray of them, the fine-lined pattern left from the blade used to cut the skin away. Hortensia paused by the lady selling gari, rice and beans, two stalls away from the orange-seller.

'Kí lẹ fẹ́, Mà?'

Hortensia shook her head. They were close enough that she was worried that, if she spoke, Peter would hear, recognise her voice, turn around. She shook her head again at the trader's furrowed brow, but stayed examining the dry goods.

'Which one do you like?' the trader pressed further, assuming the problem to be one of language.

'No. Thank you,' Hortensia blurted, panicked.

But Peter was distracted. Oranges forgotten, he was now bent forward, his ear near the woman's mouth as she whispered something. His hand was on her neck, his thumb pressed just beneath where her earring dangled. He smoothed down her hair, which bounced and twirled along her back. Hortensia's eyes stung, grew hot and cloudy, so she couldn't see a passing trader proffering up her okros and freshly shelled kobiowus of egusi. Her knees were weak and to avoid falling down she leaned against one of the wooden poles supporting the stall.

'Ẹ pẹ̀lẹ́, Mummy. Are you okay?'

Hortensia blinked. Peter had said something funny. The woman stretched her head back and her mouth widened, her lips, the red of her tongue. He said something again and reached for her. She yelped, swung out of his grasp, upsetting a neat arrangement of plump tomatoes.

'Ah-ah! Careful now,' the trader said, then turned to

mumblings in Yoruba to finish her insult. She bent to collect the muddied produce.

The admonition went unnoticed. The game of catch between the two continued, their tight little dance.

Hortensia moved to the side of the dirt road, watching. Two motorcycles went past. A man pulled a wheelbarrow stacked with white bottles and a gramophone on repeat, announcing the cures, the potions and miracles. Someone bumped Hortensia from behind, an old man on a bicycle with rubber piled up behind him.

'Ẹ má bìnu. Ẹ pèlé.'

She was unhurt, assured him of this.

When Hortensia looked again, Peter had caught the woman. Their chests, their bodies heaved from the exertions. She caught her breath. He put the tips of his fingers on either side of her face, along the sharp line of her jaw, and he tilted her face upwards; she licked her lips and he used the back of his hands to tickle them. Hortensia wondered what it felt like, the hard metal on his ring-finger moving along the soft wet skin.

An old woman sat watching, a wrapper around her waist, her dry breasts hanging, weary from use. She took a rag to her neck, damp with sweat. Swatted a fly. Peter and the girl stood kissing, oblivious as only white lovers in Banga market could be. 'Aṣẹẁó!' the old woman hissed. 'Shio!'

In the weeks after Peter's death, wondering about some child somewhere called Esme, Hortensia came to the realisation that the quality of her life would have benefited greatly from more anger and less resentment. Resentment was different from anger. Anger was like a dragon, burning other things. Resentment burned a hole in your stomach, burned your insides.

Peter and his lover had made a baby. How? Hortensia asked herself stupidly. When?

At night the house seemed to know there was one less person in it. Hortensia couldn't sleep. Since Peter's death she'd returned to their bed, which she'd vacated when his disease started taking up so much room. The sick and their medicines require surface area; when death rounded the corner, she demanded a lot of space. Being back in the bed was strange, back on her side of the bed, deferring now to a ghost. A ghost so real she was unable even to fling her leg across the middle of the bed, lie on his side. It didn't feel right.

After turning several times to find an elusive comfortable position, Hortensia rose and attacked the pile of books by the bed. She'd moved the pile from the guest room and installed it back here, where she would sleep till she died. Towards the bottom of the pile were the design tomes. There was a stash of thick magazines, the page corners curling. Peter had once chided her for worshipping magazines with not one human on any page. Even the advertisements relied on images of things. Beautiful things, she'd retorted. And there was nothing wrong with that.

She fingered the spine of her beloved textbook. Hefting it out toppled the pile. The book sat like a boulder in her lap. She scanned the pages. The sweet rapture of a perfectly replicated pattern, the simple beauty of a design that was complete, that had everything already, too much and too little of nothing.

It had been days since Hortensia had been up to the Koppie. It felt good to stand high and look down. However, coming back, along Katterijn Avenue, her mood soured. There was Marion, puffing towards her with that damned dog at her heels.

'I need to speak with you.'

'What?' Hortensia folded her arms.

Spring was still almost a month away but the days were longer, the time between rains seemed to be lengthening. Marion was showing off the results of a recent trip to her hairdresser. 'What's that truck doing there?'

Hortensia looked over to where Marion was pointing. A builder's truck was parked just by No.10.

'It's parked.'

'I know that. Don't play with me, Hortensia.'

'Marion, I am not in the mood. My husband is newly dead, I'm in mourning.'

Marion said nothing.

'The truck is there because I contracted it to be. I have a meeting, in fact, and would rather not be late.'

'You're doing some work on . . . the house?'

'Not that it's any concern of yours.'

'Well, you ought to have let us know at least. The committee. Good faith.'

'Marion, there is no such rule. And you may not realise

it, but Katterijn is not a block of flats and you are not the chairperson of the body corporate. That house is mine and, yes, I'm making some . . . improvements.'

Happy to have landed a lasting blow, Hortensia side-stepped the woman and her mutt.

'What sort of improvements?' Marion called after her.

'Obvious ones,' Hortensia responded.

The truck was there because it was a welcome distraction, a sensible alternative to thinking about Peter and this child.

Initially, especially when Hortensia had not yet realised that No. 10 was designed by Marion, she viewed the house favourably, or at least she thought it acceptable. It cost an obscene amount of money, but they had that much and many times more. Copious interior and exterior pictures had been sent to Ibadan by the estate agents. There were of course permits to apply for and papers to sign – whenever are there not? They signed them, they came. And soon enough Hortensia heard through the Katterijn ramble of gossip that No. 10 had been Marion's first-ever design. Apparently Marion had been vying to own it herself. This explained the kind of reception Hortensia had received from Marion when they first arrived.

It was a hot day and the walk up the Koppie had left her thirsty. Hortensia chatted briefly to the builder, explaining her ideas. After she left, Hortensia sat in her study and asked Bassey to bring her a glass of ice cubes. She liked to dip her fingertips in and run them along her temple.

The heat was welcome, though, as was the lack of rain. The weather was encouraging for the works that were about to commence. The fewer rain-days, the better. No delays, no gaps leaving room for all the thoughts she was trying to keep at bay. The building works were to be Hortensia's opium. To this end, ever since the idea had occurred to her, she'd been busy with it. Knocking down walls would mean new plaster. The chore of trying to match a new can of paint to the existing was hopeless. So new paint it was. A few sheets of wallpaper for special places. She took the samples to bed. During the day Hortensia made labelled and dimensioned sketches for the contractors. Today she was preparing a work schedule; it gave no consideration to rain-days.

She sat back in her chair, looking over the drawings she had made, her plan showing exactly what needed doing.

There were certain problems with the design of No. 10. Not an infinite number. In fact just one problem repeated several times, at least according to Hortensia, and she regarded her own grasp of design with unwavering certainty. No. 10 had many windows onto things that Hortensia didn't think needed seeing, and none onto the things she thought were important to notice.

She would direct the builders to start with the bricking-up of certain windows, two specifically. One, in the lounge, looked out onto Katterijn Avenue, but what was the use of that? And the second in the upstairs guest bedroom looked appropriately towards the vineyards but, by just a few centimetres, avoided the view of the old Katterijn well.

After the bricking-up, there were three windows Hortensia wanted added to her home. The first was a view, from her kitchen, into the garden. The second a window one could look through as you climbed the staircase, to notice the old church and its cemetery. And lastly she wanted a view of the Koppie from her study desk.

And while she was at it, why not put in a pool? Hortensia, despite being born on an island, did not much care for water. No, the addition of a pool was to tip the insult to Marion and her design from red to flaming.

Amidst the preparations, Marx called. Two of his gently prodding emails had landed in Hortensia's inbox before she trained her Gmail to relegate them to Spam. Now he'd tracked her down. Perhaps Mrs James had not quite understood her duties as per the will, he'd begun in a tone that made Hortensia want to swat him. She'd understood perfectly. Had she contacted Esme? No.

He'd sighed. He sounded older on the phone.

'Mrs James, I appreciate this is . . . all rather strange. I'll tell you, it's certainly one of the strangest wills I've ever handled.'

Strange was the right word. A man who had spent the last year of his life immobile and mute suddenly had a voice, clear instructions, power – all from the grave.

'Are you there, Mrs James?'

'Not for long, I hope.'

'I appreciate—'

'I know, you said that already.'

He sighed again. Hortensia was accustomed to being sighed at.

'I must go, Mr Marx.'

'Will you be contacting Esme? The thing is, there are implications.'

'You made that perfectly clear.'

After her first meeting with Marx and on studying the paperwork, Hortensia had concluded that Peter had drawn up this last will and testament to play some sort of game. She couldn't quite work it out, but hated him for it all the same. Not only was his will his means of breaking it to his wife that he was a father, but he'd clearly stipulated that Esme was not to be contacted by anyone but Hortensia. Peter had apparently never revealed himself to his daughter in life, and it was Hortensia who was to now communicate to this person who her father was, and so on. His estate would then be apportioned out in varying fractions to herself, Esme, a distant cousin in Sussex, the damned hunting club and a constellation of charities. But he hadn't stopped there. If Hortensia did not contact Esme, her inaction would render his will invalid. He would be regarded as dying intestate (at this point Marx had elucidated her on the meaning) and the South African Law of Succession would proceed. After paying whatever debts he had, the law would divide his remaining estate amongst his beneficiaries, of which Esme, having never been legally recognised, was not one.

'The implications are that the girl will get none of his money.'

'Mrs James, I don't assume to counsel you on what is good and proper, but—'

'Thank you for that, Mr Marx. For not assuming. If that's all.'

'I will be in contact, Mrs James. We shouldn't delay. The whole process can be quite lengthy. I'd prefer to really get going with this. You need to start, though, I cannot make any moves until Ms Esme is notified. I hope you understand this?'

Hortensia explained to Bassey: if Marx calls, take a message.

On the appointed day, Hortensia waited on the kerb for the works to start. An excitement caught her, a fever of energy. Marion too was about. Hortensia nodded a greeting that was met with a scowl. The builder, a woman with no eyebrows and the name Hannie, arrived and stood with Hortensia for a few minutes. They compared schedules, then Hannie went inside to prepare, her workers following. The brick delivery truck arrived and parked. Hannie came back outside and had a brief conversation with the driver. Hortensia, standing close by, had the sense not to attempt to understand what was being said – Afrikaans (apparently a simple language to learn) had always eluded her. Not that she'd tried much. While they talked Hortensia walked up to the truck to study the crane used for lifting the pallets of bricks. Hannie went back to her workers.

Funny how many bricks such a small job involves, Hortensia thought as the operator cranked the crane to start depositing the bricks by the roadside. Then, much later when she woke up in hospital, she had to retrace the events to make sense of the pain in her leg.

She didn't like thinking of herself sprawled on the Katterijn Avenue pavement, Widow James Knocked Down by Delinquent Crane. But most of all she hated the piece of news she was given by the nurse. That not only had she been knocked unconscious, the fall further damaging her already-weak leg, but the damned crane that had caused all this had also swung a blow at No. 12. Part of the front of her neighbour's precious home was in rubble. Hortensia had once heard Marion complain that the façade of her home was too near the street – might she now take some comfort in having been right?

Agnes had a piece of debris glance off her cheek and was stitched up. Marion, who had been in the back garden at the time, had fainted from the turmoil but had, otherwise, been uninjured.

The Constantinople Private Hospital staff didn't take long to fear Hortensia. She'd arrived at the hospital on a stretcher but, on waking, had immediately managed to insult the paramedic. Within hours she was in theatre. The brakes of the truck had failed, or perhaps they had not been fully engaged. The truck had slid down the gentle slope and Hortensia, this yellow mass coming towards her, had scrambled and fallen. The machine had continued careening, made twigs of Marion's fence and jammed into her home, the crane arm pivoting and slapping into the façade. Hortensia had broken a femur. She also had several gashes, the biggest of which was on the side of her head, above an eyebrow – it would leave a scar and a particular sensation of a headache approaching.

After the operation the surgeon explained that she'd performed an open-reduction internal fixation, words that meant nothing to Hortensia. Fancy word for a pin, she presumed, but she didn't care enough to confirm. She liked the part of the explanation that promised quick mobility. She didn't so much appreciate the 'person of your age' comment, which was used to explain the lack of a cast; it would be too heavy for her, impede mobility, and so on. They'd given her a minimum of twelve weeks for the bone to heal.

The crane-driver was a man who hadn't quite grasped what it meant to apologise. He visited Hortensia in hospital and, in a clipped English accent, spoke about the distractions of the day, the glare in his eye, massive oak trees with branches that should have been trimmed; he mentioned the faulty machine and only then did it dawn on Hortensia, as she reminded herself that a workman never blames his tools, that she was being awarded an apology. Except it lacked the one thing all apologies require in order to be called such – an admission of guilt.

As Hortensia listened and silently critiqued the poor job the crane-driver was doing, a sick feeling reminded her that she also had an apology to make. If Hortensia James hated anything, it was needing to apologise. She could barely remember a time when she'd had to. For a few seconds this pain surmounted the agony of her broken limb.

Sleep in the hospital was fitful. Hortensia regarded hospitals with suspicion. Her left leg was a throbbing mess. She opened her eyes and grimaced.

'Ah, you're up,' the nurse said, shutting the door behind her.

'I wasn't sleeping. My eyes were closed.'

Hortensia could smell the odour of superiority when in the company of nurses or doctors. After three days under the observation of such people she wanted to go home.

The nurse wavered at the door. 'There's the matter of a care-nurse, Ma'am.'

Hortensia stiffened and looked in the nurse's direction. 'No. Thank you.'

'Doctor is coming to see you before you leave. She did ask that I arrange for a care-nurse, Ma'am.'

'I. Said. No.'

The nurse waited outside Hortensia's room while the doctor entered and attempted, with her best bedside manners, to convince Hortensia about the necessity for a day-nurse. At Hortensia's age it was too dangerous not to have someone qualified observe the healing process, to guard against gangrene.

'How long have you been doing this?' Hortensia asked into the silence that took over the conversation.

'I completed my internship two years ago.'

Hortensia rolled her eyes. 'I meant this.' She waved her hand. 'Forcing nurses on people.'

'I don't understand the question.'

'I'm old, not incapable. You've assumed I can't care for myself. How long have you been ramming this assault onto unsuspecting patients? I do not want your miserable spying nurses in my home. I've met them already and I don't want them. If I am to have a nurse, I will order one myself.'

The doctor opened her mouth to speak but the words stuck to her tongue.

'Now, please let my driver know that I am ready,' Hortensia directed, meaning, to anyone who could over-hear, that the interaction was over.

On departure she opted for the motorised wheelchair, mentally arranging that she would now occupy the east-facing study on the ground floor, at least until after the eight weeks the doctor supposed it might take her to climb stairs again. On the drive home, ignoring the mountain as well as the beggars, Hortensia rearranged the furniture in her study; she placed the Imbuia four-poster bed where the sun could reach it. She moved the writing bureau where the curtains would shield her laptop from the glare. She would buy another bar fridge. She wondered if she'd left the window to her study open, if the room would be freshened by crisp air or cloistered when she wheeled herself in. Maybe she would move some of the books into the hallway, use the glass cabinet that had stood empty since she'd donated the porcelain lamps, acquired at a Turkish auction, to St Winifred's Girls' High School. Hortensia had always adored the antique lamps, until she walked past them weeks ago and, inexplicably, experienced deep offence at the crudeness of their design. That was old age, Hortensia thought, drawing her attention back to the scene around her as the driver made a jerky turn onto Katterijn Avenue. Then, pulling up the driveway, regret flooded in as Hortensia realised she'd spend the next few weeks staring at the egg-cracks in a fresco she hadn't got around to restoring. For the second time that week the circumstances surrounding the injury were more upsetting than the injury itself.

SEVEN

'Am I dead?' Marion asked the glare of light she could just make out through squinted eyes.

'Marion Agostino, can you hear me?'

'I'm not dead.' She couldn't keep the disappointment from her voice. Her head hurt. There was noise. 'Where am I?'

'She's come to. She's fine.' The man had turned away from her.

'Where am I?'

'You're on a stretcher, Ma'am. We're outside your house. There has been an accident.'

What accident, she thought, but then the events slowly came back to her.

'The painting?'

'I beg your pardon?'

'Where's the painting?'

'Something about a painting.' He'd turned away from her again. The manners on these people.

Marion made to move and a pain shot through her.

'Ma'am, you need to stay lying down for a while. You'll be okay, but just stay down for me, please.'

Marion wanted to hit him but found her muscles unco-operative, her body like jelly.

'The painting,' she said one last time and woke up hours later inside a dreary room at the Katterijn Guest House.

In a daze Marion phoned reception, half-expecting them to reassure her that the painting was fine, but instead a woman's voice explained that Marelena had checked her in. Marvelling at how she had no recollection of all this, Marion phoned her daughter.

'Darling . . . I see . . . Not good enough for your own house, I suppose . . . Don't start what? . . . I'm just saying . . . And I can't afford here, by the way. Anyway, I can't natter on, do you have the painting? . . . The painting . . . The one from Dad, the . . . Yes, that one. Tell me you have it . . . So you didn't see it? Wrapped. Well, did you check in the . . . Yes. Well, this is very important, I need you to . . . What? . . . Alright, alright, but call me back as soon as you're done.'

Marion wasn't an expert and Max hadn't been one, either, but a friend had advised them. Investment art, he'd called it. They'd purchased the Pierneef some twenty years ago. A genius, the dealer had said. And look at this colour here, the light just in that corner. It was of the land, Northern Transvaal. Charcoal-blue mountains in the backdrop, a line of trees through the valleys, yellow-green grass, shadows and dirt. They had thought of it as a backup plan, but now it was to be her salvation.

The painting didn't hang on a wall in the house. It took a tour of the cupboards until Marion, first checking with Max that it could really be worth *that* much one day, wrapped it in paper and string and bundled it into the attic.

Marion checked her phone to make sure it wasn't on

silent, that she hadn't missed Marelena's call. It was important that she confirm the painting was safe and whole.

Marion didn't feel up to dinner but she ought to eat, ought not to starve. She lay on her back on the guest-house bed. There was a stain on the ceiling, not a new one; they'd fixed the leak, but left the mark – nice, real classy. This is what it feels like to be an old woman, discarded by your own family. Money. The only thing with the power to bring some respite to old age. And maybe love. Although Max was a bastard and, for all the children she'd gone and had, not one of them gave a toss. Feeling desperate, Marion, staying horizontal, reached for her cellphone and punched out Stefano's numbers. His mailbox was still full. And his voice-message pointedly unfriendly, as if he'd recorded it especially for her.

The phone rang. Sarah Clarke. As if there wasn't enough to worry about, now there was the upcoming committee meeting. Should she send out a cancellation email? Sarah wanted to know. Marion fretted. She felt in no state to head up a meeting. And yet there were pressing committee matters. After the claim notice in the *Gazette*, mediations had commenced between the two parties, the Samsodiens and the Von Struikers. Marion had explained to Ludmilla that it was crucial the committee be kept up to date with the events – the outcome of the claim would affect them all. The first mediation had taken place and Marion had convinced Ludmilla to attend the upcoming committee meeting and give feedback. Meanwhile Beulah Gierdien had written another letter. It felt like such sore luck to be indisposed at such an exciting time in the committee's history. Marion had been head of Talk Shop club in high school several years running and fancied herself an under-exposed orator.

'Well?'

'Huh?'

'Should I cancel?'

'Oh . . . damn that woman!'

Sarah chuckled.

'What's so funny?'

'It's not her fault.'

'Whose – Hortensia's?'

'Yes. That you were knocked unconscious.'

'Don't be naïve, Sarah, of course it is. Whose else fault could it be?'

They opted to postpone the meeting for a few days.

Marion ate her dinner, glancing, worriedly, at her phone every few minutes. No Marelena. Had she forgotten, or was she avoiding giving her bad news. Marion found it difficult to call her and find out.

After the lousy meal she walked down the guest-house corridor, her footsteps dampened by the carpet, which was in a colour she had no name for, mildewed in the corners. Her skin crawled. Literally, as if it was crawling away from the onslaught of ugliness. Since she'd arrived at the guest house she'd seen the back of the head of a guest and a couple at dinner – too in love to notice that they were in a dump. Apart from those encounters the place was deserted.

Marion reached her door and her cellphone rang. The lawyer. Marion walked into the stifled air of her room and took the short call, updating her on what her ridiculous life now hinged on – a pathetic string of insurance claims.

After the lawyer, Marion dialled Marelena's number but

it just rang; she didn't leave a message. Her stomach knotted, but she couldn't work out whether that was the regrettable meal she'd just eaten or fear. If the painting was destroyed, maybe she could make a claim. Except there was no record of the painting. Which was why she'd concocted the idea to hide it from the sharks in the first place. Now the lack of a record of the painting meant she couldn't claim for it. Anyway, even if she could claim for it, the sharks would get that in the end. Since the botched attempt at Peter's funeral Hortensia had presented a solid wall, with no holes for Marion to slip a request for a favour through. Why was she stalling when so much was at stake? And around and around and around. Why didn't she, Marion, just die? Why couldn't something kill her – she'd lived long enough, surely.

In another year she would be eighty-two. Her parents had died before then, living separate lives in the same old-age home, quiet in their bitterness and hate. Why couldn't she have followed their example? Why did she have to live longer? What was the point anyway? You can't die, but you haven't got the money to live properly, the money to act as balm to your misery. What was the point of it all? You needed money – life was much too glaring without the shade of lots of cash.

Marion left the lights off, she walked to the dresser. It wasn't yet properly dark outside and some light beat its way through the washed-out curtains. The photograph on the shabby surface looked at her, its frame scuffed, a scratch through her father's face, but otherwise fine. Apparently Agnes had gathered the stuff into a small box. The same box Marion found upon waking up at the guest house.

That and a hurriedly packed suitcase of clothing and toiletries. Why had she taken out the portrait and put it here on the dresser? Here where her parents could watch her the whole time. She smiled. What did it matter where she put it, they would always be watching her, regardless. And although divided in almost everything else, her parents, dead or alive, watched their daughter with the same singular emotion – fatigue. She'd made them weary.

Marion remembered the information, hard and small like bird droppings, that she massaged out of her parents, but mostly they had nothing to say about where they had come from. When they claimed not to remember she understood, even at four, that they were lying. And in the easy logic of children, lying became an alternative to remembering. It became a thing in the world. The way walking had become a thing. The way words and speaking had. Lying became something else to master.

Marion knew some things about the past. She knew that her parents felt lucky to have got away when they did from a Lithuanian village they never named for her. They settled in District 6 in Cape Town, her father learned English and encouraged her mother to do the same. He traded well and soon could afford to move the family out to Wynberg, where Marion had the experiences that would become her first memories. She grew into the kind of girl who liked ribbons, but only brown ones, and she hated wearing shoes and preferred not to brush her hair.

Marion knew her mother disliked the fact that they lived not far from Mortimer Road where the shul stood.

She disliked that she could see the roof of the shul from the kitchen-sink window, where she spent most of her days standing. Having moved away from the most horrifying danger, her mother would have liked very much never to see another shul or say another prayer. Like closing your eyes so the monsters can't see you.

The house in Wynberg had not been large. It had a tin roof and thick white walls that were always rough and cool to the touch. There was a leak that never stayed fixed and a half-step up into the kitchen that Marion banged her foot against on a weekly basis. Once, running for an unremarkable reason, she knocked her foot on the step hard enough to bleed. Her mother put on the plaster. Girls don't run, she said. Girls never run. There were many versions of the same admonition. Girls don't chew gum. Girls don't whistle. What did girls do? Marion once asked her mother. The question stumped her mother for a few seconds. She was shelling peas, she was showing Marion how to shell peas. Girls crossed their legs when they sat. What else? Marion had asked. Again a long silence. Girls shelled peas.

That Marion undid her mother had always been evident to her. You don't need to be an adult to understand the concept of 'bothersome'; you don't have to be able to spell it, either. From very early Marion realised she could upset things. Her unsweet self remained so, despite being clapped in pressed lace blouses that became almost instantly unpressed, and dainty velour booties that never stayed clean. She realised that she was failing. She failed to be petite, failed to enjoy pink. She failed without trying. In just waking up, walking in a straight line, opening her mouth to say something, she could annoy her mother. And because she wanted love – what six-year-old did not? – she said quiet prayers to a God her parents never introduced her to and tried to negotiate with him to garner more favour. She learned how to sit still. She made a point of mastering how to shell the peas.

Time outside the house was what Marion enjoyed most. Inside was cloistered, regulated. From the age of eight she was allowed to walk up the street if her mother was on the stoep. This was her favourite thing. Marion counted the houses and she talked to them. Little whispers, little secrets that no one else had to know. And it was her love affair with those houses that made the one story that both her parents would go on to tell friends, or even just anyone they met. For instance, when Marion, much later, graduated from university, her parents, already divorced, came to the graduation dinner. They used whatever bravery they possessed to survive each other's presence at the event. Even though they sat apart, Marion heard them at the exact same time telling the people they were sitting next to the exact same story. We once asked Marion what she wanted to be when she grew up and she said a house. We told her she couldn't be a house, because a house was a thing and she was a human. She cried for a while. And then later she came to us and said she'd decided what she wanted to be. We asked her what. And she said – a human house. It always brought laughs, the story. When she was younger Marion hated to hear it, but as her parents grew old and dutifully told the story at every opportunity they could, she understood it was a kind of anthem for them. Like a psalm. Her parents were both uptight people. Marion had never seen them hug or kiss each other. Her mother touched Marion's skin to scrub it, her hair to tidy it, her cheek to de-smudge it, her bum to smack it. Her father touched nothing, except on the odd occasion he would lay his hand on the top of her head, although Marion never understood what that was for. Much much later, only when Marion had children of her own, did she understand that for her parents the story, the remembering of it and the telling, was a deeper kind of touching.

She spent childhood managing herself. Despite sincere attempts, she frequently couldn't help stepping over the lines her mother so carefully drew out for her. Her parents seldom had gatherings at the home, but there was one dinner party Marion remembered – not the reason of why, and not even who was there and how many. She recalled that it was a stressful occasion for her mother, who spent most of the evening in the kitchen and cried at the end after everyone had left. Marion remembered wearing powder-blue with frills, her mother in heels that she couldn't walk in and her father quiet but smug. Marion remembered the actual meal. Delicious. And she, all of six years old, remembered feeling compelled to utter a sentence into a silence that presented itself: Ma said black is the same as Kaffir.

A few of the guests tutted their disapproval; mostly people laughed as if Marion had told a joke. Regardless, after everyone had left her mother gave her a hiding. Smacking her daughter was easier than feeling ashamed.

Adolescence was a tug-of-war. Sometimes it seemed like Marion was in fact a little lady, the kind her mother required her to be. And other times she burst out from the stitches, tore the seams.

When Marion was eleven, old enough to make accusations and old enough to know fear when she saw it, she asked her mother. Why hadn't they given her anything – not even a religion, not even some uncles or aunties, nothing to remember, no rituals? The question had come from a place of loneliness, from a feeling that three did not really make a family.

Her mother decided to talk about something she'd never spoken of. She told Marion that she – Marion – was born on the twenty-first of June in 1933. Marion, of course, knew this already. When she interrupted to say so, her mother raised a hand in a gesture that was unfamiliar and so, for this reason, Marion hushed and listened.

Her mother had been pregnant on the ship. She and her husband sailed for South Africa from London, leaving behind the dormitory house they had lived in, with so many others, for a few months. It had all been a jumble of nightmares and rain. On the *Blue Mary*, her mother had been sick often. Sick with the sea, but also sick with the baby. Sick too with fear and a close sense of what is ugly about the world, what it is like to be hunted. She stood on the deck, Marion's mother explained to her, when the seas calmed and she saw the shining waters of the Atlantic Ocean.

No one could ever know but, standing on the deck of the ship one evening, she'd considered jumping. Her bits of sick were bobbing down below on the waves. She felt a madness, like a fever, and the only thing to end it would be to jump, fling herself and the unborn child over the edge, give them both a simple kind of peace. She held onto the rails and, as if it was a fast wind, the feeling passed. She reasoned that if she could get away from the dark place they'd come from – not just physically – then she could be alright. She decided to make herself forget and she vowed that, henceforth, for every remembrance anyone, even her husband, attempted to inflict on her, she would slap it away. Because this would be a new life, away from a land that had turned on itself. And in the new life there would be no need for remembering. She wanted to forget and she wanted to be forgotten. After all the horrific attention, she longed to simply slip through life unnoticed.

Marion was surprised to hear her mother say so much, but it was a carefully made story with nothing fraying along its edges. Marion never asked again.

In the guest house in Katterijn, as the sun began to drop, Marion put the portrait of her parents back into the brown cardboard box full of worthless trinkets and forgettable memories. Stupid portrait. How ridiculous, the painting – worth something – and this photograph survives. This stupid picture that was irrepressible. She shoved the box with her leg and her heel complained.

From the window she could see the highway. Apparently if you looked carefully into the thicket you could pick out the Von Struiker Gardens, so said the receptionist. Marion narrowed her eyes as she glared at the view. Too little light, really. But the room was too quiet, and it felt less quiet if she stood at the window and looked out of it. She missed Alvar. Of course, apart from the painting, that had been the first thing Marion had wondered. She feared the worst but, like an exclamation mark to Marion's failure as a parent, Marelena had taken Alvar in. Imagine. She'd taken the dog in and she'd put her own mother into a guest house. Marion bristled, but she found it difficult to despise Alvar for being favoured.

At last Marelena's number shone on the screen of her cellphone.

'Darling, have you found it? . . . The painting! Marelena, I don't think you fully understand just how important this is . . . I'm not shouting! . . . Well, can you check? Please . . . I'm asking as sweetly as I can – I won't sleep otherwise . . . Thank you. I spoke with the lawyer earlier. It's all a mess, but what can I do? The lawyer thinks the whole incident might buy me some time with the debt collectors; meanwhile I'm waiting to see what the insurance pays out for the damages – it better cover the repairs . . . What do you mean? . . . I don't know what I'll do afterwards, Marelena, I don't know – sell the house . . . What? . . . Yes, I realise I can't move in with you, I gathered that, darling . . . ' She made a laugh devoid of humour. Sighed. 'Yes, darling, I'm sure it will all work out. Please don't forget about the painting . . . Yes, well, goodbye.'

Marion took out her teeth. She slept curled with a hand on her face, turned upwards. Parrying what, she couldn't say.

In the morning Agnes brought a note.

✻   ✻   ✻

The letter had been hard to compose. A few days on and Hortensia was still juggling the words in her head. She'd already received notice of the insurance claim for the damages. In fact it was a whole chain of insurance claims, like dominoes. She called off the building works, thinking Marion would be happy to hear that. From Bassey's account – he'd heard from Agnes – Marion was staying at that disease of a guest house down the road and was not in the least bit happy about that.

'Why not with her family? She has a soccer team of children,' Hortensia asked Bassey, who'd brought tea and then stood in the doorway of her study for a while, indulging her with gossip.

He shrugged. 'Agnes says the two kids live overseas. The other two are in the country, but may as well not be.'

Hortensia snorted, ignored Bassey's look of recrimination. There were fewer and fewer pleasures – why not enjoy the Vulture's misfortune?

'Anyway,' Bassey said, the word he used as a means of taking leave.

'What happened? With her and the kids?' Hortensia was keen to have him stay and talk. What else was there to do – she was bed-bound.

'Agnes says the only thing that kept her a Christian was working for that family – that it is tribulation that builds faith.'

'Dreadful!'

'She said you need Jesus in your life if you're going to work for the Agostinos.' Bassey turned and Hortensia, indulging an old habit, counted his steps back down the hallway and into the kitchen.

The hospital had insisted on their blasted nurses. Hortensia did her best to make their work unpleasant, and she happily noticed that the same nurse never returned the next day. She imagined there were a finite number of Constantinople Hospital nurses and that soon enough they'd run out and leave her be. Let her get gangrene and die, for God's sake, what of it?

Amidst the fog of the pain-medicines they plied her with, Hortensia tried to design her apology. With the recent example of the crane-driver vivid in her mind, she could not ignore adding the ingredient he had omitted. Somewhere in the crowd of things she meant to tell Marion, there had to be an admission of guilt. She, Hortensia, was complicit. She was sorry. Sorry. The word alone was an assault to her sense of herself. Waves of nausea visited her during the day and the miserable nurse on duty thought it had something to do with the pain. Each time Bassey came into the room she worried he had news that Marion was back next door or, worse, right outside her own door. But of course Marion couldn't come home; her house was in disrepair, no works could begin until the insurance chain was worked out – who did what to whom, what was damaged and who was utmostly responsible, who owed whom and how much.

Maybe she should phone Marion but, as much as she would have liked this she knew it would be a cop-out, the coward's way.

On a particularly miserable morning, when the previous night had been a succession of bad dreams (Marion sitting on Hortensia's head, Marion asking Hortensia to pick her teeth with a plastic toothpick, Marion making Hortensia floss her own teeth with strands of Marion's grey and greasy hair), Hortensia decided: enough. She shouted for Bassey, thinking as she did that they must call the electrician and have a buzzer installed by the bed.

'Yes, please.'

'I need to speak with Mrs Agostino. Don't look at me like that. What do you know?'

Bassey, of course, knew that the women hated one another. Everyone did.

'Nothing.'

'Well, I need to speak with her. I mean I would like to . . . I can't really go to her, you see?'

'Yes.'

'So you can talk to Agnes, yes?'

Bassey nodded.

'Think I can send her a letter? Marion, I mean. Through Agnes. I don't even know if she'll come. She'll probably see my name and reach for a blowtorch.'

Bassey smiled. Hortensia had always liked the fact that he enjoyed her scathing humour.

'Pass me my writing paper, it's in the second drawer. It's not locked. My pen is over there.'

Dear Mrs Agostino

Hortensia crumpled the paper and started again:

Marion, I know I've caused you some difficulty. I would prefer to speak in person. I would come to you if I could, but I think you know I am confined to my bed. It is unreasonable, but still I thought to ask – will you please come, so that I may apologise to you in person?

HJ

Hortensia wondered if Marion would see this as Hortensia's comeuppance – come and see a weakened Hortensia, come and see her grovel. Or would she be incensed that she was being summoned? Or some strange combination of both? Would she come? The nightmares continued. For many days no reply arrived.

EIGHT

It was good to be at a committee meeting without Hortensia the Horrible around to snap and carry on. Marion waited while the minutes from the last meeting were passed around to be signed. It was also good to be out of the dreary guest house and to forget her financial hassles for a couple of hours.

'Sorry I'm late, Marion, everyone.' Ludmilla took a seat.

When they'd bought in '64, the Von Struikers had already been living in Katterijn for a couple of years. Marion remembered envying them at dinner parties. Jan (Jannie), tanned, with a flick of blond hair falling forward into his left eye; Ludmilla certainly stout (and she'd got stouter) but contained, apparently in no need of making a good impression. Because she didn't like them, Marion had made them her friends, attended all their soirées, noticed that behind the money their marriage was a sham and took comfort from this.

'Jan not joining us?'

'We decided I'll handle this.'

'Okay, well, we should focus on the claims, but first, Agatha, you said another letter from the Gierdien woman arrived?' Agatha was in charge of checking the post-office box.

'Yes, this time she's requesting a meeting.'

'Really we should just put her in direct contact with Hortensia, Marion,' Sarah Clarke said. 'Let them have it out. It's got no legal ramifications, unlike the Samsodiens, which we really ought to be focusing on.'

'Could you pass the letter, please?'

Agatha leaned across the table and handed Marion the envelope.

She scanned it. Marion still harboured hope that she could torment Hortensia with this Beulah Gierdien business. She didn't feel like simply handing it over just yet. 'I'll hold onto this.' She put the letter in her purse. 'Agatha, do you still have that section in the library with the history of Katterijn? Maybe I'll come round, check on the validity of Ms Gierdien's story.'

'Can we move onto the Samsodiens' claim? After the first mediation our lawyer has advised us on how to proceed,' Ludmilla said, impatient. That she thought the committee a nonentity was no secret. In fact she only ever referred to it as 'the club', giving Marion the impression that she thought it was a place old women gathered to gossip.

'Lawyer?' someone asked.

'But it's still at the Commission stage, Ludmilla,' Marion said.

'I know. But just in case it gets to the Land Claims Court, we want to have all our ducks in a row.'

'What does your lawyer say? Do they have a claim?'

'They do have a claim, but we can refute it.'

'They have a claim?' Marion couldn't hide her shock and then blushed when she saw the pity in Ludmilla's eyes. As if Ludmilla had looked at her, seen a child who understood so little of the world and felt sorry.

'But we can refute it,' Ludmilla repeated. 'The Samsodiens have a lawyer too. The Commission is proposing monetary compensation, but it looks like they'll refuse. Very likely we'll end up in court.'

Ludmilla spoke about the strategy going forwards. Marion only half-listened. She was disturbed by the possibility that the Samsodiens had a claim.

'How did you acquire the land?' Marion asked.

'Auction. They were desperate and needed the money. We bought it fair and square.'

Marion only nodded.

The nurse was heffing; it wasn't really a word but it was a term Hortensia used. Maybe her mother had used it? It certainly described the kind of thing people did around Hortensia a lot. She'd say something – something simple, more true than offensive – and the person would heff. For some, heffing involved physical traits like a downturning of the mouth to show displeasure or a shaking body to show general unhappiness.

'I expect an apology, Mrs James. No one talks to me that way.'

For others, their heffing meant they said things like that. Demanding apologies with no regard for how difficult they were for Hortensia to manufacture.

'And I intend to report you to the head-nurse.'

They threatened. And all for what? What had she said? He, the nurse, had made the mistake of trying to make small talk, to unburden himself of his whiteness by suggesting how non-racial he was and how many black friends he had and how wonderful Nelson Mandela was. He seemed, on entering the house, to have been struck by a kind of PC-diarrhoea and, almost immediately, he'd begun to produce a litany of anecdotes to absolve himself of any sense of responsibility for the wrongdoing that white people have been known to inflict almost everywhere they have been.

'I see nothing to report, but do as you think best.'

She'd caught him unawares; he'd been telling her about his 'buddy', the guard at his bank, who had taught him the 'African handshake'. Which is it that makes him your 'buddy', she'd asked, punishing him with his own choice of word. The fact that he's black or the fact that he's poor – or is it both?

Hortensia wasn't being mean for its own sake, she was genuinely curious to know. She'd witnessed the scene the nurse described many times already. A fraught eagerness that played itself out in close, uncomfortable spaces. The security guard and the blasted cumbersome handshake white people had decided was the password to being down. A shortcut is what it was.

'You must know he's not your buddy?' Hortensia asked. She'd done her own study of the nation, post-'94. Cheap tricks like handshakes and cute localised expressions to hide what was really needed. Slogans in place of the real dirty slog required if unity was truly the goal. 'You can't be stupid, surely?' she asked the nurse. 'Which leaves the conclusion that you must be a liar.'

He was now packing up his little nurse-bag, which could only mean he was leaving. Hopefully this was the last nurse they would send her.

'How dare you speak to me like that? I have never been

spoken to in this way.' Spit flew as he enunciated the words.

Hortensia nodded. She was lying on her back, her legs elevated on a stack of pillows. She was, obediently, rotating her ankles. The nurse looked bruised, as if she'd thrown stones at him. But Hortensia seldom needed stones, her words were enough.

'I'm leaving these here.' He grouped the medicines onto the side-table, then he collected his bag and stepped out of the room.

He would be the fifth nurse in three days to walk out. Hortensia groaned.

Her mood lifted when Bassey entered. Luckily Bassey never required her to admit it, but Hortensia felt grateful. He had never managed, in the almost twenty years he'd worked for them, to anger her, to incite her to want to diminish him to dust. He was a quiet man who parried all of Peter's attempts at friendly employerness. He did, however, assent to play chess. He embarrassed Peter, the first time they played, by beating him, Hortensia recalled, quite brutally. And then curiously never won again.

Bassey's eyes were deepset, two sharp slits, his skin shiny.

He held an envelope with its flap unsealed. Inside was a folded piece of paper with the name of the guest house along its top edge. It said:

Okay.

Hortensia figured that meant Marion was coming. She was instinctively peeved that Marion hadn't taken the trouble to specify a day, or a time, but then she accepted this was the only bit of control Marion had left in the whole arrangement. She would show up when she pleased, confident that Hortensia wasn't really going anywhere. All Hortensia could do was wait.

Sure enough, the high-pitched voice at the front door, the merciless piercing of heels into the Macassar-ebony floor – it could only be one person. Bassey poked his head through the gap in the door to announce the guest, but Marion pushed past into the room before he could utter a sound.

'Hortensia.' She was stiff, perfunctory, which made Hortensia realise anew the intense difficulty of the task ahead.

'Marion, please do sit down.'

Bassey ducked out, but Hortensia called him back, asked Marion if she wanted anything. She asked for lemonade and Bassey left to fetch it. Hortensia thought it sensible to wait for him to come back with the drink before commencing. Once she started, she had to just go with no interruptions. Marion sat quietly, uninterested in the seeming trifles of the sickbed – where does it hurt? How long will it take to heal? And so on. Bassey entered into their tight silence and, after arranging Marion's glass on a side-table, retreated once more.

'I was quite busy. I couldn't come immediately.'

'I'm glad you're here.' Hortensia could not remember the last time she was this intent on being agreeable. It felt like play-acting.

'Yes, well, what did you want? I'd rather not discuss paperwork with you, but I'm glad there've been no shenanigans from the insurers.'

Hortensia wasn't entirely sure what this meant. Best to ignore it.

'Well, as I said in my note' – typical, Hortensia thought, that Marion would make such a show of not remembering – 'I wanted a chance to apologise in person.'

Marion sat to attention, as if the National Anthem was about to be played and she was required to put hand to heart. Hortensia swallowed. She'd promised herself she'd keep it short: the more you spoke, the less apologetic you sounded.

'I realise I have done you a wrong. Your house is in tatters, and that is my fault. I am sorry.'

Whether due to its brevity or, Hortensia hoped, its startling honesty, somehow Marion became angered by the apology. Maybe that's true of all apologies, Hortensia considered, giving permission for the wronged party to rant. Maybe that was all the crane-driver had been avoiding. But she, Hortensia, was enjoying the fact that she'd upset Marion by apologising with integrity, it felt like a double victory.

'. . . and we all know how that can go,' Marion was saying. 'I cannot afford to compromise the sale – everything must be perfect. And to top it off, forget the house, let me tell you. On the other side of that wall, by the way, was a painting. An original. Possibly somewhere destroyed.' Marion raised herself up in her seat. 'A Pierneef. So you can't just blurt out three sentences and think you're done with that. You have caused me so much trouble. So much.'

Hortensia had never been a fan of landscape art, but the expression on Marion's face did not invite discussion on the topic.

'Marion,' she said, lowering her voice to the softest she knew how to. 'I am truly sorry.'

Marion stood up. She'd only drunk about half of the lemonade, but Hortensia could tell she was now going to leave. And she did. The whole episode gave Hortensia a sense of longing that she had nowhere to put.

NINE

The Constantinople Hospital called to ask what had happened between Hortensia and the last nurse. Hortensia wished they wouldn't. She had said, from the very first sniff of the suggestion, that she neither needed nor wanted a nurse. Well, the head-nurse huffed (a much more toned-down version of heffing), they were having some difficulty scheduling another nurse. And did Hortensia know that they'd never experienced this before and, well, they had to see to it, because they were responsible for her health and they were only trying to help. Alright, Hortensia said. Hoping the less she said, the shorter the call would be, the sooner the annoyance would end. Well, the nurse continued, she would have to go away and then come back. Okay, Hortensia ended the call, liking the first part of the woman's statement and hoping the second would never come to pass.

In the meantime she devised her own plans.

'Bassey!' she called.

Bassey walked in.

'Now,' Hortensia started, 'I am going to need a bit of . . . help.'

She had solved the matter of ablutions in two ways. The easier activity only required that Bassey place the low table and the steel bowl of warm water within arm's reach.

A clean sponge, white soap on a wooden tray. For the more private activity, Hortensia grabbed as much dignity as she could; she pointed Bassey towards the bedpan and explained to him what to do when she (thanks to the exercises she'd been doing daily since leaving the hospital) bridged and formed a gap between her bottom and the bed, through which he could slide the pan. Employer and employee came closer than they had ever been. An intimate smell embraced them.

'I'm ordering a commode,' Hortensia called after him as he walked down the hall to dispose of her waste. 'And a nurse.'

She reached for the private-care brochures, dialled the number. As she waited for the receiver to pick up, she ran her fingers over the duvet cover. She'd missed her fort-nightly call with the House of Braithwaite head-designers. As her age had advanced, Hortensia had grudgingly stopped insisting that all designs go through her for approval. When they'd moved to South Africa, she'd sold her share of the studio to her partner Adebayo and opened a Cape Town branch. In addition House of Braithwaite still operated out of the studio in London. It was only in 2000, seventy and tired, that Hortensia stopped going into work every day. Advances in technology meant she could conduct meetings from home and she prided herself on knowing everything that was going on in her company. Sometimes on the calls, though, she wondered if she detected a sense of condescension, as if her design staff were humouring her, a terrible habit the young have when relating to the old.

On the other end of the line, someone finally picked up. Hortensia cleared her throat. 'Hello? . . . Yes. I'd like to order a nurse. About five-foot four-inches, 52 kilograms or thereabouts. Age between forty and fifty. Preferably unmarried. No children. I don't want someone who ta— Hello?'

Her physiotherapist was a tall woman with short yellow hair that curled back off her forehead and around her ears. She had large feet clad in the plastic Crocs Hortensia abhorred. She – her name was Carole with an e – had a rough manner which Hortensia was grateful for. The woman, who looked to Hortensia like she was pushing fifty, had no sympathy for her patient's condition. Rather she seemed annoyed that a stupid old woman had broken her leg – all this suited Hortensia.

'I see we can't seem to find you a nurse,' Carole said.

Hortensia smiled to indicate her innocence in the matter.

The physio had been visiting three times a week, although she'd explained that these visits would wane as the fracture healed. Hortensia relaxed with Carole, allowed her to conduct her work of taking her body through a series of exercises. She especially obliged with the exercises, eager to be strong again and capable of doing things for herself.

The only hazard she had to endure with Carole was her insistence on explaining everything to Hortensia as if she were a child. It wasn't as much what she said as how she said it, her tone dragging – all the easier for the dim-witted Hortensia to grasp.

'We need to get to weight-bearing strength,' was Carole's mantra through all and any exercise regimen.

There was a set order to Carole's visits. She arrived and, after no pleasantries but several questions as to the state of Hortensia's leg muscles, they started the bed exercises. Usually, after the bed exercises, Carole would struggle along and manage to get her patient into a chair, but on the third visit she relented.

Carole hefted Hortensia into a sitting position on the bed, then after a few minutes she asked if the big black man who'd let her in could help get Hortensia into the armchair.

'His name is Bassey,' Hortensia said, with a tightness in her jaw as she pressed the button she'd had installed.

Bassey arrived and obliged.

Carole assembled the commode. Later she leaned against the wall in the hallway as Hortensia walked its length, manoeuvring the walker – a new addition to her routine. She hated it, found it offensive. A metal thing with no class.

'See,' Hortensia said as she walked along with great difficulty and little grace. 'I don't need a nurse.'

'We can't just leave you, Mrs James. It's been bad enough that so many days have passed with little supervision. What about the night hours?'

'What about the night hours?'

'What if something happens? You fall, you need something. I asked, and the big . . . Bassey doesn't live on the premises.'

'I don't follow you.'

Carole rolled her eyes. 'We will be contacting you, Mrs James. Another thing: next week I won't be here.'

'Oh dear,' Hortensia said and meant it.

Carole made a face. An attempt, Hortensia felt, at a smile.

'It's all rather sudden, but I'm getting married this weekend. I'm going on my honeymoon.'

'How nice,' Hortensia said, not meaning it. 'So, what? I'll hear from the hospital?'

'Uhm, they should call, yes. All the best, Mrs James.'

The hospital did not call. Instead, Hortensia could hear the voice of . . . Dr Mama? She listened to the sound of two people walking down the generous passageway.

'The doctor is here,' Bassey announced and closed the door behind him.

'Dr Mama!' She was genuinely surprised.

He'd been Peter's GP. She hadn't seen him in almost two years.

'Mrs James, what terrible circumstances, but . . . still it's good to see you.'

He was bifocals-wearing, grey-hair-having. Hortensia put a smile on her face. She'd learned, especially in Cape Town, that a smiling black woman was a dangerous weapon in its apparent innocuousness. It was what she thought of as a decoy, something to distract people with, while she worked out where their weak points were.

'What a surprise!'

'Well, news gets around – I had to come.'

'Nonsense. How kind.' Right then she remembered his voice. Explaining her husband's disease, warning and preparing her.

'You look too happy for someone with a broken leg.' He came to stand close to the bed.

And the next surprise was that she found him handsome. Where had that come from? She hadn't thought that two years ago.

'I'm always happy,' Hortensia lied and was pleased to hear her own laughter follow the preposterous claim.

Dr Mama laughed too. He had one dimple on his left cheek. His eyes were clear. His skin was dark and smooth and reminded Hortensia to add 85-per-cent Lindt to Bassey's shopping list.

'How's the pain? Is this the medication you've been taking?' He perused the medicines on the bedside table – a collection of Celebrex, the anti-inflammatory, paracetamol and an analgesic.

'What pain?' Hortensia said, laughed again. She was enjoying the laughing; there was seldom a reason, but Dr Mama seemed a good enough one.

'You know what they say,' he continued. 'At our age, if you awake with no pain you're probably dead.'

Again laughter.

'On a more serious note, I'm sure you're a strong woman. But if the pain's too much, it'll affect your rest. How's your sleep?'

Hortensia rearmed herself. Doctors were not as bad as nurses, but still, you had to be wary. If he even so much as glanced at her in a . . .

'Hmm?'

'Pardon, sorry I didn't catch that.'

'Sleep, Mrs James.'

'Hortensia, please.'

'Hortensia, do you go for eight hours unbroken – seven at least?'

She laughed, this time with mirth. 'I haven't slept for seven hours straight since I was a design student. Come on, Doctor.'

'Gordon.'

'Gordon.'

'Okay, well, we'll need to do something about that, then.'

'I won't take sleeping pills.'

'I understand, I wasn't going to propose any.'

'Good.'

'Maybe some relaxing thoughts before bed? Do you find you sleep during the day?'

'Sometimes. Not much else to do.'

'Try and avoid this. I think of it as saving up the hours for the night-time rather than spending them in daylight.'

She smiled, a clean one with no malice.

'I'll also change your pain-medication. And I'll prescribe some probiotics. Who's been administering the daily injection – the Warfarin?'

'Ah, highlight of my day. Carole showed Bassey how to do it.'

He nodded. 'So, I'll take these away . . .' He juggled things, replacing bottles with bottles as far as Hortensia could tell. 'You'll keep taking it at the same times – here, I'll leave you this label. I'll explain to the gentleman before I leave.'

She'd never really looked at him. She was too busy being married to Peter. But there was something 'messy' about Dr Mama. It was strange because this was the last thing you might want in a doctor. Except what Hortensia detested most about those in the health industry was the way all the things they knew built up between them and you, like a mountain. Dr Mama – Gordon – had none of that. He seemed to somehow be a doctor by accident, as if it wasn't his fault and he was sorry about it. He seemed helpless but intelligent all the same, nonchalant that he had happened to know some stuff, so they made him a doctor; he didn't look like he'd ever have to shove that in your face. He was more the type to get you to forget.

'Okay. Now, anything else? How's the movement? – bowels, I mean.'

'I beg your pardon.'

'I understand. Just find a respectable way to let me know in the case of constipation, would you?' He winked.

Hortensia relaxed some more but her guard wasn't totally down.

'I'm confused, are you *my* doctor now? Did the hospital send you?'

'Not quite. I'm here as a concerned friend.'

'Liar!'

'Carole is your physio, am I correct?'

'Ah, Carole. Good girl. Decent.'

'She told me about you,' Mama said.

'Bad things?'

'Not at all, but she did explain the "difficulties" they've been having with you at Constantinople. I agreed to . . . well, I said I'd come and see you,' he smiled affably. 'I think they hoped you'd like me.'

'I see. And was all this at the secret doctor-sect meeting?'

'Still so funny, Hortensia. I remember you as being very funny.'

No one found Hortensia funny. Caustic, yes, but not funny.

'And I also wanted to say: I'm sorry for your loss. I heard Mr James passed away some weeks ago.'

She reached back for her smile, her armour. Hortensia held her face. Holding was something she was good at. Holding was a way of staving off being ambushed by the kindness of strangers.

'. . . you call me,' he was saying.

Except Hortensia couldn't work out if he'd just said she could call him for sex or if he'd asked her out to the theatre. She nodded.

'Then there's the final matter of the care-nurse.'

'I can take care of myself, Doctor. Gordon.'

Dr Mama was buckling the brown leather bag he'd walked in with. For that bag alone, the elegant cut and the audacious red stitching, Hortensia felt she ought to kiss him.

'I understand that, Hortensia. But there's something about the care-nurse that wasn't explained to you.'

She straightened up.

'The care-nurse is something we doctors put in place that is not really for the benefit of our patients.'

'What!' Hortensia laughed in disbelief.

'Well, of course it is to the patient's benefit. But in cases like yours where a doctor cannot see you every day, cannot monitor you, that nurse is more for us than for you. He or she will help us ensure that we give you the best treatment possible. There are too many dangers otherwise.'

Hortensia had listened attentively. She liked Dr Mama, he had a soft way of talking. She realised he was only telling her what she needed to hear, but appreciated it nonetheless.

'So you really think I need a nurse.'

'Absolutely, Hortensia.'

She puffed.

'I hate nurses.'

'I'm sorry to hear that.'

She looked out the window and got annoyed that her building works were on hold. Blast!

'So will you assure me? No more ill-treatment of your nurses? They mean no harm, Hortensia.'

'You just want someone here with me, is that right?'

'That's right. Someone with some ability. Even just another body for . . . well, in the instance of an emergency, for example.'

Hortensia nodded. She'd already asked Bassey. He'd declined in that way that was annoying but that she respected; she did not own him, he did not owe her.

'There's a great nursing sister – I've had the chance to work with her before. Trudy.'

Trudy? What kind of name was Trudy? Hortensia forced what she hoped was a smile. But she felt helpless, put-upon.

'So, is that settled? You happy with that? She'll come in from tomorrow and, at least for the first week, I'll have her stay nights. Then we look again – how's that?'

Hortensia flicked her fingers, a sign of defeat.

'I'm glad we could work something out.'

She felt nauseous for the rest of the day.

The unfortunate person named Trudy was black. She said she was Zambian, spoke with an American accent and was so short and pudgy that after the first week Hortensia felt Trudy was the perfect comedic foil to Bassey's largeness. Put the two of them onstage and laughter would happen spontaneously. Trudy was also disappointingly young. After her first day Hortensia called Dr Mama.

'You sent me a Lilliputian.'

He laughed and Hortensia pointed out that she wasn't joking.

But it was Trudy or nothing – there were no more nurses. And perhaps her youth helped. Hortensia disagreed with the prevailing wisdom that the young were somehow quick-witted and savvy. On the contrary, in her older years Hortensia had discovered young people (generally speaking) to be cocooned in a special fluff of obtuseness, which made them immune to the world and could easily be mistaken for intelligence, but only if you, the onlooker, were a little less than sharp in your observations. Trudy had this coating, which was just as well because Hortensia's bite had little effect on her.

'And that name of yours?' Hortensia had started in on Trudy within hours of her arrival.

'I hate it,' Trudy had said in a whine that wore on Hortensia like wire on glass.

There the volley ended. Hortensia, for once, without a response.

On the bottom floor of No. 10, apart from the common areas and Hortensia's study that had now been converted into a sickbay, there was also Peter's study, which he hadn't used since his illness. There too was a laundry room that led out to a granny flat. Bassey stored his day-bag there and Hortensia threatened him with it as a place to live if he agreed to stay nights, but in all the years he'd worked for her this had never happened. Adjacent to the laundry room was a small en-suite guest room, which is where Trudy slept.

Without knocking, Trudy walked into Hortensia's study. 'You slept later than normal today, it's almost nine a.m. Wonderful progress.'

Hortensia wished she could reach her to slap her. Where did these people find these tones of voice? That particular lilt that could only mean they thought they were talking to someone they considered mentally deficient.

'What do they teach you?'

'Pardon?' Trudy was constantly hard of hearing, which was both good and bad.

'What, are you deaf?' It was bad because Hortensia actually wanted people to hear her, but good because it allowed her extra room for particularly rotten insults.

'Yes, I'm deaf in my left ear actually. Sorry, I often forget to mention it. I lip-read. Let me put this down and give you my full attention.' Trudy placed Hortensia's exercise file on the desk and turned to face her charge. 'You were saying?'

Hortensia, her lips pushed forward in displeasure, shook her head.

'What I meant was sleep is good at this stage. Doctor would be happy to hear the small change in medicines is working. You ready for your ablutions? And then today we'll walk the hallway. I've set up a little obstacle course for you to make it fun.' At this Trudy giggled.

Hortensia cursed God.

Lawyer Marx called. He asked if she'd contacted Esme. And she said no, she hadn't contacted Esme. To hell with

Esme. What, was it a crime to take her time? An old woman like her.

The medication took turns making Hortensia feel like a superhero and making her want to punch everyone. In other words, it had little effect on her. She felt she owed Trudy a daily battle when it came to the time to swallow the pills.

'What's this now?' Hortensia asked, although it was the same dosage of medicine she'd been taking for the past couple of weeks. 'They giving me morphine again?'

'Nothing's changed, Mrs James. We stopped the morphine – Carole stopped that, as far as I can tell from your chart. This is jus—'

'And no sleeping pills. I expressly asked for no sleeping pills.'

'Absolutely, Dr Mama made that clear to me. He'll make a call tomorrow by the way. Check in on you.'

Trudy handed Hortensia the cup of water and then passed her the pills one by one.

'What's that noise?' Hortensia asked, alarmed.

Trudy swung her head.

'Bassey!' Hortensia called out.

'I'll get him.'

'Bassey!' she called again, pressing the button at the same time.

When he appeared, Hortensia questioned him.

'It's next door,' he explained.

The mess of insurances had been sorted out, Marion the Vulture was repairing her nest. Hortensia felt a pang of jealousy. Her builder had wanted to know if she'd be continuing with the works to No. 10 and she'd had to decline, had to accept that in her state she didn't have the energy for managing the project just then.

Hortensia spent the day tuned to the sound of what she guessed was rubble being cleared, the occasional call of one worker to another, bits of broken house scraping about. Then, with late afternoon approaching, came the doorbell and the sound of Marion herself. Hortensia tried to make out what was going on in the front room. After she heard the front door shut, she prised an explanation from Bassey. Marion had simply needed a drink of water. Next door, her water had been switched off and while the workers were drinking from an outside tap – linked to a borehole – Marion, who'd come to visit the site, didn't think that suitable drinking water. The hag, Hortensia said. Bassey frowned and excused himself to make dinner.

TEN

Marion hadn't been on a building site in longer than she cared to remember. It felt good. The builder had not been on-site when she dropped by, but she'd phoned and made an appointment with him for the following day.

She awoke uncertain what to wear, even from her limited supply. The phone went, reception said Agnes was downstairs to see her. Marion rehearsed in her head. Only when walking down the dank stairway did she realise her buttons were misaligned.

'Agnes.' Marion walked up to where her maid stood at the reception counter.

'Good morning,' Agnes said.

'Your key, please, Ma'am,' the receptionist said.

Marion placed the key attached to an oblong piece of wood on the counter. She walked towards a grouping of chairs. Agnes followed. The woman was still shapely at her age, in a way Marion had always envied but never had the strength to admit to herself.

'Sit down, Agnes.' Marion liked the sound of her own voice. She was relieved it sounded stronger than she felt. She was relieved at being able to give orders. Bring command to chaos.

Agnes settled herself on a weary couch and Marion sat

beside her. She looked around; she'd keep her voice down, say as little as possible. Agnes wouldn't make a scene.

'As you know . . . things at home have changed slightly.' Marion coughed into her hand for no reason.

Agnes's face had always surprised Marion. Two eyes, a nose and mouth, yes, but the composure. Where does someone, especially without much money, buy that kind of peace? And even, as here and now, about to hear bad news. She must know surely.

'Agnes, I—'

'I found this, Ma'am.' Agnes pulled a long chain from the pocket of her skirt.

'Oh, gosh.'

Marion had thought it lost for ever in the rubble. She'd searched for it, racking her brain to remember what the last valuer had offered. It was a thick spiral of gold links. A gift from her father before her parents divorced, before life got more tangled. The rope of gold had always seemed inelegant, but Marion was grateful for it now. That and the large sapphire.

'Where did you find it, Agnes?'

Agnes shrugged. 'I went back. After the accident, Niknaks came with a bakkie to pick up my things. I wasn't with her and when I looked I saw I'd left something, so I went back. A picture of her when she was still a baby, with her father. And then, I don't know, one of those things, while looking at the damage I saw something shiny. There's a small break.' She stretched across to show Marion where she meant. 'But otherwise good.'

'You went back. Oh, did you . . . perhaps see . . .?' She wanted to ask without letting on how important it was, although this impulse embarrassed Marion – after all these years, to think Agnes would steal from her. 'I had wrapped a painting. Just before the accident. But Marelena can't find it. Did you see anything like that when you went back?'

Agnes frowned, thinking.

'I mean, thanks for this. Thanks for the chain, but did you see a painting?'

'No, Ma'am.'

Marion felt like crying; in a few seconds she'd convinced herself that Agnes had the Pierneef in her back pocket. 'Well, okay. Let's get on with it. I actually don't know what to say. You've been with us so long.'

'It's fine, Ma'am. Ag, Niknaks has been saying I must retire anyway. For some years now.'

'Oh.' Why did Marion always feel like she had to fight so much in Agnes's presence. Fight for her own dignity.

'She sends her greetings. And says she's sorry about all the . . . for the accident.'

'Yes. Thank her.'

They sat. Marion had no money to give Agnes but felt thankful, for the first time in her life, for the government and that Unemployment Insurance Fund business. She'd been sluggish in registering when they first employed Agnes, but the woman had pestered her and, now, Marion was glad she had.

Both women sat with their hands in their laps. Marion looked at her loafers – good enough for site?

'Well . . .' Agnes made to stand.

'What will you do, Agnes?'

'Niknaks is about to have another little one. Her business is doing well, which is why, I suppose . . . why she kept asking. She wants me to be a grandmother.' Agnes sighed in a way Marion hadn't heard before. 'But . . . my boyfriend asked me to go with him on holiday . . . to Mozambique. He was in exile there back when . . . Anyway, I think I'll do that first.'

A boyfriend. A holiday. Marion nodded to convey an understanding she didn't feel. Her tongue wouldn't move.

'Will you be alright?' Agnes asked and Marion nodded more vigorously.

Shaken, inexplicably angry, Marion took the short walk from the guest house to her own home, still worried about her choice of shoes, unable to erase the image of Agnes's face from her mind. She fingered the jewel in her pocket, wondered why she wasn't happier to have had it returned to her.

A man in a once-white shirt greeted Marion at her gate and said his name was Frikkie. She blinked – someone that black called Frikkie, come on! When they'd spoken on the phone, his English had been so good. She'd been impressed that an Afrikaans person could sound so Brit, she'd never have thought she was speaking to a black man.

'Well,' Marion said, stopping and standing, arms akimbo, at the bottom of what used to be the porch steps.

Someone had set up a ramp. There were two workers on-site. One man with his shirt tied around his waist was separating a pile of rubble. Useless and useful, Marion supposed were the two categories. She took a breath: that site-smell, dust and metal and sweat. She'd missed it.

'We'll spend today and maybe part of tomorrow preparing the site. And I ordered a portable. Should be here any moment.'

Marion nodded. She'd asked that her toilets remain off-limits, which seemed a reasonable request.

'I'm sorry I wasn't here yesterday. I thought we could discuss the works now, if you have a moment.' He indicated a bench and two chairs, some papers held down with stones.

'Yes.' Marion joined him at the makeshift office. 'So this is *your* business?' She'd owned a business once.

Frikkie nodded. Marion attempted to sit down on the low chair. She managed it, but not without some strain. Frikkie touched her elbow by way of support; she snatched her arm back and lowered herself.

Whose idea had it been to leave the practice? Marion wanted to heap the blame onto Max, but she couldn't forget her own pressing need to prove herself as a mother. She was already two kids in and still working, when Selena's difficult birth had put her in hospital, drugged and horizontal. The doctor's 'slow down' coupled with the increase, over the years, of Max's insinuations about her mothering quickly translated into two-day working weeks and ever shorter conversations with her partner, Harry Cumfred. Damned fool! Long before he bought her out, he'd already started referring to the company as Cumfred Architects. Baumann and Cumfred was no more. There was a time after giving up the practice when Marion thought she could still bully Harry into allowing her back in, then another bump appeared – Gaia. The result of careless sex, Max returning home after an extended conference, feeling guilty and eager to please. After the birth of her fourth child Marion's head got fuzzy – four children shouting different things at you, the world creeping in, getting in through the holes. It became too much. By 1972, almost twelve years after launching her practice, Marion stayed home.

'Hold on a minute.' Marion rose to answer her cellphone, walked some distance away from Frikkie and dropped her voice. 'Darling? I'm in a meeting . . . Yes at the house . . . We haven't spoken about how long yet, we were just getting to his schedule. Honestly, though, I think it'll take several weeks, plus the rain-days – just under two months, my guess . . . I understand you're using your own money for the guest house . . . Yes, I realise you're a stay-at-home mom . . . Marelena . . . Marelena, can I get a word in? No, I'm not suggesting your husband *bankroll* me . . . Two months is long, I realise. I wasn't planning on being at the guest house all that time, by the way . . . Well, I could stay here the minute the roof is fixed, for instance . . . Yes, of course I see that . . . Yes . . . Well, goodbye then.'

What had set her off? Was it the over-assured Frikkie – why did she hate him so much? – or the spite of her daughter, once the size of a worm in her belly, completely helpless and dependent on her. Marion couldn't decipher, but she dropped her phone into her handbag and placed her fingers over her face. Thank goodness she knew how to cry quietly.

The woman was crying. Marion the Vulture was crying. Hortensia strained her neck to see; she pushed her weight, through her arms, into the walker and stretched until the gentle cold knock of her head pressing against the window stopped her. Couldn't have been an ordinary phone call to reduce Marion to such a puddle. Unless Hortensia had overestimated her adversary. She stayed watching. Such a long crier too – wouldn't have guessed it. She was watching so intently that Hortensia didn't hear Bassey behind her. He cleared his throat and she jumped.

'You scared me.'

He walked to where she stood by the window. Took in the view. Marion had stopped heaving. She'd taken a mirror from her purse and was arranging her face. Hortensia swivelled her gaze between Marion and Bassey.

'Heard anything?' Hortensia finally asked, feeling dirty for prying.

'What do you mean?'

This man, always the epitome of decency.

'You know.'

'I think there have been some . . . difficulties.' He coughed. 'Financial and what-have-you.'

The following day Hortensia heard the bell go.

'Bassey,' she shouted from her bed, simultaneously pushing the buzzer. 'Bassey!'

His head appeared.

'Call her in. Don't look at me like that – call her in.'

Marion came in, talking, 'Hortensia, I am not someone you can summon at will. I'm actually quite busy and cannot visit. I merely wanted a drink of water, which this kind man obliged me with.'

Bassey left them alone.

'So?' Marion folded her arms, jutted her chin at Hortensia.

Hortensia wished she was standing, felt too easy a target flat. Oh well.

'I wanted to ask you something.' Hortensia hated having to be careful with words. She was so bad at it.

'What?'

'Marion, I . . . saw you yesterday.'

Marion looked puzzled, so Hortensia gestured with her hand towards the window. Marion moved to the window and looked out into her garden. Probably regretting the low country-style walls. When Marion turned back to Hortensia her face was pasty. Hortensia longed for a bigger sense of victory. It wasn't there.

'So?' Marion said, but her voice was quiet.

'I hate gossip.'

'Yes, well, if there's no real reason for me being here, I'd better go.' She moved to the door.

'Marion. You should come here.'

'What? What do you mean? I am here.'

'No, I mean . . . to this house. You should come *here*.'

Marion stayed rooted.

'I'm responsible for all the damage, the turmoil. You come here, you stay in your own quarters – the house is big enough. You don't have to shuttle back and forth between the site and that dreadful, sorry excuse of a guest house—'

Marion snorted; at least they agreed on one thing. She opened her mouth to say something, but Hortensia raised a finger.

'Think about it. Don't answer now. We aren't friends, Marion. I'm just—'

'I'll think about it.'

She left the room. Hortensia didn't hear the front door bang.

To ensure her plan would work Hortensia called Dr Mama, asked if he would stop by. She felt she was bothering him but didn't care.

'Any complaints?' Dr Mama asked after the initial physical examination was complete. It wasn't why she'd called him, but Hortensia had played along.

She lowered her voice, 'I don't like Trudy.'

Mama smiled.

'She's a good nurse.'

Hortensia nodded slowly. Marion hadn't called yet.

'I mean, what does she really do?' she continued.

Mama stood up and walked towards his bag. 'No complaints then,' he said and they both laughed.

'Seriously, though. You said even just another body.'

Mama looked perplexed.

'In case of emergencies.'

'Hortensia, I hate to put it to you, but there is no one else. Trudy is actually one of the nurses from my own practice. I spoke with the folks at Constantinople – none of their people will come here.'

He looked the most serious she'd ever seen him and she was sorry to be the cause of it.

'Gordon, what I'm trying to say is . . . what if someone *else* was available?'

He looked relieved at the thought. 'A friend?'

'Well, I wouldn't quite call it that.'

'You have someone that you'd like to come and stay?'

'What if I did? Would that be . . . acceptable?'

'Absolutely.'

'As in no Trudy?'

Mama's face relaxed and he shook his head. 'You really don't like her?'

'It's not personal, you understand. I mean, it's more out of compassion. Such a nice child, Trudy. No one like that should have to look after me.'

'But there's another person.'

'Oh, this woman is truly awful. Perfectly suited for someone like myself.'

Mama laughed.

'Well, I'd need to meet her, this woman. I mean, I know I said "another body". I was trying to be agreeable at the time. I'd run her through a few things. It isn't a joke, you know, Hortensia. It's your health. Your well-being.'

He was so earnest that for a moment he seemed younger than he looked. A little Boy Scout. A delicious one.

'Grandma?'

It was the little one knocking. She'd phoned from reception. Caught off-guard, Marion had barely had time to straighten her blouse and refresh her lipstick.

'Come in, Innes.'

Neither of Marelena's girls had Baumann in them, not the way their mother did. They looked – one simply an almost exact but miniature copy of the other – like their father: dark hair, fine eyebrows. Lara was prettier in that beauty-magazine kind of way. And Marion noticed how

Lara was the one who wanted Barbie dolls, make-up kits, and Innes, with thick glasses, her hair cut short, her nails clean but unpolished, asked for books. As if life itself was a cliché.

'Where's Lara?' Marion guessed the older girl was exercising her disgust by staying away.

'She dropped me. She'll phone on her way back from Grandpa.'

Marion frowned for a second, then relaxed. She kept forgetting that the kids still had a rather dull-looking paternal grandfather. He lived in a neighbouring suburb – she forgot which.

'Ah, I see.'

Marion indicated for Innes to sit on the hastily made-up bed while she took the chair. One leg was wonky. Guest house indeed. As she balanced her weight, Marion watched Innes take in the room. Their eyes met and Marion smiled. She could only imagine the chutzpah Innes would have needed in order to be allowed to visit. The stories she'd have had to endure from her mother, specific recollections well suited to showcase Marion's ineptitude as a parent and possibly as a human being.

'Can I use the loo?'

'Over there.'

Doubtless big sister Lara would have butted in with some first-year lawyer-speak. Human-rights-type stuff. She disapproved of Marion's treatment of Agnes. Always had done.

'What's this?' Lara had asked one day while visiting, many years back.

'Utensils. Cups. Plates,' Marion responded, eyeing the large Tupperware that Lara held aloft.

'Why are they packed away like this, Grandma?'

'They are for Agnes,' Marion had said, her mouth set. 'For Agnes.'

And Lara's eyes widened. She went crying to her mom. It might not have been so bad if a few days before (this was when Marelena still visited) Lara hadn't run to the pantry to replace a roll of toilet paper and returned with the one-ply.

'That's for Agnes,' her grandmother shouted, before muttering, 'Why on earth is she keeping her stuff in my pantry?'

The child looked confused. Why was her grandmother buying two different kinds of toilet paper? 'Because,' Marion said.

Because two-ply was more expensive and, considering her station in life, it seemed perfectly reasonable to expect Agnes to manage with one-ply. The child was asking questions about things Marion had never had to reason through, but there you were – there was your reason.

But the damage was already done. Lara was upset, Marelena was upset. She comforted her daughter and pursed her lips at her mother. 'I thought, after all this time, that you would have stopped with such things.' Marion was judged. Bitter about being misunderstood, she took it up with Agnes.

'Why are you keeping your toilet rolls in my pantry, Agnes? When the shopping comes in, when you unload the bags, take your things and keep them at the granny-flat.'

'No, Ma'am.'

'What?' Agnes seldom had cause to use the word 'no'

when speaking with Marion. In fact Marion couldn't remember a time she'd ever heard her use it.

'This is not my toilet roll, Ma'am. I buy my own.'

'Why do you buy your own?' Marion asked. Whatever could have changed? She'd been working there for decades and understood the rules.

Agnes, wiping down the speckled marble kitchen counter, shrugged. 'I needed something better, Ma'am.'

One day, soon after this conversation, when Agnes was distracted with laundry, Marion stole into the granny-flat to inspect the bathroom. There was the offending toilet paper. Three-ply. It turned her cheeks crimson and (never to be outdone), on her next trip to Woolworths, Marion selected a large supply of white three-ply toilet roll for herself.

After all that, Lara took Marion on as a project – her untransformed grandmother. Marelena was doubtful, and Marion even overheard her one day explaining to Lara not to expect too much from Marion. Why not? Lara had asked. She was around twelve at the time. Because she is old and stuck to old, bad ways. Marion would always remember that sober summation her daughter had given of her. Old and stuck.

'Tea, dear? Rooibos?'

Marion rose towards the kettle.

'Thanks, Grandma.'

'Some cookies.'

Each night, in an unnecessary and ineffective pretention, a pack of biscuits was placed on her pillow. Brown in see-through plastic. They looked vile, but she hoped Innes would like them.

'Sorry I missed your birthday, love. I was just . . .'

'I know. It's fine, Grandma.'

'Twelve suits you. Milk?'

'Yes, please.'

Marion pulled the bedside table closer and set the tea on top. She sat back down. Innes had a chip on her front tooth. Marion put her hand to her heart, remembering the day the little girl had fallen. At the park.

'How's school?'

Marion had tried to persuade her daughter to send Innes to St Winifred's, but Marelena believed in co-ed. Marion had taken it upon herself to look out for Innes, certain the awkward child would be putty in the grips of public-school children.

Innes pumped her head, her mouth full of biscuit. There was usually more activity when Innes visited, Alvar barking, Agnes fixing a sandwich. Grandmother and granddaughter smiled, shy. Innes had only taken three sips of her tea when her cellphone chimed.

'Ah, your sister's here.' Marion could already see herself, alone again in the room.

Innes scowled at her phone. 'Aw, man, only just got here.'

'Thanks for the visit, dear,' Marion said, moved by the sight of her granddaughter's irritation.

The chime again.

'Come, take the biscuits with you. Lara will be upset if you make her wait. Come, Innes, hurry. Hug!'

Her small bones crushed against Marion's belly, her bosom.

'Oh, I nearly forgot, Grandma. The woman at reception asked me to give you this.'

Innes handed Marion a white envelope, then ducked out the door. After Marion closed the door, she pulled out a folded piece of paper. It was Hortensia's handwriting:

Hello, Marion. I wondered if you'd considered my offer. If you wanted to take me up on it, would you agree to come by tomorrow and meet with Dr Mama?

Who in Heaven's name was Dr Mama? And why would she need to meet with him?

Marion stormed into the study where Hortensia was standing, her weight on the walker, receiving instructions from Trudy.

'Marion, you're early.' The design was very careful – one wrong move and it wouldn't work. Hortensia needed each to play their part.

'I don't appreciate being summoned again, Hortensia. I thought I'd made that quite clear.'

'Yes, well. Trudy, do you mind?'

The girl left the room and closed the door behind her.

'I get it: you've hurt your leg and you've caused some trouble for me and now you're trying to be helpful, but . . . I do not like being summoned.'

'I apologise.'

The apology tripped Marion. She took some seconds to find her feet again. Hortensia stood and waited.

'So, who's this Dr Mama? Why would I need to meet him?'

'Well—'

The bell went. A few seconds passed before Bassey appeared, announcing the doctor.

'Oh, how wonderful,' Mama said, walking in. 'This must be your friend that you told me about.'

Hortensia saw Marion's face fall. How to recover this – how to avoid a mess?

'Gordon, this is Marion. Marion, Gordon, Dr Mama. Marion lives next door.'

'Oh. I see your house is in a bit of disarray then.' Mama smiled. 'How perfect that you move in here.'

Marion's eyebrows jumped.

'Well—' Hortensia began.

'No explanation needed, Hortensia. I'm sure she'll have a cheering effect on you.'

'I don't—'

'Please, take a seat, Marion.' Dr Mama signalled to an open chair. He sat down as well. Hortensia stayed standing, gripping the walker, for once grateful that she had the stupid thing to hold on to.

'I wanted to meet you, Marion, just to ensure that you are comfortable with the arrangement. And, sorry to be distasteful, but I had to confirm you were fit for the task. Able-bodied, if you catch my drift.'

Hortensia had given up. She waited for Marion to work it out, for Dr Mama to talk long enough that she'd understand.

'Not on any medication yourself, are you?'

Marion shook her head.

'How long have you two known each other?'

The women looked at one another. Hortensia spoke first. 'About twenty years.'

Mama whistled. 'Precious! I admire you both. Really. And, Marion, your willingness to sacrifice.' He turned in his seat to face Hortensia. 'I see no reason why your idea can't work. Start as soon as you prefer. Trudy will stay on for the first few days Marion moves in, go over the odd procedure – nothing major – and then, once everything gets into a rhythm,' he cracked a wide smile, fanned his hand in the air, 'you're free.' He rose. 'Now, I must run to my next appointment.'

Perfect, Hortensia thought. Bingo!

'Call him back and tell him he's mistaken about you.'

'I will do no such thing. You call him back and you tell him he's mistaken about *you*.' Hortensia felt high, now that it was all out in the open.

Marion scoffed. The mist of Dr Mama lingered in the air. She was worried that if she stood up, her legs would buckle.

'But this is ridiculous. I haven't agreed to come here, and I certainly have not agreed to be your nursemaid.'

'Well, you had your chance to say something and you remained silent. Too late now. Or you can call him and tell him you're not really able to "sacrifice" after all.' Hortensia grinned, pleased with herself. She'd used her secret weapon – Marion's pride.

'I won't do it,' Marion said. 'Because he is not mistaken about me, I'm always willing to sacrifice. Now, you, on the other—'

'Well then, prepare to move in. Because I certainly am not requesting True-dee stay on, which seems to be his only alternative.'

'So what? Why do I care?'

'Well—'

'Oh, damnit! You tricked me, Hortensia.'

'Nonsense. The way I see it, we help each other. I don't need to know the details of your financial or family situation, but I suspect that if you stayed here, less stress, less *tears* would occur.' Hortensia arched her brows. 'The house is big – we never have to see each other.'

Marion said nothing.

'You do your things and I do my things, and we stay out of each other's way.'

'The only reason the doctor is agreeing is because he thinks I'll look after you.'

'Who's going to tell him?'

Marion shook her head, weary. 'Hortensia, you seem to think yourself invincible. You are injured, you need care. And you're sending away the only person who has been giving it to you.'

'I can manage perfectly fine on my own. If you ask me, she's more of a nuisance than a care-er. Darn pest! I can't wait to be rid of her. I don't mind dying, you know.'

Marion sighed. 'I don't know about all this.'

But she said it in a voice that suggested defeat.

ELEVEN

The arrangement was simple. While Marion's house was being repaired (builder promised six to eight weeks) she was to move into No. 10. A few weeks had passed since the accident. Carole the physiotherapist had predicted a maximum of twelve weeks for Hortensia's bone to knit sufficiently, eight weeks till Hortensia could move without aid.

The house was apportioned out. Hortensia would remain downstairs in her study-cum-infirmary. Marion upstairs in one of the guest rooms. Bassey served meals on a tray. He took Hortensia's to her room and Marion's to hers. As far as Hortensia could discern, besides her daily site visits, Marion went nowhere. She barely left her bedroom.

Trudy's last task was to organise for a contractor to raise the toilet seat, install handlebars (the ugliness of which Hortensia and Marion agreed on) and slip-proof the shower. She had written down a series of exercises; some Hortensia could do sitting at her desk, some she had to perform along the length of the hallway. Occasionally she needed Bassey to set up what Trudy called the obstacle course. A chair midway to sit on. A table in the middle of her path, forcing her to navigate around. The toilet could be tricky, but very little lorded it over Hortensia and certainly not her bladder. Dressing was a chore, so often it was tracksuit top, skirt (easier to pee in) or her favourite cerise nightgown with matching housecoat. The azure one, when the cerise was in the wash. With Marion about, Hortensia had wondered whether to dress up more, but hadn't the strength to attempt it.

On waking, Hortensia kept her eyes closed. A wind blew the oak, she could hear the prattle of the leaves against the windowpane. A band of finches twittered and Hortensia felt glad to hear them. She admitted to herself that she missed the Koppie. That her walks up there weren't just some masochistic ritual, but also a chance for total quiet, to spot bulbuls, for birds to chirrup, for branches to twist in the breeze.

Hortensia grunted, which made the effort of rising out of bed less painful. Ablutions took several minutes too long but, once ready, Hortensia, manoeuvring the walker and cursing it simultaneously, began her exercises along the hallway. Bassey stuck his head out of the kitchen and asked if he could make her breakfast. Concentrating on the task at hand, she nodded her consent. The house phone rang, way at the other end of the hallway. She muttered under her breath as Bassey went to answer.

'For you, Hortensia.'

'Message,' she said through clenched teeth. Was it her or did the pain increase each day?

Bassey spoke into the receiver.

'He says it's urgent. It's Mr Marx.'

'Blast!'

Bassey brought the cordless. Hortensia moved to the wall and leaned her shoulder against it. She took the phone. Bassey hovered, pointed to the chair some steps away from where she stood. She shook her head.

'Marx. I don't appreciate all this badgering. I'll do it when I'm good and ready, not a minute before.'

'Time is running out, Mrs James. If you don't act soon I'll have to assume you're rejecting the will, I'll have to—'

'I don't care, do you understand? I don't care!'

'I'm not sure there's reason to shout.'

'I'm not shouting!'

'I'll call back when you're less agitated.'

She could not press the red button hard enough; she just managed to stop herself from flinging the phone. 'Oh my God, you startled me. Don't do that!' She hadn't noticed Marion come down the stairs.

'Good morning,' Marion said.

'I suppose.' Hortensia took the few steps towards the chair, where she set the phone down. She continued her walk, wishing Marion would leave instead of stare.

'Was that the phone I heard?'

Prying.

'No, it was the bells of Notre-Dame.' This was pain. You live so long you think you've felt it all. 'Excuse me, Marion. If you don't mind.'

'Oh, sorry. I'm in your way.'

Understatement.

'What are those?' Marion asked as Hortensia walked past her.

'What are whats?'

'On your legs.'

'Stockings, Marion, what else could they be? Compression stockings, they call them. Damned nuisance.'

Marion stifled a laugh. The phone rang again. Bassey answered, grimaced and looked at Hortensia. He covered the mouthpiece and dropped his voice, 'Him again.'

'Take a message. No, tell him I'm dead. In the few minutes since we last spoke I . . . damnit . . . I kicked the bucket.'

Bassey took the cordless into the kitchen, he spoke in hushed tones.

'Whoever could that be?' Marion asked, her eyes wide.

Hortensia turned around at the front door, took a breath, eyed the length of the passage back towards her study. Her thumbs hurt from pressing down so hard. She decided to ignore Marion for as long as humanly possible.

'And,' the woman continued in a voice appropriate for reading fairy tales, 'whatever could they want?'

'Nothing. They want nothing. Now leave me be – out of my way.'

She laboured past, upset that Marion remained standing, spritely in fact – what was there to be so happy about? Hortensia had been looking forward to a beaten Marion, vanquished, come to drink at her enemy's waterhole. She leaned forward to rest and stared back at Marion, keen for some kind of win, however small. Marion looked away first.

'I see,' Marion said. But then continued with that grating tone of joviality, 'Well, while we're talking, Hortensia, you missed the last committee meeting. Perhaps I could update you.'

'The what?' They were talking – there was the problem right there. 'Marion, I have broken my leg. Do I seem to you like someone who gives a toss about your miserable committee meetings?'

'Oh, Hortensia. And here I was, thinking we could mend fences.'

'No. We absolutely cannot mend fences. I said you could stay, I didn't say we had to make conversation.'

'All I wanted to tell you . . .'

She nattered on. Hortensia made a point of not listening. The usual barbs didn't seem to make a dent in Marion, and Hortensia experienced a wave of regret. The plan had seemed so good at the time, Trudy so thoroughly unbearable.

'So what do you think?'

'Marion!'

'Just say "yes" or "no".'

'No!'

'Darn it!'

Marion jiggled her arms in annoyance, but it was a non-committal annoyance. Hortensia panicked at the thought that she'd lost her ability to upset Marion Agostino. Maybe the woman was on drugs.

'So you stand by your refusal of Beulah Gierdien's request?'

'Of course I do. And we're not discussing it. Marion, you're interrupting my exercises.'

'Well, she wrote again, requesting a meeting this time.'

Hortensia clicked at the back of her throat.

'And, while we're on the subject, Ludmilla was at the last meeting. They have the lawyers involved. The Commission has now appointed a mediator between the Von Struikers and the Samsodiens. We're hoping the whole thing gets thrown out.' It sounded hollow. 'And that the courts don't get involved.'

'Well, no surprises there. You and the other backward people of Katterijn are worried you'd get cooties, if the darkies move in.' Aha – there was the glimmer of madness Hortensia was used to provoking.

Marion straightened the front of her dress. 'Well, I see you're in no mood for company. I'll leave you be.'

God! If only Bassey was not just a chef but an assassin too, they could do away with Marion the Vulture. Dig a grave in the back yard. Forget burying the ashes of someone's miserable grandmother – bury Marion. No one would look for her.

As if he could hear her thoughts, Bassey appeared.

'Everything okay?'

'All good, thank you.'

Bassey had been twenty years younger when she'd interviewed him for the job as their housekeeper; his right leg had since found a limp and, a few years back, he'd started wearing spectacles. Hortensia had carefully curated her relationship with him. This compulsion had come with having money, with being called 'Madam' in Nigeria by the housekeepers; it had come with the weight of money. Her parents had had almost none, even when they made it to London from Barbados, where they'd had even less. They'd just worked and put everything towards their daughters' education. Hortensia remembered her mother coming in one day, that first year after the move. She must have been twenty-one, home from Bailer's for Christmas. And her mother came in late from work. It was hailing and Hortensia recalled the cold air that entered with her mother and how it stayed in the room. Funny how cold air could preserve itself in a room where it was not welcome. Her mother made tea, as she normally did when she came in from work. It was about 4.30 p.m. but dark outside. Her mother wouldn't stop shaking, and Hortensia kept waiting for the cold air to die out. She and Zippy sat at the table and were served their tea: salt biscuits and an apple to share.

'It's cold,' Hortensia had said and her sister and mother agreed.

But then when her father came home – not yet diagnosed, but slow in his movements, weakened – her mother turned on him, she'd stored up all her frustration for him. With her daughters looking on, Eda let Kwittel know that a rich white woman in an animal's skin had bumped into her on the pavement and raised her nose at her and told her to get back on the banana boat. Hortensia had never seen her mother so furious. And yet it wasn't just anger, it was shame.

When Hortensia found herself embraced in money, from Peter's considerable salary but also from her own successes, she understood that this was something she would need to manage. She would never allow money to turn her into someone who could make a woman come home shaking and shout upsets at her husband.

Bassey had answered a simple advert. Several others had too but, during the interviews, they had fawned over Hortensia, the way honest people had to in order to get work from those with more fortune. Bassey arrived on a motorbike. This surprised Hortensia and, when she asked, he said he needed to be able to get around and that he could not afford a car. He looked much the same as he did now. She'd noticed his pronounced Adam's apple, his darkened nails, perhaps telltale of a past as a smoker, although he declared that he was not one. Peter had begged off the tedium of finding a housekeeper, so Hortensia conducted the interviews alone. It was summer; she sat with potential employees on the stoep and ignored the occasional stares from neighbours passing by. What struck her about Bassey was that, on greeting him and settling in front of him on a crochet-covered cushion set upon a wicker chair, she immediately wanted something from him. Not sex. Not housework. Not even loyalty. It was something imperceptible, something she would never pin down in all his years of service. But one thing was clear: she would never get it. And this was the reason she hired him.

He'd answered no to all the questions: children, wife, live-in. Over the years, Hortensia calculated that he could well be homosexual. She also had times she thought he was simply celibate, but not for religious reasons, rather something philosophical. Or perhaps a disregard for shared nudity, the exchanging of bodily fluids. She could not imagine him having any capacity for the carnal. If it happened at all, Hortensia thought, sex with him would be in straight lines. There was something eternally tidy about Bassey, held together. It played out in a mild disdain for herself and Peter, she had always sensed it. Not a dislike though, something else – not pity, either. She'd noticed it that very first day when he'd sat across from her. A discreet weariness in his eyes like a tired king. And while Hortensia had been confused by Bassey's regalness, his haughtiness, she'd also liked him for it. He spoke as if his words were precious and he knew the person he was talking to couldn't really afford them. His facial expressions bore signs of forbearance – the quiet, long suffering of those who tend to others.

Marion could not keep herself from fussing. At night while Hortensia slept she walked around No. 10. Checking. Like a mother, after a long separation from her offspring, looking for birthmarks. It had been her idea to expose the concrete lintels, adding grey to the palette, adding weight. And there: the wall, running from the entrance down the passageway. She'd come to site and it was up . . . and straight. It's wrong, she'd told the builder. It's supposed to be skew. He, a burly guy, old, had said he thought she'd made a mistake. And did she know what she was doing? He'd called her 'girlie'. It's supposed to be skew, she repeated, calling for the site drawings. Why? he'd demanded, his eyebrows twitching. The workmen were looking on. Because that's how I designed it. It caught the view, it caught the light, it fanned out the hallway, making a perspective that she found delicate. He gritted his teeth. You need to redo it, she said. Do it again, do it skew. And they did. Marion grinned, remembering. There was a swell in her heart, a mound of pride.

Coming to No. 10 was what she'd always imagined. A feeling of rightness restored to life. All the reasons to fret forgotten. Marion slept as if returned to the womb. She was home.

This sense of ownership also stirred up an interest in

the decor of No. 10. Hortensia was, thankfully, mostly out of the way, so Marion consulted Bassey, who was puzzled by her behaviour but polite. For instance, she asked him about the choice of curtains in the lounge.

'A rather dirty yellow, don't you think?'

He turned his head to the side and dropped it just an inch. He seemed to be waiting, then he carried on with his vacuuming.

Once she cornered him in the kitchen.

'I'd played with the idea of a fireplace here, but I think this was the right decision, you know? The stove is a kind of fireplace really – that was my concept at the time. In the centre like this, the hearth.'

There were small details she'd not really forgotten, but filed away, and it brought her joy to notice them again. The views of the mountain from the guest bedroom upstairs. The wooden lattice of uneven squares separating the entertainment space from the lounge. A series of holes in the wall, filled in with coloured glass and little concrete shelves jutting out.

'You could put something nice out. A vase or something, Bassey. If she has one. The idea was to catch the coloured light, refract it. The sun comes up that side – can you just imagine it?'

There was a knock on the door. Hortensia knew it could only be Marion because it wasn't Bassey's knock. His was urgent business. Quick successive knocks. Hers, three generously spaced-out raps.

'Yes?'

Marion closed the door behind her and stepped towards the bed. 'Sorry to trouble you, Hortensia.'

'What is it?'

'I'd just wanted to ask if someone could visit.'

Finally a contrite Marion. A grateful Marion. A seeking-permission Marion.

'Visit you?'

'Innes, my youngest granddaughter. We're quite fond of each other.'

Hortensia doubted very much that anyone (perhaps apart from that ridiculous dog) could be fond of Marion, but she let it go. On account of how timid the woman appeared. She even seemed smaller, somehow. Cut-down. Hortensia smiled.

'Why not? I mean, please, Marion, be at home here. Do as your needs dictate.'

At the door Marion lingered next to a portrait photograph, heavily framed, that Hortensia had been wanting to take down.

'May I?' Marion asked, which was silly. Asking for permission to look at something plainly visible.

She studied the picture. Hortensia didn't mind so much. After all, they were young there, and still beautiful.

'I've been meaning to take it down,' she said.

Marion turned to look at her and they held eyes.

'Thing is,' Hortensia continued, but looked away, losing the stare-off, 'it hides a stain.'

Before she left the room Marion reached and lifted the photograph to check. She noted the stain on the wall and nodded.

* * *

When Innes visited, Agnes was with her.

'How surprising to see you,' Marion said.

'My sister hasn't been well, so she asked if I'd take her place for a few days.'

Marion regularly forgot that Agnes had a sister, whom Marelena had hired soon after she got married and started having children of her own.

'Oh.'

Innes hugged her grandmother at the waist. 'Mum was busy, so Agnes came with me. I rode my bike and she rode Lara's.'

Marion hadn't noticed the bikes propped on the stoep. 'You cycle?' she asked Agnes.

Innes moved through into the hallway. 'So this is the house. Grandma, show me around.'

'No rush,' Agnes said to Marion and went into the kitchen, calling for Bassey.

Dazed, Marion went after Innes, cautioning her to be quiet because an old, sick lady was sleeping.

'I heard that,' shouted Hortensia. 'What do we have here?' She emerged from her sickroom.

'Good afternoon.'

'Yes, you're Innes and I'm hungry.'

The entire afternoon seemed intent on baffling Marion. First Agnes, buxom and maladroit, on a bike chaperoning her granddaughter. Then Hortensia being . . . charming? Marion realised she'd never seen her with anyone under fifty and the effect appeared to transform the woman into . . . someone nice.

'Come,' Hortensia was ushering Innes. 'Bassey makes a mean hot chocolate.'

It became crowded in the kitchen, in a warm sort of way. Bassey and Agnes chatted. Hortensia leaned against the central island, teased Bassey about his hot chocolate and ordered that he make some. Marion remembered dimensioning her kitchen drawings, the plans. Reasoning out how the spaces would be used, where the cook would stand, how far from the fridge. Innes wanted to know whether Hortensia had cried when she broke her leg, and could she see the wound, please, please – she promised not to scream.

The visit went surprisingly well. Marion vacillated between being jealous that Innes and Hortensia got acquainted so quickly, and being relieved that Hortensia was being so kind; no jabs, no goading, not even a suggestion that this was a woman accustomed to striking people with her tongue. When Innes left, Marion spent some seconds wondering how, after such civility, she and Hortensia might slip with dignity back into the antagonism that was known and comfortable between them. Her concern was unnecessary.

'Lovely little girl,' Hortensia said, standing beside Marion on the stoep as the two bikes pumped away, up Katterijn Avenue. 'If not that she *calls* you "grandmother" I would never have imagined a familial connection.' She turned and went inside.

TWELVE

When they met, Peter, twenty-six, had just completed his studies at the Imperial College of Science and Technology where he read chemical engineering. Hortensia wanted to know what he was doing tutoring at Croydon. Peter mentioned his father, a man Hortensia would eventually meet, large like his son, but unsmiling – the only man she would ever confess to being afraid of. He had organised a job for his son at a prestigious firm of engineers and Peter was stalling.

'You don't want to work?'

In the early days they didn't so much date as walk beside each other and talk. It was an unspoken caution of theirs not to visit pubs together or restaurants. An attraction was growing, but sitting across from one another at a table, arranging a specific meeting, was too solid a gesture. After the incident with the Teddy boys, Peter's daily presence at the entrance of the college when she exited the building at the end of a day's work left a tickle in the area where her belly button was. But there was the fact that she wasn't imagining the glares they received, walking side by side down the streets. A woman (many women with many faces that eventually became one), her hair beneath a scarf (or in a hat, or pinned up), tutted (or scrunched her nose or spat) as she walked past them – Peter didn't always seem to notice, but Hortensia could never forget.

'I wish to work. I intend to work very hard, but . . . we don't get along so well. I want to find my own job, on my own steam.'

Hortensia nodded. There was something stiff and deliberate about Peter, the son of a war-man, he referred to himself as; but that was the only detail he offered about his father. Later, when they finally understood that they were in love with each other and ought to (Peter's words) marry, and when they finally worked up the courage to tell their parents, Hortensia met the war-man. He shook her hand, looked her in the eye and asked if they intended to have children.

Father, what a question, Peter said. But later on in the visit the question came up again. What would they be, though? What would you have? As if, Hortensia thought, Peter's parents were breeders wondering about the outcome of mating their prize stallion with a questionable mare. What kind of pedigree could they possibly get from such a coupling? She would regret not speaking up, not silencing them. She was accustomed, from her days at Bailer's, to being called names, being openly mocked. This was a thinner, sharper knife. The parents had a way of looking at her that told her who she was, where she truly belonged. They were accomplished at this, had learned it from their parents who'd been experts themselves, and had learned it from theirs and so on.

But so much came before that. The slowest of courtships. A wooing measured out in footsteps.

'And you?'

She wasn't shy, had never been.

'I like the lines of things. Forms.'

He wanted her to explain more. She'd decided, long before being awarded the scholarship to study in England, that the world was divided into three different parts. There was the space. Peter smiled while he listened to her and it played with her heart that he was amused, but not in an unkind way. He interrupted to tell her she had strange ideas and he liked it. She continued.

'In addition to the space there are the people, yes – the animals and so on?'

He nodded.

'And then there are things. I'm really, really interested in things. The lines of things, you see? The forms.'

All that talk, but done side by side, never front-to-front. The first time they sat down at a table, a year had passed. Hortensia had gone back to Brighton, completed her second year and then returned again to London for the summer and to work at Croydon. Peter had turned down his father's contact and had interviewed for a job at Unilever; he'd been working for almost six months. While apart, they had spoken on the telephone a few times and a letter each had passed between them. The idea to sit down for a tea was his. He'd given her directions to his office. When she arrived, she found that she was out of breath.

'Hortensia,' he said, entering the reception area.

He looked composed.

'Hello, Peter.'

They shook hands and she detected in his face some

small pleasure at seeing her. He watched her for a few seconds and she liked this.

The desk-lady went back to her seat, but Hortensia could tell her presence was a kind of disturbance, a wobble in the balance of things.

'It's so good to see you.'

She smiled, dropped her head to the side. This was a youthful habit that in only a few years she would lose.

'Am I too early?'

'Not at all. I have a break, now. After you.'

They walked along the Embankment. There was a building site nearby and the noise of drills, post-war efforts of remaking, gave a good excuse not to talk; Hortensia had nothing to say. People watched them walk, many turned around, and she decided that was because they looked handsome together. She moved closer to him and toyed with hooking her arm into his. Decided against.

'You look . . . lovely,' Peter said.

'Pardon? Oh. Thank you.' She checked the ground, watched her feet, watched the paving. She wondered where her courage had gone.

There was a tea room at nearby Charing Cross, Peter mentioned, and they turned a corner and walked towards the station.

He asked for coffee with milk and she said she wanted black tea. They sat in the corner of the cafeteria away from the window, from the stares of passing commuters. There were sconces along the cream-coloured walls and Hortensia fingered the cheesecloth on the table, the soft fuzzy skin of it on the tips of her fingers. It was warm in the corner, but she still rubbed her hands together as she sat. Finding her courage again, she started,

'You look so . . . like a proper working man. It's good.'

His eyes were a very grey-blue and sometimes, if he looked at you in a particular way, you could be fooled into thinking there was something green there too.

'It's not the best money yet, but there are prospects. Maybe they'll send me to Africa.'

'Goodness!'

The time they'd been apart seemed to have done something to them. She felt a woman and, finally sitting down together, across a table, he seemed a man who didn't just happen to be wherever she was; it had been planned and arranged – on purpose.

'How are the lines. The forms?'

'Two more years.'

The conversation found its stride. It seemed easy to tell Peter that she had been cheated of a mark because she was black and a woman. He nodded, frowned and apologised as if he'd committed the slight. He knitted his eyebrows, which were a darker brown than his hair. She'd thought he would ask her to prove it, ask for a clear explanation. In fact she'd been afraid he'd do that, not only because it would mean he didn't understand, but because she had no proof. She had only a feeling that she trusted and it meant something to her that he trusted it too.

They sipped their beverages, both warming their hands against the mugs.

'And your parents?' She was asking after their health, but inside she was asking: what are we doing and, if we do it, how will it all go?

'The same.' He smiled into his cup, took a gulp, set the mug down, looked around the teashop.

She walked him back to his office.

'So, have you ever thought about travelling around. The world, I mean?'

Hortensia frowned. 'Not really.'

'For instance, going really far, somewhere like Africa, for instance.'

She smiled.

'Well?'

'It would be like going home. For the first time.'

He nodded. 'True,' he said, a little pink with embarrassment. He scuffed the underside of his shoe back and forth along the pavement. They stood to the side as his colleagues walked by. 'I have to get back,' he finally said and bent to land a kiss on her cheek.

It took her by surprise. Later she would tease him about taking a year to make up his mind.

'See you,' he said as he went in through the door. He didn't look back.

They saw each other a few more times before Hortensia returned to Brighton, her address securely written in neat lines in Peter's address book; his, put to memory in her mind. They wrote to each other and where before even their most friendly of meetings had maintained an air of formality, the letters were flirtatious, loose, even steamy. Peter had noticed a mole, black like the ink of his pen, just beneath her left collar bone. Distracting, he confessed. And two letters later he wondered about it, what it felt like to touch. Hortensia was initially more practical. She wanted to know whom he had exchanged letters with previously. Was he courting another? Her suspicions were there without having to be conjured – no doubt the result of growing up in the fog of Eda's endless sense of present or coming injustice. As the year went along, the frequency of Peter's letters, his jokes and his passion gave Hortensia the courage to allow love to bubble up, to scatter and pop along the surface of her life. He asked that she draw him pictures – their ready joke about forms, lines. Peter sent Hortensia scribblings of chemical compounds, which he would name and explain to her. Why the fascination? she once asked. His answer was cryptic in its brevity. He liked to study 'combination'; he liked to dwell upon the science of it. She enjoyed this about his mind, the intensity with which it considered these scientific details that remained abstract to her. He seemed to apply the same intensity in studying her and, late at night, this thought made her skin hot.

The following year, in May, Kwittel died. Hortensia attended the funeral but returned to Brighton and stayed through the summer, unable to face London. She felt guilty, but couldn't find the courage to return to a home without her father sitting inside it, reading. Peter drove down to see her. He came to comfort her, to hold her.

Marion hadn't got around to the library. She'd told herself that Beulah Gierdien was in the unfortunate position of needing something from Hortensia James, which she would never get. The spite that had initially motivated Marion's need to vindicate Beulah's request had diminished. In its place Marion found herself curious about

Hortensia, about her strange regard for history, her solitary life.

At the end of the last committee meeting Marion had stressed to Ludmilla the importance of keeping her informed. It was that self-contained Scandinavian quality of Ludmilla's that had made Marion nervous, made her worry that her committee meetings would be sidelined.

Instead of an update, Ludmilla called and asked if Marion had been to the library already – if not, could she please look up some details for them. She was interested in the history of the Koppie and its surrounding lands, since it was looking possible that the case would settle out of court and the Samsodiens would be granted a parcel of land, within Katterijn, as compensation. I doubt we can stop them, but you never know, Ludmilla had said, and Marion had the uneasy sensation of feeling both nauseous and flattered. She agreed to go.

When Marion told Hortensia she was going to the library, she also thought, in a rare moment of care, to ask if she could get her a book.

'From that sorry excuse of a library, with countless Wilbur Smiths pouring from every crevice and not a single book by Walcott, Lamming or Aidoo?' She sucked her teeth. 'Ignoramuses.'

Marion took that as a 'no'. She gathered her book bag and walked, enjoying the sun on her neck, the fact of not needing a scarf. She missed Alvar, but when she'd raised with Hortensia the possibility of having him at No. 10 – out of the question, she'd said, shaking her head for extra emphasis.

On account of its three gables, Marion assumed the library building had once been a wine cellar although Beulah's note said 'stables'. Its foundations dated back to the eighteenth century. The thatch roof had since been replaced by slate, but the entrance still had the original stone floor.

'Agatha.'

She was a woman with the requisite brown bun on the top of her head, a white-bone comb holding it there, and thick glasses that made her eyes look like large black-and-white buttons.

'Afternoon, Marion. Returning?'

Marion pushed her stash forward. The Jilly Cooper was forgettable. Her cheeks grew warm as Agatha scanned the three Wilbur Smiths. She hadn't had the strength to challenge Hortensia on that.

It was midday on a Tuesday, the Katterijn library was empty, but then again Marion had rarely seen it full.

'Here are the magazines you requested.' Agatha moved a pile of glossies along the counter. 'You taking out some more? I can keep these here for you.'

'Thanks, Aggie. I'm actually here for some research, but . . . you know, I was also wondering, where do all the books come from?'

'The collection? Donations, really, Marion. And some funding from Council.'

'And the ones that get bought – who buys those? I mean, who decides for the library?'

'I do. And I take suggestions as well, based on what people around here would like to read.'

'I see and . . . do you have anything . . . diverse.' There was really no need to whisper.

'You mean black?'

'Aggie.'

'We have a special section. In the corner over there.'

Marion nodded. She was picturing Hortensia being sent to *a corner* for the authors she preferred.

An old woman and a little boy came through the swing door. She had a cane and the boy dragged his school bag behind him, like a dog on a leash.

'Hello,' Agatha greeted them and they walked past the counter to the children's section. 'You were saying, Marion?'

'Research. The historic materials. Remember I mentioned I'd come through . . . for the Beulah business. I thought I better get on with it.'

'Yes, of course. It's nice to have some interest. I stumbled on the materials when I took over and tried my best to sort them out.'

Agatha seemed excited. She rose off her chair to come around the counter. She had the walk of a heavier person, her steps suggesting a weight her bones didn't carry. She put a hand to Marion's arm by way of leading her.

They walked through the main room of the library, with its runs of benches and a few reading alcoves with dormer windows. The back room, a large storeroom, smelt of dank and mould. It was dark despite it being a bright day outside. There were two high square windows, but apart from that no natural light got in. One desk and a narrow chair waited for Marion.

'You can sit here. Some are in files and some of the stuff is back there still in boxes. Wait.' Agatha's tone was hushed.

Marion pulled the chair out and balanced her weight

on it. Agatha shuffled towards an arrangement of book-shelves and sealed boxes.

'I hardly ever come here any more,' Agatha said, breathless with pulling files off the shelf. She set them on the desk. 'Careful,' she said catching Marion's eyes. And then she left.

Marion shook her head. Agatha was known for being dotty, an odd sort. The files left a film of dust on the tips of Marion's fingers and her eyes watered from it.

Beulah's dates – the deaths of the babies – matched the documents Agatha had produced. There was no mention of a Jude, but there was a pile of medical records as well as death certificates. Marion leafed through and her fingers remained light, unaffected, until she realised she was leafing through pages documenting the death of children – so many. Annamarie's children, if Beulah was to be believed, could be amongst these. Marion felt ashamed. A woman wanted to perform a ritual ceremony, fulfil her grandmother's last wish, and here she was fingering through history with no purpose. She wasn't here to corroborate Beulah's story – she didn't care enough to – and she wasn't here to refute it, either. Ludmilla had wanted her to sniff around, find some reason why the Samsodiens shouldn't be granted land in Katterijn. Marion suddenly felt tired, unfit for the tesk.

In another pile of documents there were some maps, hand-drawn and labelled in what must have been Dutch. A file of just numbers, some kind of ledger. Another with names, with the odd sheet of paper in Arabic script. At the bottom of the pile were a series of drawings. There was a sketch of Katterijn vlei. A diagrammatic map of the whole neighbourhood with some of the buildings labelled, in

English this time. Marion's eye searched for Katterijn Avenue; there was No. 10 on that stretch – the original manor house, which had burned down. There was the post office which used to be a barn, the Katterijn well that City Council wanted to reinstate as a monument; and there must be the library, except it was labelled as the slave quarters for one Van der Biljt farm. How many incarnations could one building have? There was a series of maps showing the topography and another with all the trees numbered. There was a moth-eaten map of the Koppie, but it wasn't labelled the Koppie. Almost three hectares of farmland that ran down the hill and abutted the Vineyards. There was a page with names, the script unclear, smudged. Marion read through some sentences at the bottom. Her teeth came together in her mouth and she tasted something unpleasant at the back of her throat. There were sketches of the different contraptions, straps and turning wheels. In a neat hand someone had explained how far to turn the handle before the first bits of bone would start to break. She folded the map over, annoyed that her hands were shaking.

Back at the front desk, Marion couldn't find a voice to bid Agatha goodbye in.

'Got all you want – information, I mean? Not taking out anything, I see.'

Marion didn't move. She fixed her stare at the cross that hung from Agatha's neck – silver, too large and trendy-looking for a woman like Agatha. She turned to leave.

'There's blood here, Marion.'

Marion walked; she heard Agatha call out about the magazines but decided not to turn back – she'd get them some other time. Outside she took five deep breaths.

Everyone knew Aggie was a few keys short of a bunch, but Marion couldn't stop trying to fix her hair even though it was already neat; she straightened her rings but the gems were facing outwards, straight already. She walked back towards No. 10, and twice she stopped to look over her shoulder.

When Ludmilla called to find out what Marion had discovered, Marion told her the truth. That the documents were old and tattered, that if Ludmilla wanted to conduct proper research she should drive into town, visit the archives. Marion was unusually short with Ludmilla on the phone and she could sense the woman's confusion. She herself was perplexed.

They planned it, practically had the conversations marked out onstage with electrical tape. Hortensia would graduate, they'd tell Eda first (Peter wrote his intentions down in a letter) and then they'd, together, visit Peter's parents. With all the nerves, the rehearsals and the overwhelming dread, the actual conversations were an anticlimax. Eda, convinced her daughter had been destined for spinster-hood, didn't even mention that she would have preferred a black son-in-law, a Bajan at that. They'd been prepared for a bigger fight from Mr and Mrs James. Peter had not had to say anything explicit for Hortensia to realise his parents would disapprove. While affronted at that first meeting, at their appraisal of her, she'd also imagined, fantastically, that there would have been spitting and hissing, swearing at the least. The civility of their prejudice, the cunning, had left a polite wound. Beyond that they seemed resigned to their misfortune – Hortensia's black-ness and the brown grandchildren she would give them.

Their wedding was a small affair at Hortensia's mother's church. Mrs James, Peter's mother, would have preferred her church, but did not insist. Uncle Leroy, retired serviceman of the Carib Regiment, ambled down a short aisle with his grandniece's bony hand in his. They walked staring ahead at the priest, at a surprised-looking Peter and, beyond, at the yellow blue-and-red stained-glass window depicting Jesus, haloed and chaste.

In the morning, getting ready, Hortensia had looked long at herself in the mirror, having never felt this pretty. She was drunk on the romantic booze of a wedding day – Zippy with a garland in her hair, the flurry of little girls with dusty rose-coloured bouquets, the shiny smiles everyone reserved for Hortensia, smiles at their highest volume; no one could have been more smiled at than Hortensia on that day and she went deaf with it.

The morning after the wedding her ears were still ringing. She was even more senseless after having made love to Peter; her first experience that pain and pleasure could coexist.

When they awoke the morning after, Hortensia had felt shy, but she had taken his cheeks and gazed into a face she adored. His ardour of the previous night had drained and instead he looked blank.

'Are you okay?' he asked. And this surprised her. What could be wrong? 'You seem a bit . . . I don't know.'

The words didn't suggest it, neither did his facial expres-sion, but all Hortensia could think was: he is scared. There was no answer to his question; he wasn't really asking her anything. It sobered her up, though, and in the few years it took the company to give Peter a raise and suggest he move to their branch in Nigeria, Hortensia stayed sober. In fact love would never again induce anything more than an ache in the centre of her belly. Peter's coolness of that morning, though, was quickly replaced with the characteristics she was more familiar with – intense, studious, quirky and warm. They honeymooned for three days.

Hortensia moved into Peter's flat in Highbury, they made love every night. Peter, seemingly recovered from the shock of being a husband, ardent and happier than she'd ever seen him.

Soon after she graduated, Mr List, whose faith in Hortensia never wavered, had invited her to submit designs for a collection he was putting together. His drawings showed lean, pointy women, fabric held at the neck with a bejewelled clasp and trailing down, scraping the floor; others cut clean at the small of the back. The clutch-purses and capes were a piece and had become a hit with a crop of rich, bored people. In an article in *Harper's Bazaar* List was honest in his praise of Hortensia's House of Braithwaite and the contribution the designs had made to the success of the collection – it was Hortensia's first sensation of spotlight.

The main feature of her designs was a series of dashes, deliberately misarranged. Once repeat-printed onto yards of fabric (her colours were variations of mud and flecks of white, egg-yolk-yellow and cobalt), it looked like someone with too much time had sat and scratched out an alien cipher. This motif became a signifier of her designs. Sometimes sharp precise lines, sometimes frenzied scratches of different thicknesses. Always dense. In later versions she varied the lengths of the dashes. In one collection she hid black stencilled birds (wings spread) amongst what now resembled foliage. In another she interrupted the pattern with bands of blank. For a special commission (carpets and curtains) she arranged the cipher into wiry-like shapes that looked like an ancient alphabet. Decades later, when her reputation in the design world was established, Hortensia's rich ciphers would be spoken of with wonder.

Peter had initially thought it trivial to refer to lines on a piece of fabric as a cipher. His rebuff had hurt Hortensia, though, and they argued about it – about the possibility that he, with his mathematics and chemistry, did not consider her work serious or worthwhile. He apologised and they slept entangled, but the feeling never left Hortensia, that although Peter was intrigued by her work and seemed genuinely pleased at her success, he didn't really comprehend its significance. Making marks was pure to Hortensia. It saddened her that what she considered the best thing about herself was a puzzle to her husband.

Soon after the article was published, House of Braithwaite won a large contract with Deutsche Lufthansa offices in Cologne, to produce wallpaper for the executive suites. She was able to join a collective of designers in north-west London. She hired a part-time assistant. Hortensia favoured block-printing and stencilling, but these were time consuming. Eventually, after receiving a commission to design all the fabrics for a yacht owned by one of List's most devoted customers, Hortensia bought a new mechan-ised screen-printer, Swedish-engineered. She moved into her own studio and hired another pair of hands.

The more celebrated House of Braithwaite became, the

less Hortensia felt the need to justify her work to Peter. For her it was easy; she had always longed to make beautiful things and now she was doing so. She liked the shining light validation throws on those who do well. She came home and loved her husband but also went out and loved the attention. Peter observed one day that she was perhaps gone too much. Between her trips to fairs in Milan and Stockholm he missed seeing her. She shushed him, but later she would wonder about the glare of success, feel the pull of the notion that a woman's true success was in the home and not out there in the world. She would feel punished and reach to blame something – her mother, Peter, the unjust God – and find nothing but herself.

In 1956, both her marriage and her business over three years old, Peter mentioned that his superiors were keen to second him to Nigeria, Ibadan, and that he was keen to accept.

Eda didn't like the idea of her daughter going so far away. Despite Hortensia's efforts, she'd continued to drive trains. She'd been puzzled at Hortensia's suggestion that she could stop working. She ignored that offer, but accepted the one to move out of Holloway to a more comfortable flat. Zippy was doing her A-levels, she wanted to go to university and then become an accountant. She considered Hortensia going off to Nigeria an adventure and softened Eda's fears with stories of fellow classmates from West Africa.

Hortensia settled into Ibadan as if it were a neighbourhood in London. The new environment and the chunky accents around her were not strange, nor were the house staff, although she'd grown up making her own tea and mopping the floors.

They still had sex in those days. Next to the kitchen sink on the charcoal-blue Italian factory tiles that the supplier had given Hortensia a discount on; or Peter standing, pressing in, Hortensia's hands spread against her favourite surface with the canna-lily wallpaper (last batch by the, now dead, textile designer). Peter went off to work, chauffeur-driven, and Hortensia worked in the shed she'd had converted, almost on arrival, into a studio. Her work was still being sold from the London studio, which she'd reluctantly surrendered to the assistant, with Zippy keeping an eye. Hortensia had seen yards of adire on a visit to Abeokuta and was in search of a local designer to join her in opening a boutique. At the end of the day Peter would come home and they would touch eyes over dinner. The heat was sticky and the love slippery, but Hortensia's uterus didn't take any notice.

Years passed. 1958, she was twenty-eight years old and her mother wanted to know why she wasn't yet pregnant. Peter said nothing. The sexual clamour of their arrival in a new place died down, though, and Hortensia discovered the loneliness of marriage.

They began to argue about silly things and she discovered that he had a temper, rare but awful enough that, each time it erupted, the gap between them widened. Gradually it became a fact that Peter touched Hortensia very little.

In bed at night they slept turned away from one another and in the daylight, on the rare occasions they walked together, they did not reach for each other's hands. Marriage was a disappointment. Colder than Hortensia had imagined, it was the sad end to her Sunday-school belief in the lore of Noah – that life was best lived in pairs. Instead, marriage had turned out to not be much after all. It was the tedium of little domestic details. It was negotiating the tiresome habits of another. Marriage also made Hortensia suspicious when she met new people. Where was the nastiness in this one? she would think to herself as she handed change to a trader or stood to be measured by a polite seamstress. She'd seen Peter cradle an injured bird so gently that the animal had managed to come to a state of calm. And, in the heat of one of his moods, she'd seen him smash a plate to the floor. Not just any plate, but the gold-leaf-painted Chinese porcelain plate that she'd spent months negotiating for and finally wangled out of a dealer in London. It had been her favourite, with four pheasants and four orchids arranged along the face, flecks of gold dancing between them like magic dust.

What happened? This was a common question she asked herself. And then Hortensia would work backwards through their time together, through the string of little and big arguments, offences taken, insults applied. Often the house settled into weeks of corrosive silence. The silence was easier than the booby-trapped mission of attempting conversation. But sometimes the silence wasn't a relief, it was a form of punishment. The spells of silence could continue for days, but they always ended unceremoniously.

'Did the paper come?' Peter would ask at breakfast and Hortensia would answer in a clear sweet voice.

Or they would be in the bedroom, Peter dressing for work, the sounds of the driver singing as he completed the morning car wash, the tinkling of the housekeeper as she laid the breakfast table. Hortensia would already be dressed. She'd stand by the window and look out into the garden, the tennis courts beyond, the pool that the gardener fought with every day to maintain the chlorinated blue of cleanliness.

'Harmattan is late this year,' she'd say.

And Peter would nod and then, understanding that she couldn't see him, with her back turned, and might take his silence to mean he intended to stretch the fight out, he'd say, 'Yes, it just might be.'

Sometimes they did make love, but it was duty. Hortensia remembered her father telling her about hurricane scares when he was a boy. When the electricity was cut off, how to keep the eggs fresh: every few days turn them over. That was how they made love. It was a domestic task to keep something from rotting.

THIRTEEN

The feeling Marion was experiencing was not one she was familiar with.

She knocked on the door.

'Marion,' came Hortensia's response – the woman could see through wood.

'May I come in?'

She heard what sounded like a sigh, which was as close to a 'yes' as Hortensia was likely to come.

'Sorry to trouble.'

Bassey was off and the house was empty.

'I felt like some company.'

Hortensia pursed her lips, watched as Marion pulled a chair up to the bed.

'Marion, with all due respect, I didn't invite you into my home in order to offer you company.'

Always terse. Always so cutting.

'I went to the library,' Marion said in a bid to ignore Hortensia's discouraging look. When she didn't say anything, Marion bravely carried on. 'I . . . I just felt like . . . Don't you sometimes feel a bit . . .'

'Marion—'

'Just let me try and explain. I remembered something.'

'Is this really necessary?'

'Yes.'

Marion had remembered being in class.

'At school, St Winifred's, in Wynberg. Maybe you've heard of it.'

Hortensia nodded, her face was set, Marion faltered.

'I . . . I—'

'Marion, really.'

Marion smoothed her skirt and rose from the chair. 'I'll leave you in peace.'

Once Marion's history teacher, Miss Siebert, wrote an address on the green board. Miss Siebert – they called her Queen Victoria behind her back, because her hair went down to her bum and her skirts to her ankles – told the girls that this was a place that sold books. And she said the girls should go and visit it sometime, that this was a good idea. And she taught the lesson and every now and then throughout the class as she gave informa-tion – something about the Hottentots, something about the British – she would mention the books in the bookstore. And then at the very end, and the class was memorable because it would be the last Miss Siebert would ever teach at St Winifred's, at the end Miss Siebert said in a higher voice than normal: 'I don't know if I've really made myself clear, girls. You should go. You should buy this book.' And she hurriedly scrib-bled the name of a book on the board. 'Because you see, this,' she indicated the orange textbook she'd been teaching from, the one Marion would later cram to score an A, 'this is not really history.'

Miss Siebert didn't come back. One of the girls told that Miss Siebert was a communist who had sex with her garden boytjie. The girl boasted that the book Queen Victoria had written up on the board was a banned book, and that her father worked with the council and she'd done a good thing and told him. The school board shivered that such insubordination could take place at St Winifred's. A more suitable history teacher was found for the girls.

Marion took her confusion home to her parents. She told them about what Miss Siebert had said, about the bookstore, about real history. Her questions were swatted away, dampened. She felt the incident ripple but there was no one to ask about what was real history and what was not. Her parents weren't in the business of telling these two kinds of histories apart; they weren't in the history business at all.

Marion's knock again. God, that woman!

'Come in!' Hortensia shouted. 'What now?'

'Actually I forgot to mention just now: the thing is, I've been considering that stain.'

Hortensia arched an eyebrow. There was definitely something wrong with the woman. One minute blabbering, the next going on about a damned stain. Hortensia rolled her eyes. 'What is it, Marion? What is it that you want?'

'The stain, you see. I wondered if you'd allow me to . . . try something.'

'What makes you think I haven't already *tried* something? I just need to get someone in, that's all. If I wasn't flat on my back, many a thing would be handled.'

'May I?' Marion decided to ignore Hortensia's protests.

Hortensia sighed. Marion went back into the hallway and returned with a white square of cotton fabric and a saucer with some liquid in it.

'Now, Marion—'

'Don't worry, don't worry. I know what I'm doing.'

She removed the portrait and set it down, on the nearby desk, with more care than Hortensia thought necessary. To her horror, Marion spoke while she worked.

'See, it's a bit complicated. Because of the wallpaper you've used. One of yours? Anyway, so I guessed it started out as a grease stain,' she began to get out of breath. 'And then someone, Bassey perhaps, had a go at removing it, smudged the dye and maybe used bleach – reasonable choice, you know, but . . . Ah, you see . . . The wall's at an angle by the way, did you realise? . . . There, just a . . . All done.'

'I won't even ask what was in the saucer.'

'Don't.'

'I can't understand why you care.'

Marion shrugged. 'What should I do with this?'

The picture had been taken in a studio. The photographer had been stern, but then had suddenly become animated, saying, 'Kiss her, you fool! Right there on the cheek' and then he'd pushed down on the button.

'Give it to Bassey. Ask him to throw it away.'

Slowly small pieces of information materialised. Her name was Valerie. She was British. She came to Nigeria every year, staying for a few weeks, and then returned to

England. Exactly what she was doing there remained unclear to Hortensia. But in the weeks when Valerie was in Ibadan, a routine was established and Hortensia trailed them.

Once, on a Friday evening, she followed them down a road. They parked outside a motel and Hortensia returned to the house. Peter came back from his conference late on the Sunday evening.

Hortensia thought of them together. The motel was grimy. Peter was clearly avoiding the better hotels where he might run into someone from Unilever or some other multinational, someone from his circle.

One day, just after Peter announced another conference, Hortensia told him she would be doing some travelling, spending more time in Abeokuta with her potential business partner. It wasn't a lie that she was going to go into business with a Mr Adebayo. They'd met at an art exhibition in a private home in Bodija, discovered their shared trade and made plans to meet again. They were not quite far enough into their plans to set up a shop, but none of their dealings required that she sleep away from home.

'I see,' he said. 'Abeokuta is close enough – why stay over?'

'Well, I know so little of the culture, really. I want to spend some time. Mr Adebayo will take me around. Even just more knowledge of the art. I know so little – it embarrasses me.'

He nodded.

For an unknown reason Hortensia continued, maybe in an attempt to revive something. In the beginning they had talked and talked.

'I mean, technically this is where Picasso stole from, isn't it?'

Peter frowned; they'd argued about this before. About the word 'stole'. Back then he'd said 'exploited maybe, but maybe not even that', and so on. They were neither of them experts on art history, European, African or any other. Their arguments had been fiery: that Africa was reduced to a 'period'; that the works Picasso was inspired by had been looted by the French; that Africa was a fad – exotic and, of course, dark. Hortensia regurgitated all this, as if the material of past conversations could be incendiary, as if love were a bonfire.

Peter was frowning at her, as if he could see through her, see the lie. Hortensia got up and walked to him, looked into his eyes.

'I'm really excited about opening this boutique. I feel we could do something new. I know you don't think much of—'

'That's not true.'

'Well, I just want to be able to do a great job at this.'

Peter nodded.

Hortensia figured they would fuck while she was away. Peter would bring the girl into their bed and they would have each other.

On the Friday evening, she waited for him to leave for his 'conference', then she packed and climbed into a rented truck. She drove aimlessly for two hours, then doubled back to the house. The problem of Fola the housekeeper had been solved when Hortensia let her off for the weekend. The problem of Sunday the gateman had been slightly more tricky. Although the neighbourhood was renowned for its safety, Unilever took no chances – they'd hired Sunday to keep an extra eye on things. Hortensia surmised that Sunday would only take instructions from Unilever or, at the very least, from Peter, whom he referred to as his Oga. Hortensia resolved this by calling Peter's bluff. I'm away, you're away; just let the old man sit with his family over the next couple of weekends – don't you think? The house is fine; all these pretensions when actually we're safer than we would be on any London street. Peter had smarted at her underhand critique of their new-found wealth and the status it afforded them in Ibadan. But he'd also agreed. Sunday was given the two weekends off.

Hortensia needed something. Something deeper than a kiss in the middle of a market, something raw. She wanted to have a clear picture of what real, absolute and unequivocal betrayal looked like.

She parked the truck some way along their street, but she could still see the gate, see who came and went. She waited. They did not come. She was dressed in the burkha; she ate two oranges, then eventually around 10 p.m. she drove to a nearby inn, where she'd rented a room. She did the same the next day and on Sunday. The weekend passed. Peter got back from his conference. Hortensia returned from Abeokuta.

'How's it going? This Mr Adebayo, will I meet him sometime?'

'Perhaps. He's very busy at the moment.' This was true. 'When we launch the boutique, we'll have a great big party. Maybe, then.'

*   *   *

The second weekend Hortensia tried again. Once in disguise, she parked the truck some distance along their street and observed from her post. Peter's car rounded the corner, paused at the gate as it swung open, entered. He had the woman in the car with him. Like a cat who traps its mouse, then ignores it, Hortensia drove to the inn and slept. On Saturday she returned before dawn. They stayed in all day. Occasionally Hortensia would stretch her legs around the block. Her scheme was helped by a nearby mosque and a large community of Muslims in the adjacent neighbourhoods. No one asked her any questions.

Hortensia waited till the clock struck 9 p.m., then she let herself in through the gate. Peter's car was parked in the driveway. The lights were off in the front portion of the house. None of the garden lights were on. Switching on the lights was the kind of thing she or the housekeeper would do, but would never cross Peter's mind. The house was a long rectangular bungalow. A succession of rooms, each more intimate than the last. A low hedge had been planted right along the external walls of the house, a thick necklace of a bush with broad, deep-magenta – almost brown – leaves. She bent low, trailed her fingers through the plant, walked down the length of the house. At their bedroom window she gathered up the skirts of the black gown and pushed her body through the hedge, parting the soft branches. There were no curtains here. She'd decided not to have curtains on account of the high walls, on account of the lovely garden. A touch of lace would suffice, she'd thought, and there it was now. White, finely holed and incandescent, which could mean only one thing. When she'd asked the mercer for lace without metallic threads he'd gone ahead and ignored her. How had she missed it? The realisation distracted Hortensia for a few seconds but then she heard Peter's voice.

Although the room was lit, it was difficult to see anything clearly through the lace. It was more like watching shadows. Someone was lying on the bed. She could see his back, the rounded cheeks of his bottom. Peter naked, an unfamiliar state. His voice again. But she couldn't see the woman. Maybe there was no woman. Maybe she'd invented the whole thing. But then she heard her voice. A figure walked into the room, said something, Peter laughed. He continued to laugh as she climbed on top of him, stretched out, flattened her breasts against his shoulder blades. Now it was her bottom Hortensia could see, her back. She said something again, he laughed again. Was that his laugh? Was that what it sounded like? They continued talking, his voice muffled by the bedding, her voice muffled by his skin. Hortensia needed to pee. Nothing more seemed necessary than to lift the abaya and squat. She did so, aiming, acquiescing to a little splatter on her Nikes. The release caused a sigh, but Hortensia was also thinking: what was the point? What was the use of marking her territory when it had already been usurped?

As she watched them it didn't feel dirty. She felt right-eous, she felt that she was conducting an important task that demanded rigour and integrity. Her job was to watch as closely as her situation permitted. She wanted to remember everything. She wanted to be able to recollect it, to be able to draw it, if such a time was ever called for. She wanted to see how Peter would hold the woman, how he would kiss her.

She stood almost through the night. All three rested very little. When light threatened to begin to show up in the skies, Hortensia crept away. Outside the compound, back inside the truck, she rubbed hard at her vagina until she thought it would catch alight. Then she lurched out from the truck door and threw up into the grass verge.

At the age of thirty-one Hortensia James started to hate. It took her some time, the way certain fads stutter before they really take off. She wrestled it for a while, resisted. She understood that hate was a kind of acid and she preferred not to burn. Also hate was unpopular and, back in those days anyway, she'd still wanted to be liked.

This longing slowly left her, though. She went from resenting just Peter, to the housekeeper, the driver, the market woman. People were slow, simple-minded; they all harboured ill intentions, seemed determined to be unhelpful, especially when their jobs required being of service. They didn't answer questions properly, spoke as if they had been trained all their lives to frustrate whoever addressed them. Hortensia's foul temper kept her mouth in a line, her brow knit, her teeth pressed together and her eyes cutting. She got good at chopping the legs off people, with no knife, with only words. She was always angry and while, initially, she noticed it (worried that it shouldn't be there), it slowly became what was normal. She developed headaches. She tied a block of concrete to her ankle and let it drag her down. Hating, after all, was a drier form of drowning.

Hortensia looked at where their portrait had once hung, hiding that stain. It would forever confuse her, how love could turn such a corner. Because there had been something once, a real thing, precarious like only love can be, but tender and sweet.

Before they married and after they declared their love for each other, those were days of a restful joy. He was long, you see. Lying side by side, their feet interlocked, she could rub her cheek against his solar plexus. She could curl and tell him what his intestines were saying. He could move his index finger along the curve of her earlobe, back and forth.

He was soft, the way men were not allowed to be. They played a lot. Silly games. One was a game of finding things.

'Let's say I get lost,' Peter would start. They'd be at the park, he'd have hidden a small bottle of beer in his inside jacket pocket. 'You lose me and have to describe me to someone.'

'Peter James. Large lumbering giant of a man. Thick fingers. Strong-looking. Competent.'

Peter would laugh. The idea was to throw in both insults and compliments. It was a game that meant you'd been looking, that you'd noticed things regular people had not. It was the kind of game you could tie your love up in, without putting your heart in too much danger. They both liked to play.

What of now – what if she played it now?

'Sandy blond hair that went white with time. The grey hides the dandruff. He wears spectacles, which he keeps on his brow or dangling from his neck with a cord that I bought him. A green cord. His skin tans easily, he has bushy eyebrows and his face, that he kept clean-shaven as a young man, he let overgrow with beard in his last years. Hard and spiky, the hairs were, when I felt them on my cheek and chin. He's wearing a simple white shirt and khaki shorts, he's got sandals. He wears no jewellery, except his wedding band and a beaded bracelet I bought him after we became lovers. Peter is an avid red meat-eater, despite the doctor's orders. He doesn't know that I know he's in cahoots with Bassey and he steals onto the verandah to eat a cut of steak every few weeks. One of his teeth, an incisor, is turning yellow. The inside of his mouth is such a light shade of pink, I'm always taken by surprise whenever I catch a glimpse of it.'

And he knew chemistry. Tr, she'd say, their bodies at right-angles, her head on his stomach.

'No, doesn't exist.'

'Tg? Tl?'

'Tl. Eighty-one. Thallium. A metal.

'Sc.'

'Twenty-one. Scandium.'

'You're lying.'

'No, true. Scandium. Used in lamps . . . amongst other things.'

'Okay. Sa. No, no, Sg.'

'Seaborgium.'

She raised her head, shot him a look.

'Truly. Seaborgium. It's number a hundred and six.'

*   *   *

Gordon Mama's laugh reverberated through the house like thunder. Marion stood at the door of her room listening. She'd never heard anyone laugh that way. Ever. She put her hand on the knob, rested there, didn't turn it. He was probably doing a routine check-up. Might he wish to see her, what with her bogus position as nurse-maid? She turned the knob and stood in the doorway. The laughter had stopped. Marion walked down the stairs, petting the banister, remembering when she'd specified the walnut. And then all the trouble to get the grain running the way she felt it must, arguing with the carpenter, the whole thing.

'Good morning, Marion,' Bassey, whom nothing got past, greeted her at the bottom of the staircase.

'Bassey,' Marion said.

'Breakfast?'

'Yes, please. I noticed Dr Mama came in.'

'He's in the study.' Bassey gestured with his hand, waving her on.

Marion knocked, feeling ridiculous.

'Yes, Marion,' came Hortensia's response.

Hortensia didn't look happy to see her.

'Ah, Marion,' Mama said. 'I was just asking for you.'

'Good morning, Doctor. Hortensia.'

'Progress is good. I'm really pleased with the healing,' Mama said to Marion with such seriousness.

She tried not to laugh. And then she felt embarrassed; since she'd moved in, she hadn't once asked Hortensia how she was.

'Good,' Marion said and ignored the way Hortensia's eyes darted upwards.

Mama buckled his bag.

'That was quick,' Marion said, wondering why she'd come in at all, why it had seemed important to see him again.

Bassey appeared through the open door. 'Mrs Agostino, will you be taking breakfast in here?'

There was silence as Mama played with an already-done buckle.

'Why not join us?' Marion asked.

Hortensia frowned.

'For breakfast, Dr Mama. Join Hortensia and I.'

Bassey outdid himself. He covered the long wooden table in the sunroom with Hortensia's pineapple-yellow chambray. A white squat vase in the middle with three sprigs of red hibiscus from the garden. Marion and Mama sat in the lounge, catching the aroma of pancakes, fried eggs, sausages and sautéed mushrooms.

Hortensia, once she'd warmed to the idea of a breakfast, had insisted on getting dressed. She appeared wearing an olive-green jacket with Chelsea collar, a pastel green T-shirt underneath and a faded blue-jean skirt. It must have been an effort to get dressed. She even wore shoes, pigskin, Marion guessed. The whole effect spoilt only by the walker.

'Shall we?' Hortensia asked.

They rose and followed her to the sunroom.

Conversation flapped about, looking for deep waters. For a few minutes Bassey worked in the background, cleaning up in the kitchen. He hovered, added a jug of water with slices of kiwi and mint leaves. Added a plate of cut strawberries and a bowl of cream onto an already full table.

'Champagne?' Bassey asked into a puddle of silence.

Hortensia shook her head and he retreated, closing the kitchen door and leaving them without the comfort of his background bustle.

'Well.' Mama arranged strawberries on top of a pancake. 'This is lovely.' He criss-crossed honey and sprinkled cinnamon.

'Do you have children, Dr Mama?' Marion asked quite suddenly. Hortensia coughed.

'One. A daughter.'

'How nice. How old?'

'Thirty-six. A young woman, really. I don't get that, though. I see her and I still see the child who wanted me to look under her bed. Check for monsters.'

They all smiled.

'And yourself?' He asked Marion. 'Do you have children?'

Marion grimaced. 'I do. I have four.'

The space was shallow for a while again. Cutlery scraped. Marion looked into her orange juice, feeling as if Bassey really had added champagne. She touched her neck, looked from Mama to Hortensia and then back into her juice. Was time here, she thought, in the room with them? Had time sat down for a short while?

'I think it's the hardest thing I've ever done, ever failed at.'

'Marion, don't start with your—'

'No, really, Hortensia.'

Mama left his cutlery balanced on the plate and listened.

'I . . . I had Stefano and then Marelena.' She looked at

Mama. 'My husband was Italian. Then I had Selena, and Gaia is my last child. I don't know. I thought giving birth would be the hard part. I don't know where I got the idea, but . . . I thought I'd be good at actual motherhood. I had no idea how hard I would find it.'

'Hortensia, you're lucky you never had any.' Mama sounded as if he was testing out a joke. Hortensia smiled on one side of her face, a practice-smile.

'I even started praying after I had children.' Marion put a piece of a strawberry into her mouth, worked it.

'Why?' Mama asked.

'Marelena. She was toddling about at the time, a small thing. And she fell. I was away from her and I heard that girl cry like . . . someone had poked her eye out. The kind of scream I'd never heard before. I ran to her, wishing I couldn't run, wanting to reach her but also not. I searched her body. Of course there was just a scratch – nothing really. I can't explain it, I felt so upset. Cheated, but I couldn't tell of what.'

'And then you prayed?' Hortensia said.

'I prayed. Me. Well, I hadn't prayed since I'd lived in my mother's house. My parents were Jewish. Or, rather, my parents were Not Jewish.'

Mama frowned. 'And you?'

'Well . . . I observe nothing.'

'But you prayed?'

'Yes, yes. I found a reason to pray again. Marelena fell. My children fell over and suddenly I needed God.'

Mama gestured and Hortensia poured him a glass of water. A slice of kiwi escaped into his cup, splashed the cloth, darkened it.

'I think I know what you mean,' Mama said.

They ate and Hortensia thought about how intimate eating with someone was. How you might not ever really know a person until you took soup with them, listened to them slurp or try not to slurp, listened to them swallow.

FOURTEEN

Peter came home and whistled. At breakfast he whistled. The ditties were unrecognisable, characterised mainly by the happiness they conveyed, a bouncing tune, something light and transcendent.

'I can't concentrate,' Hortensia said.

He stopped, but then started again after only a few minutes had passed.

'Peter,' Hortensia lowered the newspaper, letting the page rest on her half-eaten grapefruit.

'Sorry – habit, I guess.'

He smiled to himself and Hortensia wondered if he was remembering some detail of his lover's body. Perhaps a mole on her upper back, maybe near her spine. When he breathed heavy, Hortensia imagined that he was smelling the woman, ingesting a memory of her through his nose, the smell of her lips or her eyelids.

'How's work going? The project you mentioned.'

There was no project, or there was one project and she was of middle height with paw-paw-sized breasts and milky skin.

'Good. Fine. It's a lot of travelling but . . . I manage.'

'Yes, that you do.'

'And the boutique? Do you have an opening date yet?'

'No, but soon. We want to launch with a whole range of decor items. Make a real impression.'

'Hmm. And how is . . . everything?'

Hortensia wasn't sure what he was asking.

'I'm okay. I'm—'

He checked his watch. 'Yes?'

'You'll be late for work, you need to go.'

'No, no, I'm listening.'

'I'm fine. Just . . . I was thinking maybe I should see someone, you know? Someone else. Dr Momodu has said one thing, but a second opinion is usually recommended.'

'Ah,' he scraped his chair out from the breakfast table. 'Did you have someone in mind?'

'Or have you given up, Peter?'

'Horts, that's not what I said.'

To stop from crying she pushed her chair out and went into the bedroom. Locked it. Peter knocked on the door, but when she didn't answer he went to work.

Hortensia didn't mention it again, but booked herself an appointment with Dr Hussein. He revealed what she had already been told: her uterus was malformed. He said it with reproach, as if she had taken the vessel herself and squashed it. There was nothing more to be done, said the doctor.

Peter continued to whistle.

Why don't you leave me? Hortensia asked him in her mind. Did he enjoy seeing her shame – was that part of the scintillation of the act? Would it be less exciting without her, the wife, waiting at home jilted? Was he evil? Hortensia would ask her breakfast plate while they sat in silence. Are you evil, Peter?

*   *   *

There was one time Hortensia decided to tell him she knew, make a quiet agreement about a settlement and leave for London. She called Peter at work.

'Will you come home for dinner tonight? . . . I know you always come home, but I meant would you come home early enough so we can eat together? I just want to sit with you, that's all.'

Hortensia and Peter sat, stiff, unaccustomed to facing one another for such a sustained period of time. They had got into a different routine. Hortensia taking meals in her studio or else in the lounge in front of a soap opera or the news. Peter coming in around 10 p.m.

'Good day? At work?' Hortensia could hear the emptiness in her voice but she pressed on.

Peter shrugged, which was a regular response to most of the questions Hortensia had for him.

'Did you want to talk about something specific?' he asked.

'I don't know. Did you?'

'I don't know what you mean.'

Hortensia sighed, focused on the chicken breast, which had more flesh than she knew what to do with. Each morsel she swallowed felt as if it was swelling up in her gut and pushing her belly button further and further out, mocking her.

'Just thought we could sit together. That's all.' But the true words failed her.

Then there was a time he tried. Hortensia was already in bed, pretending to sleep. Peter came home drunk. Stumbling and falling through the house towards the bedroom. When he entered she could smell him.

'Awake? Horts?'

She stayed pretending in the dark. Shocked at the touch of his hands on her arm. She remained still, breathing deeply.

'Hortensia?'

But Hortensia was determined to mimic the sleep of the dead; the stupor of one truly given to the most vacant dreaming. Peter undressed, falling a few more times. In his underpants, he got into bed. She didn't scrub the bath that night, she didn't fall asleep, not even for a few merciful minutes. She went over in her head, too many times to count, what the thing was Peter had wanted to awaken her for. The thing he'd had to get sloshed to be able to mention. How would he have said it? she wondered. In what tone? Would he have tried to seduce her somehow, in the same voice he used to use for sex, then tell her that he'd taken a lover? Try and cajole her into seeing that he'd had no choice? Or would he have employed his office voice, something measured and uncomplicated? Saying: it is over. The kind of voice that prohibits begging.

Over time, over the years that the affair continued, Hortensia stopped seeing life as a good thing. In a cold church in London she had said yes to him, to be the only one person always there to be safe with, to bear the weight of her when her weight needed bearing, to respond to questions that no one else would care to. Someone to say the unsayable, to be scared with, together. And here she was, scared alone. Night was the real measure of love, Hortensia thought. Anything can sparkle in the daylight.

But night – that was when humanity got tested. It was always at night that she saw things between them were decrepit and ugly.

Hortensia and Mr Adebayo opened a small boutique store near the Secretariat on Lebanon Road – a new trendy area of the city. The new business was a welcome distraction. Adebayo, a small man, teeth a shade of orange thanks to his penchant for kola-nut, and stained fingers, the tattoo, Hortensia thought, of an honest tie-and-dyer. His voice was gravelly and his life seemed to revolve around his art, no mention of children or wives. His single-mindedness and brusque manner suited Hortensia. His designs had captivated her when she'd visited his studio because they looked so old. She envied him his shades of indigo and newsprint-white, the neat squares of his 'Ibadan-is-sweet' design.

Gradually, as the business took off, Hortensia stopped following the lovers. She spent her days in the shop or the adjoining workshop. She sent pictures of the fabrics to Mr List along with her sketches and he used the material to launch a new range of bejewelled handbags. Adebayo raised a shaggy eyebrow but nothing more. The bulk of their customers were expats who delighted in the combination of Adebayo's ageless designs and Hortensia's modern spin. She suggested he take lace and dye it like he would the cotton, she cut up the fabrics into bedspreads and tablecloths, curtains and cushion covers.

And then overnight Hortensia went from considering smocking to sitting by the radio, reading the newspapers of a country splitting, warring. On the thirtieth of May 1967, Lieutenant-Colonel Odumegwu Ojukwu declared the Eastern Region of Nigeria, the Republic of Biafra. Like a soundtrack through the almost three years of war, Eda begged Hortensia to come home, her voice filled with pre-emptive horror at the thought of having to bury her own child. But despite talk at Peter's office (a few resigned, some took unpaid leave) they stayed on.

It would later embarrass Hortensia that when the war ended all she could notice was that her husband looked less happy, less rosy in the cheeks, no whistling. Yes, the war was over, millions were dead and her husband's lover had apparently disappeared from their lives, as surreptitiously as she had come into it. Shameless, having allowed herself, as a cheated-on wife, to become oblivious to the true horrors of war, Hortensia fantasised that the woman had been caught up in the conflict somehow, been shot in the chest or, better yet, beheaded.

By the middle of 1970 the Zonta women's society opened a branch in Ibadan and Hortensia joined up. With the boutique thriving and an end to Peter's extramarital activity, Hortensia had expected happiness. She would later feel stupid for this. For thinking they would simply pick up from where they left off, wind back some years, cuddle in bed and laugh again. Peter's mood darkened, reminiscent of their first morning after marriage. His mood darkened sufficiently that it stopped being a mood and started being simply who he was. Occasionally when she arrived home from work and he offered her an orange or asked if he could rub her feet, she shivered; these slivers of good nature would last some hours and then slip away – their fleeting nature made them less bearable than his regular unpleasant tempers.

There were moments when Hortensia daydreamed about running away. Adebayo, she'd decided, had no interest in any sexual relations, whether with her or anyone else for that matter. On sad days, to make herself laugh, she plotted her seduction of him, imagined backpacking through the south-west up into the north. There were days her scheme brought tears of laughter, aching stomach muscles.

Every few months she would awaken and find herself enveloped in Peter's long arms. They would make love, fierce, intense, as if despite their unhappiness they understood that the infrequency of their sexual relations demanded explosiveness, fire.

They were not happy, they were not unhappy.

In 1990 at the ripe age of sixty-six, Peter retired. Soon after, he started to complain that he couldn't see so well. He visited the optician for a pair of glasses. Hortensia made fun of him, she'd always been the near-sighted one. They were out walking one day, in a market not dissimilar to the one she'd tracked him and his lover in almost thirty years before. Hortensia was musing on this, walking leisurely several paces behind her husband, when he fell to the ground. Her immediate thought was that he was dead, and tears came in the few steps it took to reach him. His eyes were open.

The doctor took various tests and the cabinet in the bathroom filled up with the tablets they prescribed. But Peter's complaints (body ache, fuzzy head) persisted. Four years later the Jameses moved to Cape Town. The location changed very little; Peter continued to suffer from a series of complaints that doctors misunderstood, misdiagnosed or suggested he ignore. In South Africa Peter spoke less and less. It was not the kind of thing that was easy to notice. In 1995 Peter spoke about a tenth or so less than he had in 1994. No one knew, but this pattern was doomed to continue, until 2014 when he died a veritable mute.

Before that, though, Hortensia endured the descent. Everything was sore but he still limped off to golf on Sundays. He threatened to go on a hunting trip and she called the club and told them he was senile, that they shouldn't let him near a rifle. In bed she read out passages to him. Sometimes he listened agreeably, but mostly he blocked his ears with his hands or he pointed out to her that her voice was unbeautiful. But he buttered her toast. He knew just how brown she liked it and tutted Bassey if he ever attempted this job. You're no good at this, ol' boy, he said. Or 'my man'. Those were the names he used for Bassey. His shoes were never side by side, instead often rooms apart. Hortensia could not work out how this feat was achieved so consistently. Neither could the housekeeper. The snoring was unbearable. He ate meat when his doctor had said no. He refused a hearing aid, goaded her about hers, even though he needed one much more than she did. He sat practically deaf and turned the volume of the television up so high that the neighbours complained. He was sick. They'd grown old together, but all that seemed to mean was that they'd borne each other and not died yet. He had nightmares sometimes; he once woke her up and said his mother was on the phone. Your mother is dead, she said. She's not on the phone, Peter, she's dead.

He still liked to cut her fruit, bring a plate of quartered oranges out to the garden while she inspected the rose bushes, trail behind her.

'You look ravishing, my tulip. I love your hair like that,' he would say. Except her hair was the same as it had always been and so the compliment meant nothing. Plus she hated tulips.

He joined her in the television room. Picked up the remote. He chopped between channels with no regard for the programme she'd been watching.

'Peter, really?'

The doctors had said just ignore him.

'What is it you're looking for, my love?'

He continued.

'I said, what the hell is the channel you are looking for?'

'Where's the sex channel?' But under his breath, like she wasn't in the room and he was talking to himself.

'The what? Peter, we don't have a sex channel.'

He flung the remote control out the open window. It fell in a puddle, she had to buy a new one.

'Stupid box.' He walked out.

But he also came home with flowers. Bougainvillea. I know you love these, he said. And he brought his nose to her neck and said, are you wearing perfume? His breath was old man's breath, sweet, rancid – he only brushed his teeth if she stood and watched and this was not always possible. There were nights, rare but beautiful, when he asked her if he could hold her in bed. I can feel your bones through your nightie, he said.

* * *

He got sicker. The time to bring up the past – the lover who had appeared as mysteriously as she had disappeared – the time to reconcile passed them by. Hortensia still did not know for sure what had made Peter lose his love for her, misplace it. It hurt her that, despite her anger, she'd loved him until he was a ravaged and lifeless body.

'Do you need some water?' Hortensia sat by the bed, the nurses having left for the day and she finding herself, strangely, walking up the stairs and into what used to be their room and was now his; she'd moved into the room next door.

The floor lamp by the door cast a shadow that hid most of the waste his muscles had become. There was a way his tongue hung out that Hortensia decided meant thirst. She moved to pour him a cup of water. His eyes followed her. She hadn't come into the room, hadn't said a word to him in weeks, over a month.

'Here.'

She helped him lift up, just a bit, so the water didn't spill down the front of his white flannel pyjamas. She held the cup for him, placed her other hand at the bottom of his back. His throat worked to get the water down, much went out the sides of his mouth. Hortensia settled him back, wiped him. The act of caring was like bicycle-riding – once learned, never forgotten.

'Pardon?'

She thought he'd whispered something. Hortensia put the cup down and moved her ear closer to his chapped lips. It would be a bit of a miracle; he'd stopped speaking months before.

'I can't hear.'

She moved so close the cracked skin on his bottom lip scratched her ear, a sensation, a tingling and an excitement that seemed misplaced.

'Peter?' Still unable to hear, she took his hand. Then Hortensia lifted the skirt of her nightgown and eased herself onto the bed she hadn't shared with him in almost a year.

He'd always been so massive.

'My love,' she said again, allowing a rare tenderness.

Hortensia let her arm fall over his body, she listened to the unrelenting labour of his breathing.

Peter kept trying to say something, but always just a dry scratch of sound came. And then he slept for several days, waking up to drink, or sometimes when the nurse was clumsy with the drip he would startle. But mostly he slept. As if, after all his days of illness and her unrelenting disinterest, as if making up for what was definitely lost, Hortensia stayed with him throughout this time, only going away to eat one meal a day. She ate because the doctor said she had to; she had no appetite. Or she would leave for the bathroom, stare at her face in the mirror, brush her hand over the tight-cropped coils on her head, wonder who she was. Who she'd become.

Once, coming back into the room, Hortensia overheard the nurses.

'Poor bastard.'

'What a way to die, hey? Someone should show mercy – you know, pull the plug.'

'You!' Hortensia shouted. She rushed in and walked up to the nurse's face, stuck her nose into her, wanted to pump her with fists. 'Don't you dare.'

'Mrs James, I was just—'

'Don't. You. Dare.'

On her frightful and violent insistence, the nurses left and Hortensia telephoned the medical care. Asked that the nurses not come back.

'What seems to be the problem?' the man on the other end of the phone wanted to know.

'They have no respect. None. And no kindness for a man so close to death. I won't have them here again. And no replacements. I would die before you humiliate us again.'

The confused man apologised, still unclear of the grievance, unsure what to write down on his complaint form.

The phone rang and Hortensia let it go to voice-message. It was the doctor calling, explaining about the drip; it was due in just under twelve hours and could Hortensia please at least let a nurse in to administer.

Hortensia climbed into the bed with Peter, holding him the way she'd grown accustomed to over the last few days. He tried to talk; she wiped the sweat on his forehead that his feeble exertions produced.

Later that night Hortensia called the doctor back to tell her they would not need a nurse to come through. That in fact no nurse would ever again come into her house as long as she lived. But certainly none was required for Peter James – he was dead and in no further need of drips.

FIFTEEN

With the committee meeting coming up, Ludmilla called Marion again.

'So the State has made an offer. Money. Let's see. If the Samsodiens decline, it could still go to court. Stubborn, these people are.'

'Ah.' Instinctively, Marion got up to shut her bedroom door. She had a picture of Hortensia listening in. She dropped her voice, 'I read an article.' A piece had been published in the *Argus*, addressing the much talked-about reopening of the claims. A few cases were profiled. The Samsodiens had been evicted in the Sixties and forced to sell their land for a paltry few thousand rand. Marion recalled Ludmilla referring to it as a bargain. The article suggested the land was now worth over 100 million. Bargain would have to have been an understatement. 'Seems a little . . . unfair, perhaps.'

Ludmilla scoffed while Marion realised she'd just referred to apartheid conditions as 'a little unfair'.

'The sale was clean. It was a good deal. Sometimes this happens.'

Marion didn't have the words ready. She wanted to suggest that the conditions were governed by a law that was . . . unjust.

'Marion, you still there?'

Marion had avoided history. Or she'd invented her own. After all, what was history but a record of what gets noticed? Noticing, it seemed to Marion, was what life was really about. Noticing and not noticing, remembering and forgetting.

Marion had studied architecture in an attempt to forget.

It was 1951, Marion's final year at St Winifred's High. She informed her parents that she would be studying architecture. It was a problem. Marion's mother would have preferred a daughter less inclined to study and more ready to marry. But prospects were dim and so, as Marion had grown into a young woman, her mother had engaged in a different fantasy. Having never studied herself, she began to hope that Marion, with her quick mind at maths and science, would take medicine, the profession to end all professions. However, Marion's father, with no sons to work with, had enjoyed his daughter's grasp of how things were put together. They had spent weekends hammering in his workshop and tinkering with the engine of the white bakkie that he carted his trade items in. A civil engineer – he had ventured in his innermost quiet dreams – and had even gone the distance of imagining a bridge in his own name.

What neither parent factored in was the will of Marion herself. She bore down on their arguments, their threats, their attempts to slather on guilt, her mother's tears, her father's sulks, their reasoning. In between their sessions of persuasion with their daughter, there was the noise of them fighting one another. Each blamed the other. It broke something in both people, brought something ugly back, served as an opening for them to raise their voices after years of speaking only softly. By the time Marion stepped onto the University of Cape Town upper campus, dressed in moss-green loafers, a red pleated skirt and a white short-sleeved shirt with a collar; by that time her parents were busy with the business of dividing their assets, signing papers.

After finishing her studies and after her company came into being, each year Marion grew in stature for the homes she designed. The question she was most often asked was: what made you want to become an architect? There were many answers, like a series of diminishing dolls, each more intricate than the other, more hidden and more true. There was the big and loud answer. It was the I-love-great-design answer. And she did. A well-executed design with all the parts that fit together, nothing sticking out.

There was the slightly softer-toned answer that was not for journalists. It was an answer for a dinner party. An answer for the corner of a room, with a worthy acquaintance. This answer was about wanting to make things, real things that could stand up. The feeling that, at the end of the day, the result of her labours had to be material and lasting. And to this Marion could tack on the story of her parents and how they had argued about her choice of vocation.

The first year of architecture school had been a daze. There was a rash of classes, a set of tests and then the end-of-year exams. Marion's headache of growing up, of the things no one spoke of, but that were there anyway; how to be blind but still see your way to walk; all the fuzziness was slowly replaced by the exactness of geometry, the rules of perspectives, two-point and three-point. Marion discovered that she liked her pencils sharp, she wanted to go to Finland and notice the architecture over there, she wanted to sit at Aalto's feet.

This was why she'd studied architecture, this was the teeny-tiny doll answer whose face was barely there, whose body was often without lacquer, without frills. It was so intricate an answer that it was difficult to explain even to herself. That the reason she studied architecture was only made clear to her after she began studying it, as if her subconscious had known something her waking mind had not. That architecture was about a construction, a made-up thing made real. That she, Marion, needed this skill. And that even though the vertigo would never go away completely, architecture would be the only thing Marion had to steady herself.

'What's that noise?'

'What?' Marion cocked her head to listen. 'Ambulance,' she said.

Hortensia continued along the hallway, planting the walker in front of each footstep. Her timing had been off today and Marion had caught her doing her routine. Hortensia hated an audience. Each time the walker hit the wood, the clank moved up her arms like a ripple of static.

'Ice-cream truck,' Hortensia said.

'No. Ambulance. Anyway it doesn't matter. How are you feeling? Can I get you something?'

Hortensia cut her a look and ambled past. After a few seconds Marion moved up further along the hallway, overtaking Hortensia, and settled against the wall nearer the front door. Hortensia hobbled closer.

'Pain?'

'Huh?'

'I saw you scowl.'

'Hmm. Haven't heard much noise lately. How are the works coming? Frikkie, the builder. Knows what he's doing?'

'Well. I suppose.'

'Gordon is coming by this week. Thursday, I think. Late afternoon.'

'Oh. I really like him.'

'I know. That's why I'm telling you.'

Hortensia, standing to pause for some beats, noticed Marion blush.

'First darkie you ever had the hots for?'

'Hortensia James, I don't appre—'

'Spare me, Marion.' She started walking again.

'I don't see him as black.'

'Of course you don't. That's what makes you racist.'

'Hor—'

'Marion! It's too early to argue. I'm sick. And besides, we're too old for all this.'

She reached the front door, spent several minutes swivelling. She cursed as she did so. Mama had promised she could start walking up stairs soon, but he'd also warned her not to push too hard. Time was a factor in the healing, not just the exercises. She grudgingly accepted that the mindless talking helped her ignore the pain.

'So, tell me, Marion.'

'What?'

'You and Max.'

'What of it?'

'Mr Straight-Down-the-Middle.'

'That how he came across?'

'Mr Suit-and-Tie.' Hortensia, her back to Marion, cackled. 'Wouldn't have thought you a Non-Black-Gordon-Mama type of gal.'

'Hey!'

'Just some fun, Marion. God! Just some damned fun.'

Hortensia got to the chair. She set aside the walker, lowered herself. Marion moved closer.

'And the land claim? Dare I ask?'

'Well, I . . . I've been thinking. Ludmilla called me.'

Hortensia grunted.

'They submitted a dispute.'

'Thieves!'

'Well—'

'You're defending the Von Struikers, Marion?'

'Did you read the article?'

'What article?' Hortensia started reaching for her walker.

'In the *Argus*. On the whole case.'

'No. Unlike you, I don't need to see an article in the paper to recognise dog-shit.' She got to her feet.

'You don't like me, do you?' Marion asked, watching Hortensia leave.

'No, I don't.'

'Then why did you invite me into your house?'

'I was desperate . . . and possibly mistaken.'

Hortensia wasn't always in the mood for Marion. She found there were days she could tolerate her and days she couldn't. She honed her skills and counteracted most of Marion's attempts to waylay her. Her current handicap was a disadvantage but, if she was careful, she could go a whole week without bumping into her. She admired Marion's restraint at not simply knocking at her door, and continued to use her special powers to venture out only when the coast was clear. At other times, when the Vulture was about, Hortensia communicated with Bassey via his cellphone. Is this really necessary? the man had asked. Yes, Hortensia had responded.

Marion, well versed in being avoided, had her own skills to contribute to the game. She crept up behind Hortensia.

'You've been avoiding me.'

Hortensia cursed under her breath. She'd taken a chance, desperate for some fresh air, and snuck out onto the patio, happy there had been no Marion in the hallway. And yet here she was. Bassey had helped set Hortensia into the chair and she'd told him she'd shout for him when she was ready to be moved again. She was ready.

'I don't understand this, Marion. Why is it suddenly so important that we speak?'

'I visited the library the other day and—'

'I do not care.'

'I'm not denying the claim any more.'

'I don't care, Marion. And I'm not going to do this with you.'

'Do what?'

Hortensia waved her hand, as if Marion were a pong she could dispel. 'I'm not well. Please, leave me be.'

'I remembered something, that's all.'

'I'm not interested.'

'And maybe . . . all this time—'

'Bassey!'

Marion startled at the loudness.

'But why? I just thought you and I could talk.'

'Talk about what?'

'That . . . well, it seems what you're always suggesting is . . . I guess I wanted to clarify that . . . I'm not really a racist.'

'Oh, but you are. Where is he? – Bassey! And I'm not going to solve that for you or be part of your project.'

'It's complicated.'

'I'm sure. I don't care, by the way. I'm not trying to make the world a better place. I'm too tired. Bassey! For goodness' sake.'

'Oh, I'll call him for you.'

But Bassey appeared.

'Please. Help me to my room.'

The problem with shame, Marion thought to herself, is that it breeds unproductivity. It is such a crippling thing, and even at a young age Marion knew this. Perhaps not to enunciate it as such (the way she was later able to explain it to her adult self), but she sensed it intuitively.

She came home and she asked her parents why. It was a question she knew they hated. It made her father sweat at his temples and her mother's eyes grow narrow. It brought back history and unwanted memories. So they said different things depending on the day – how much energy they had. They said 'because they're different', 'because they broke the law', 'because they want to kill us'. They said 'because they caused trouble', 'because they are not good people', 'because they want what we have'. They said 'we don't know' sometimes. They said 'that's just how life is, that's how things are – don't bother about it'.

What Hortensia didn't seem to understand was that sometimes we have to honour our ancestors and side with them. This meant we justified what was horrible and turned away from what needed scrutiny. This life of ignoring the obvious required a certain kind of stamina. The alternative to this was to set on a path to make rubbish of what had gone before us. This approach – of principles, activism and struggle – required stamina too. All the same, she'd chosen the other one.

'I know I've made bad choices,' Marion started in on the conversation, no warm-up. She'd caught Hortensia as she came out of the toilet, the best place she'd thought, but Hortensia didn't look too happy about it.

'May I? Can I at least walk? Can I get past the bathroom? Can I sit?'

Marion pinked. She let Hortensia walk past her and followed. Hortensia propped herself at her desk and Marion stayed standing; after several seconds when Hortensia said nothing, Marion sat down on the edge of the bed.

'I thought we—'

'Let me speak, Marion. I can't absolve you. I don't want to do this thing with you. This let's-talk thing.'

'I thought we were becoming friends in a way.'

'I don't know what that means and I prefer not knowing.' Hortensia squeezed her eyes. 'Do you hold yourself in high regard?'

'What do you mean?'

'Do you think of yourself highly?'

'I think I'm not bad, that I'm okay.'

'Precisely. Well, I think very lowly of myself. And I am under no illusion that I am anything close to "okay".'

'I see.'

'And what's more, I don't think you're okay, either. I don't hate you, Marion, I just think you're a liar. And I can't get involved. I don't care enough and anyway I think it's too late. I don't want kinship with you. I don't hate or like you. I don't really consider you. I'm also dealing with things. But I don't want any kinship. And we don't have to get in a car and drive off a cliff or anything. You stay here. We keep out of each other's way. Your house gets fixed, my leg heals, we carry on with our separate lives. I think, at this far-gone stage, that's about as much as people like you and I can muster. Please.'

Marion stood up and left the room, her steps measured and heavy.

The conversation made Hortensia feel at home again. The worst had been said, she'd explained herself. She no longer needed to avoid Marion. She hoped she had cured her of any notion of any form of connection between them. With this sense of freedom, when evening came, she went to sit in the television room to watch the news – something she hadn't done in a while and had missed. On account of it being the twenty-fourth of September, the pictures were full of South Africa's history. A documentary was on, discussing Heritage Day, and its predecessor, Shaka Day.

Hortensia wondered about Marion's attempt at comrade-ship. Had she heard something on the radio, some call to humanity, the kind of thing that had lurked about in South Africa in the heady days of a new democracy?

After they'd arrived in South Africa, Hortensia had turned to Peter and said, this place isn't well. The country? he'd asked and she'd nodded. And the people. The best of them know they are sick and are trying different medicines. Some know, but are inert. And the worst think they are fine, that they are in need of nothing.

Of course she herself hadn't been well in years. And she hadn't had the strength or the inclination or any sense of responsibility to promote healing either in herself or others. Not then and not now.

She went to bed feeling sorry for Marion. Sorry that Marion hadn't found herself living in a better person's home. Or at least a person more prone to delusions about the human capacity for real, lasting truth and reconciliation.

When she was already in her nightgown and pulling on her compression socks, Marion knocked on the door.

'Come.'

'I wasn't sure if you'd still be awake.'

'Yes.'

'I'm not okay.'

'Yes.'

'I just wanted to say that . . . to you.'

'Alright.'

She started to close the door.

'Marion, wait. You want to know things? Past things? You really want to know? I was thinking of this story my mother told me. You remind me of her, by the way. But, anyhow, I was thinking how, before she died, we didn't get on very much and before she died there was this thing she told me. How she regretted leaving home, leaving Barbados for England. They took an Italian boat, which stopped off at Tenerife and Genoa en route. Docked at Dover, then took the train to Waterloo. She told me she'd wanted to come back even before they docked. There'd been a few of them travelling from the Islands. They'd stayed in the section of the ship for the workers, they shared sleeping quarters with some of the ship's greasers and female entertainment, should we say. I was along already. I'd won a scholarship for school and gone ahead, but Zippy, my sister, she was travelling with my parents. There was a young family on the boat with them, husband, wife and a baby of a few months old. Apparently there was this debacle that took place. My mother, Zippy, the woman, with her baby in her arms, were walking on deck. The baby was light-skinned. There came these white women, they saw the child and decided that she had been kidnapped.'

Marion put her hand to her neck; there were no pearls to hold on to.

'They seized the baby from her mother and wouldn't return the child until papers were shown, proof sorted out. My mother said she knew immediately that she was going in the wrong direction, towards the wilderness, away from civilisation.'

'That's a terrible story.'

'Yes, it is. And there are many more – too many.'

'Why did you tell it to me?'

'Because I want to upset you.'

'You think I don't know that people suffer? That life is unfair, unequal?'

'I don't know what you know. But here's what I think: that you want to convince me of something. That you want to talk to me and talk around what is true, circumnavigate whatever horror you prefer not to address. And I'm not here for that. I've got my own horrors.'

Marion made to leave.

'There was a time,' Hortensia said, 'when you didn't give a damn. I liked you much better when you didn't care so much what I thought.'

'Yes. I liked that time when I didn't care. I liked that much better, too.'

SIXTEEN

Marion had not meant to eavesdrop and yet here she was, at the top of the stairs listening to what was clearly meant to be a private conversation.

'God Almighty!' Hortensia said, putting the phone down.

'Is everything okay?' Marion asked.

'No, everything is not okay.'

'You were shouting.'

'This is my house. I can shout if I so wish. You want to know what that was? Here's some nice juicy information for you. My husband had a lover.'

'Oh no.'

'Oh yes. And he had her for several years – that's not the news, though. You know what he and his lover did? They made a baby and, what else, that baby is now a woman and heir to Peter's inheritance. And I'm supposed to call her up and let her know that, so his money can go where he wished it to. In fact he wants me to meet her – can you imagine? And that person on the phone that you heard me, rightfully, shouting at is an idiot lawyer by the ridiculous name of Marx. I—'

'Hortensia—'

'No, let me finish. I am worn out. Between Peter and

his cryptic will, you and your prodding, your Thelma-and-Louise bullshit, some woman somewhere with my husband's blood running through her. I've . . .' She walked and sat down. 'It's too much. I am – what are you doing?'

'Just coming to stand a little closer.'

'Well, don't.'

They stayed quiet in the hallway.

'That was supposed to be my child.'

'Pardon?'

Hortensia was whispering and Marion had never heard that before.

'That was my child.'

'I'm not really—'

'I was supposed to have children. Many.'

Marion's legs felt tired, but there was only one chair in the hallway and Hortensia was sitting on it.

'I'm sorry.'

'Many. And they come after me. A nursery of ghosts.'

'Like a haunting?'

'Every day.'

Marion bent down, her bum found the floor. She didn't mind appearing inelegant. She stretched her legs out in front of her; they wouldn't stay flat, hadn't done so in many years.

'I'm sorry.'

'You said. Did Max leave a will?'

'He left a bill.'

Both women surprised themselves with laughter. They seemed startled, like newborn babies, surprised that a joke could live in such dark waters.

'Seriously, though. You should read it. As if Peter . . . as if he . . . I don't know, I actually don't know what he was thinking.'

'Do you know where the child is? Does he expect you to go out and find her?'

Hortensia shook her head. 'It's all there. Marx gave an email, a phone number.'

'I don't mean to . . . Tell me if it's none of my business, but why do you think he put all this together like this, Peter?'

'I can think of two reasons. One, because he hates me and wants to punish me. For what, I cannot imagine. Control the scene, boss me around?'

'And two?'

'Because he wants us to meet. He loves me and he loves her, and he's sorry.'

'Are you worried you're doing the wrong thing?'

'I want her – the child – to not exist. Why would I want to send her an email?'

'To tell you the truth, I don't know what I'd do, either.'

'But then I think: what if she's destitute? I can't imagine it – never knowing my own father, his love. What if this is her chance to know that he thought of her?'

Marion couldn't help it when her jaw slackened. Hortensia, for just some seconds, resembled a soft-hearted woman; she could bake cookies and smile at Girl Scouts. It felt naked and made Marion uncomfortable. 'I feel like I'm forcing you to talk.'

'Oh, come off it.'

Someone blasted a horn and Marion suddenly missed her binoculars, felt blown off her perch as Queen of Katterijn.

'One thing,' Hortensia started again. 'One thing I'll always hate him for was this time in Brighton. My father had died and I couldn't leave Brighton. I don't know – I just couldn't go home. As if going home would make his absence permanent. Normally I'd work in Croydon over the summer, but that year I stayed on in Brighton and Peter came to see me. His effort was so . . . tender. I was already in love with him but, somehow, this gesture did something. Anyhow, one day he suggested we go to the beach. You realise I grew up on the best beach there is; Brighton was a joke to me. I'd been several times alone but never with him, so we went. A picnic. It was his idea to watch the sunset. We had a blanket, Peter draped his leg over me. I remember that I struggled to breathe but didn't say anything. Having the weight of his leg on me seemed more important. It grew cold and we spread another cloth over us, night came. He proposed to me. "I want to take care of you," he said. Can you believe that? "I want you to know that you can depend on me." Depend, he said.'

Marion grunted her understanding.

'And there is where I shall never forgive him. Because, you see, I really heard him that day. With something deeper than ears. Maybe you can listen with your spleen, or your pancreas. Because it felt like that, Marion. I heard him deep in some part of my body.'

'Hmm.'

'Of course he couldn't have meant it. Not with the way things turned out. And then I made a joke about the whole thing to myself. Decided marriage was like ordering in a foreign-language restaurant. Thinking it's fish, too embarrassed and proud to confirm in English. And then your heart drops when the waiter puts a plate of something bleeding and unrecognisable in front of you. Something you are absolutely certain you are not going to be able to eat, no matter how hard you try.'

Hortensia sat in a chair, she leaned forward to pull on her skirt, lifting one buttock and then the other, feeling tired even though it was morning. The strain of getting dressed – who would have thought. She also felt annoyance at having unburdened to Marion. She had no interest in it, no inclination. She rejected in herself the urge Marion displayed. The need to talk, the need to have someone listen. Her nose scrunched up. Those who talked and those, like her, who calcified. All those years in Ibadan, stalking lovers, all that time spent grieving, this was the direction her broken-hearted logic had led her in. It was not wise, but it was, like a fossil, self-preserving. She'd survived. The machinery of her body had kept going, hatred's venom for oil; her skin was taut, no one ever guessed her age. Surely if she'd lived that other life, a life of unburdening and revelations, if she'd stayed delicate, run after him, begged and pleaded, she'd have let life use her, not the other way around. And used things grow old. She had Peter to thank, then, for her flawless complexion, her beauty.

Hortensia stood. She eyed a jumble of shoes in the bottom of the closet. Of course beauty had not been what she was after, nor agelessness. She had wanted love. She fitted her feet into a pair of loafers, brown suede, not striking, but not repulsive either. Unqualified love. She reached for the walker. She'd had such a time; a time when she'd loved him, his tongue in her mouth, along the grooves of her teeth or his hand cradling her neck. Soft times. When she'd allowed softness. Remembering such a time made her feel foolish. She'd felt foolish back then too. Hoodwinked. She remembered deciding to be tough, hardening, making the trade between fulfilment and not being duped. She would use all her powers to have him endure her suffering, and by proximity he would suffer too. They went on to have an okay marriage, an okay life. Like an okay house, with just that one room you don't go into. Not because it's unfurnished or ugly, but because it's haunted. And there are no haunted rooms, really, only haunted houses.

Still, snivelling Marion was upsetting a really good system that, up till now, had been working.

Hortensia entered the kitchen. She left the door ajar so she would see when Marion came down the stairs; she intended to call out to her.

Marion had woken up with a crick in her neck, and she knew that the pain was not there because she had slept in a bad position. It was there because it was the nature of pain to show up whenever it liked.

She felt shy about seeing Hortensia, felt she ought to hide from her. She had nothing to compare this feeling to, except her wedding night, pulling the covers to hide her thighs from her husband; needing the bathroom, being scared to mention it.

When Marion got out of bed and looked around for her slippers she felt light-headed, she'd bent down too fast. She showered and wore a camel turtle-neck, feeling chilled despite the good weather.

'About yesterday,' both women said, paused. 'You first,' they both said, paused. Sighed in unison. Marion moved from the doorway and sat opposite Hortensia at the kitchen table. Ever-discreet Bassey, stacking the dish-washer, left the task incomplete and excused himself.

'You were saying?'

'I was just going to say that – I don't know how to put it – I was thinking of what it must feel like, to have read Peter's will . . . Thinking how I would have been.' That wasn't what she'd wanted to say.

'Hmm.'

Marion laced her fingers. 'What were you going to say?'

'How are you feeling?' Which hadn't been what Hortensia had wanted to say, either. The question seemed to surprise Marion as well.

'I'm fine. My neck hurts. You?'

'Everything hurts after a certain age. Dr Mama told me that, but he said it in such a way that it sounded funny.'

Marion smiled. She had something to say.

'I've been thinking a lot. Oh God!' she covered her face with her hand.

'What now?'

'I'm going to cry and you'll be upset with me.'

'Why are you going to cry?' Hortensia felt her body

move between impatience and compassion; she settled somewhere in the middle.

'Because I am ashamed.'

'Okay.' She moved towards practicality. 'You cry, Marion. I'll make us some coffee. Did you notice this beautiful piece of machinery in my kitchen – ordered it, flown in specially, delivered yesterday. It's a Blumenthal. Just you wait.'

'How do you do it?' Marion emptied her nostrils into a handkerchief.

'Do what?' She assembled two espresso cups on the counter.

'Keep it all together.'

Hortensia liked to press the buttons; such a simple transaction: push some buttons and make delicious coffee. 'I don't keep anything together. I lost everything long ago, I don't have anything left to keep together.' She put one steaming cup in front of Marion, took a sip from the other. 'That's how I do it.'

'Good coffee.'

'Excellent, you mean.'

They sat like that. Somewhere in the house a vacuum cleaner started up.

'Did you know, I was born in District 6. Did you know that?'

Hortensia shook her head.

'I don't remember it really, my parents moved the next year. To Wynberg. Then we moved to Plumstead – we kept creeping southwards.' She took in the coffee aroma. 'I wish old age would make me senile. I wish to really forget. I was just now thinking, remembering. Before he died, my father used to do this thing. They were divorced by then, my parents. And old. I'd arranged for them to stay at the home, full of Jews, the people they'd spent their lives avoiding, but they bore it. A decent enough place. So I'd visit every Sunday and we'd all three have breakfast. And my father would do this thing with the newspapers. It never really hit me before. I thought he was just losing it a bit. We'd all be sitting, and Father would start reading out a few headlines from articles in the *Cape Times* . . . or was it the *Argus*? I can't remember. He'd say – my father had a really deep voice – you know he'd be reading to himself and then suddenly he'd shout out something, like *So-and-so backs colour bar in factories* or *Challenge to Nats to keep South Africa white*. He'd say *Police out as rebellious miners protest, such-and-such street disturbed by gunfire*, and on and on. Thing is, this was the early Nineties – these weren't the actual headlines. He was making them up, remembering, perhaps, from days gone. He spoke in a certain tone. As if trying to make a point maybe. Trying to say, look at what we called a country . . . Just look.'

Hortensia stretched her legs, leaned forward on the chair to massage the length of them. She had to keep her blood moving, otherwise she feared she would not be able to stand up. Ever.

'Just blurting that stuff out. Like he was calling up the ghost of something, of apartheid. Saying . . . or rather feeling sorry. I think so, anyway. I remember now that my mother would get upset and ask him to stop. Maybe one or two would be violent-sounding. Please, my mother would say, and my father would stop but do the same thing the following Sunday. Such a feeble thing, you know, but I started thinking: maybe he was trying . . . I really like to hope that he was trying.' Her eyes glistened.

Hortensia said nothing. Her fingers massaged her leg.

'We were able to move southwards because my father did well with the shop. Trading in jewellery. A cousin would have the right contacts, a shipment would come in. I don't know – I didn't pay attention much. In 1951 we moved to Constantia; the house wasn't large, but the address was right – we'd made it. Alberta came to work for us. Her name was really Bathandwa, but my mother asked if we could call her Alberta; she liked the name, although she never explained why. Bathandwa seemed to agree.'

It happened so long ago that Marion had taught herself to think of it as something she'd once read in a book. Bathandwa had been older than Marion, mid-twenties or so. The regular cleaner of the Baumann household, Hettie, had died the year before, sick with tuberculosis in a hospital for blacks with not enough medicines, no beds. Marion was at first surprised at how young Bathandwa was. And then she was surprised by Bathandwa's ragged ear, an ear that looked as if a dog had tried to turn it into lunch. She never found the courage to ask Bathandwa what had happened to her ear.

There was a period when the Smiths next door had no one and asked Mrs Baumann if they could borrow her girl, Alberta. For two weeks she shared her time between the Baumanns and the Smiths, and then Marion never saw her again.

One day Alberta was taking out the washing, she passed Marion in the hallway and asked if she knew that Mrs Smith next door had only nine toes, and did Marion know what had happened to the pinkie on her left foot? And that the nail on Mr Smith's ring-finger was rotten – soon he'll have no nail. Whitlow. Alberta said Marion's mother had rings on her neck, red welts: did Marion know how they got there, did she notice how they came and went? So-and-so had a wooden leg from an accident at the border. So-and-so drank, her liver was finished. On it went, an inventory of scars. It made Marion, who never said anything in response, uncomfortable, but the passing remarks became a ritual of Alberta's. Once, Marion went into the kitchen to make herself a sandwich. Did you know, Alberta started, glancing over her shoulder as she stood at the sink, that Mr and Mrs Smith couldn't fuck? He had no cock, she no pussy. 'The children are borrowed, gifts from the gods who take pity on the weak.'

Marion had been friendly with the Smith girls, and frequently went round for tea. One day she was over at the Smiths', eating crackers and Marmite with her friends. A commotion deeper within the house, the sound of a loud banging and Mr Smith shouting, made the girls get up and run to where his voice was coming from.

'Dad, what's going on?' one of the Smith girls asked.

'Alberta was in the bathroom.'

'I was just cleaning up. I've finished work, Sir. I'm going home now.'

Bathandwa was dressed in dark-blue jeans and a red fitted top. Marion noticed the more familiar powder-blue uniform poking from the tote bag Bathandwa carried.

'Why are you wearing my wife's earrings? Give them.'

'These are my own earrings, Sir.'

Slender things speckled with diamantés, dangling and almost touching her bare shoulders.

'Nonsense. You think I'm stupid? Give.'

They all stood frozen in the passageway. Marion and the Smith girls tried to get a good look at Bathandwa, but the mass of Mr Smith was blocking most of their view.

'But they are mine, Sir.'

His hands shot through the space and slapped her cheek.

'And the shoes as well,' he said.

They were new shoes, heels Bathandwa had bragged about to Marion earlier in the week.

'Take them off.'

Mr Smith stripped the girl who cleaned his house. Near the end, when she was almost naked, he said, 'And what's that smell? Who told you you could use my wife's perfume?'

Afterwards, no one spoke about it. Mrs Smith came home and raised only an eyebrow when Mr Smith told her he'd caught the girl stealing. He handed his wife the things that wouldn't fit, shoes that were not to her liking. The Smiths finally got their own maid and the Baumanns found someone new as well. Before the woman could tell them her name, they asked if they could call her Alberta.

'Apartheid happened, you see? Hortensia?'

'I'm listening.'

'All those things happened and I didn't do anything about them.'

Hortensia noted a smell in the air. Sweat and face cream.

'Even when it happened right underneath my nose I did nothing. I walked past people and didn't see them. I blanked out an entire population, a history. I still do. You know Agnes, you know she once asked me whether I thought she was too old to finish her matric? Gosh, it was years ago now. The kids were all born, Agnes would have been – can't remember – in her forties maybe. And she said one day . . . I don't know, she was washing the dishes and I was asking why she didn't just use the dishwasher. I was always chiding her like that. Why, after many explanations, did she still not use my appliances properly, still not get how to fold a wet towel, how to fold a fitted sheet. Anyway she asked me if I thought she should go back and study, told me how she had always wanted to be a teacher. Know what I told her? I told her it was . . . I said to her that it was too late.' Speaking this out loud made Marion catch her breath. 'You say I'm a hypocrite. I have to be. I have to pretend it happened somewhere else; that I read it in a book. I would not be able to get out of bed otherwise.'

Marion bent her head down, turned it away. She cried for not long, then she smoothed out her skirt that never needed any smoothing and stood up, left the kitchen.

The *Constantiaberg Bulletin* covered a story about the case: 'Last attempts to reach an out-of-court settlement in Katterijn land claim.'

The Samsodiens had rejected an offer from the State based on the consumer-price index for translating past loss into present-day value. The solution that now seemed the most probable was for the State to apportion state-owned land (within a certain mile radius of the contested land) out to the Samsodiens. It looked like the Von Struikers would get to keep their farm and the Samsodiens receive a portion of the Koppie as fair compensation. Talks were being held.

'Well.'

'Why doesn't it feel like a solution?'

'What do you mean?' Hortensia asked. She put the *Bulletin* down, collected her glass of lemonade. They'd taken, sometimes, to sitting in the lounge together. Tripped into the habit.

'The Von Struikers don't actually have to do anything. Doesn't seem fair.'

'I think "fair" has been lost and forgotten for a while now. Besides, who are you to say what is fair or not? When the Samsodiens move in . . . or whoever, go over and ask them. Was it fair? Do you feel compensated? Is all forgiven?'

Marion was quiet. Hortensia started searching for the remote control. She ambled about without her walker. She wasn't supposed to, but she hoped if she acted like she didn't need one she eventually wouldn't. She found it underneath a decor magazine, started clicking.

'One of the . . . a grandmother, a Samsodien grand-mother died. Not died, well, died but . . . hanged herself. After everything, after the move and the family trying to settle . . . with a belt.'

Hortensia stopped chopping channels. She thought of being at a set of traffic lights. Waiting for cars to pass.

'She was our age, Hortensia. Could you . . . I mean, I couldn't. What would she have been thinking? How could she have felt?'

Hortensia turned the television off and set the remote aside. She blew air from her cheeks.

'I suppose there are so many like that. I suppose you think I'm stupid or ridiculous.'

Hortensia frowned. 'We had a guest once. Not someone we knew well, but a friend of Zippy's whom she asked us to host. Maria-Louisa was her name, Florentine woman. Of course Cape Town is accustomed to being fawned upon. Maria hated it. We took her along Beach Road. Camps Bay, Bantry Bay – the whole toot. The vineyards. Lovely, lovely, she said, but there is something I cannot abide. She cut her trip short. Now,' Hortensia sat back, pleased with how much she'd captured Marion's attention. 'That's not something that happens often, but it does happen. And weeks later I called Zippy to find out what it was all about. She said Maria had . . . Now you have to understand her English is alright, but not brilliant – Maria's, I'm talking about. Well, Zippy confessed that she wasn't sure she'd understood it all but, apparently, Maria had 'struggled'. That was the word she'd used. The best Zippy could get out of her was how she'd never felt so white before. And so special for being white. Mi ha fatto male, she'd said. It made her sick.'

Marion's face was drawn.

'Of course there should have been enough in her own European history to make her want to throw up. She shouldn't have had to come to South Africa for that, but all the same . . . Discomfort, Marion. If you want to look and look honestly, then prepare for discomfort. To be sick. I met a woman once. A white woman. "I feel terrible" she said. "Rotten." That's no good, I thought. What she ought to feel is responsible. But then again, look at me . . . I can't preach . . . I'm not brave, myself. I'm a coward. I looked away as much as possible.'

'Did you do anything wrong, though? It doesn't sound like it to me. Your husband broke his vows.'

'After everything died down. The affair ended and we just carried on, tolerating each other. That's a sort of crime, don't you think? I took his life. And I squandered my own.'

Marion looked sad, but Hortensia was relieved to see that she was not crying.

'You and Max. You fell pregnant easily? Just like that?'

'I'm sorry, Hortensia.'

'I'm asking.'

'Yes. Yes, we did.'

'I did get pregnant, you know. Just couldn't keep hold of them.'

Marion thought to seek out Hortensia's hand, surprised at how little it was, how delicate and lined. She thought Hortensia might pull away, but she didn't.

'The first time was different, though. I didn't tell Peter the first time. We'd been married barely a year. House of Braithwaite was up and running, a real success. I was busy and I was happy. And when I realised I was pregnant I didn't tell Peter.'

Marion felt that bony hand squeeze hers.

'You ever have clear moments, Marion? Conviction.

You ever have that? The first time I conceived a child I had this force, this clarity that I had to be rid of it. And once I had that clarity, everything else was easy. I could lie. I could find the money. I found a place.'

'Hortensia, I—'

'Wait. Nobody knew where I was. You know how lonely that is. My mother and Zippy. Peter. It was easy to name some design exposition. I mean, they were happy for me and all the attention, but they weren't keeping up with where I ought to be and when. I took the money from my business and went away for a week.'

'How—'

'I don't remember anything,' Hortensia said, looking at Marion in a way that made it clear that the exact opposite was true. A few seconds of terror in her eyes when she stopped looking like Hortensia and looked like some other person entirely. 'When I returned, Peter was home. I'd complained some time back that he wasn't taking me seriously. Wasn't taking my work to heart. And I came home and all I wanted to do was lie down under two or three blankets. I wanted something heavy on top of me, something that could cover me. But he wanted to see what I'd exhibited. I pulled out some designs I had and he wanted me to talk about them. He pored over the work, asking questions. All I wanted to do was lie down with a blanket over my head.'

And years later when the pregnancies, one after another, poured through her body, Hortensia would torture herself with the notion that she had brought this upon herself. In the days when they still lamented together, she would always know that her lament was different to Peter's and each new time she would hate that distance, hate him, hate herself more.

'I'm so sorry.'

'And someone was laughing at me. Someone was saying: "You see?" Taunting me.'

Marion shook her head.

'I felt I had to fight that. Each time I didn't carry to term, if I didn't fight that voice I would just have got smaller and smaller until I disappeared altogether.'

'It wasn't your fault.'

'Each new time, each failure, I felt the anger coming. You know how tough you have to be? To fight a voice in your own head. I couldn't let anyone else see, but when I was alone I'd bang my fist. Against a hard surface. For the pain. I don't want to let him off the hook, but sometimes I think: maybe that's it. Maybe that's why he took up with someone else. It was easier than coming home to me.'

'Hortensia.'

'Oh, don't worry, I know he was a selfish bastard. There's no escaping that, but sometimes I think perhaps I gave him a good excuse.'

It had started to rain outside.

'And you know what? You know, I didn't really *want* children. Not really anyway. Not until just that moment when I realised I would never have any.'

The following day Marion, brave, ventured.

'I know it's not my place . . . but do you suppose the things are connected, the—'

'What things?'

'You . . . the . . . children you didn't have,' she whispered. 'And Beulah's request – about her grandmother, to be buried near her dead babies. Do you suppose?'

'You—'

'Hortensia, I don't want for you to get upset. I'm coming . . . in peace, I'm coming because, well, we've been talking a bit and you said that, and I suddenly thought maybe I understood.'

Marion waited, her heart beating fast. The woman stayed sitting up in bed, a magazine open in her lap, her back pressed against the headboard.

'Do you suppose you're angry at Beulah and even . . . Oh, what's the grandmother's name, Annamarie? Everything about what Beulah is asking has to do with family and love and children – lots and lots of children, some dead, yes, miscarried; but some that survived.'

Hortensia was staring at Marion, boring through her, but Marion continued.

'I know I'm the last person to have an opinion, but why say no to her request? Why, really?'

After some seconds Hortensia spoke. 'I don't owe her anything.' What she was thinking, though, was: I have no peace, why should she?

Marion felt sad. 'Hortensia.'

'What, Marion? What more?'

Marion didn't know what she was going to say. She felt like crying but knew that would only make Hortensia think she was weak and, right in that moment, she needed Hortensia to look up to her, to follow her and do as she said.

'Why would you say "no", Hortensia?'

'Because it's my land and I can decide what I want to do with it. If Beulah Gierdien has a legitimate claim on it, not some sentimental nonsense, then she should call my lawyer.'

The argument Marion wanted to put forward to counter Hortensia was cogent in her head, but none of the words formed. She wished she was like Hortensia, always ready with the words, with the argument. Tears seeped out from both her eyes; she could almost hear them apologising as they did so.

'For Heaven's sake, Marion.'

'I'm sorry,' she snivelled, pulled a tissue from a nearby box. 'I wanted you to say "yes".'

Hortensia ground her teeth, shook her head. 'Why does it matter so much?'

'I needed you to be . . . better.'

'I don't know what you mean.'

'See, I'd have said "no" too. If it was my land they wanted. I'd have told them no, go away.'

Hortensia looked ashen. And annoyed.

SEVENTEEN

It was a small ceremony, although Marion imagined that Annamarie's funeral would have brought half of Lavender Hill running, and the surrounds. Wasn't that what the funeral of an old woman was supposed to be like? An old man even.

Beulah carried a brown earthenware bowl. She came with an old stooped man who didn't say anything. Marion guessed he was Annamarie's second husband. Beulah's mother was there and Beulah's younger brother. Hortensia and Marion met them at the gate, they thanked Hortensia in unison and then they and the small group of friends who joined them, all together, walked in a jagged line of procession towards the Silver Tree.

The brother dug the hole, Beulah said a few words.

Hortensia stayed for the ceremony, then said she had a headache and went back inside.

Others mingled around long wooden trellises laid out in the garden. There were cupcakes and koeksisters and hot tea, normal and rooibos, and small pies and samoosas and little squares of fudge. Some chairs were spread around, but people mostly stood. Marion got to talking with Beulah.

'Your brother mentioned that you are a lawyer.'

Beulah nodded. She'd taken a gulp of milky rooibos tea.

'Do you follow all the claims? On the land by the . . . people?'

'Some of it. There's a lot.'

'We have one going on here. The Von Struiker farm.'

Beulah took another koeksister. Finished it and took a samoosa. She smiled.

'I'm expecting.'

'Congratulations.'

'My grandmother used to talk about when they moved people off the land. She said about how a lot of the old people died. Broken-hearted. Some lived on, heartbroken but alive. Which is worse?'

Marion didn't know.

'Sorry to say this, Marion, but it was a wicked thing – scattering people like that. It undid a whole culture of people. Made pride difficult.'

Beulah rubbed her tummy and Marion noted that there was a small bulge to it.

'Your people . . . white people say to forget it and move on. But . . . we must also get better. Sometimes you move on and you remain sick, and then what is the point of going forward? We must get better too. My grandmother didn't want to forget. I always thought it's because forgetting would be the same as getting lost, not knowing where you are. She told us about this place.'

Marion's face grew dark.

'There was a wheel, this big,' Beulah raised her hand over her head. 'Runaways. Or a slave man caught with a white woman. Or any slave that maybe hit a white person.

Stole something, perhaps. Food. A spoon from the big house. And they'll tie the slave, the person, to the wheel . . . It was basically designed to break bones.'

Marion excused herself.

Week after endless week, it was good to have a site to visit. The works were progressing, in fact almost complete. Marion picked her way across the yard to the front door. Frikkie walked from sitting with his workers and joined her.

'Afternoon, Mrs Agostino.'

'Frikkie.'

Marion was struggling, hitting up against something.

'Can I walk with you?' he asked. 'Then if you have any notes.'

Marion nodded. Frikkie opened the front door, let her pass. She walked, placing each footstep, afraid she'd fall, but actually the real struggle was metaphysical.

'Should we start in the kitchen?'

She'd once been watching a TV recording of her favourite opera – *La Traviata* – when, in trying to adjust the picture, she pressed the wrong button and landed on a channel she didn't know existed. There was a young black girl on the screen – dressed wonderfully in fuchsia – and she was complaining. It was some kind of youth programme, the kind that began choking television after '94. Black youth, this and that. Anyhow the girl was deciding to move from Cape Town to Johannesburg and her sole reason was the absence of a black middle class. It was all quite strange, the way such things were always strange to Marion. The girl referred to Cape Town as 'closed'.

'I'm sick of being an oddity in my own country,' she'd whined.

She cited the fact that on visits to restaurants the only other black people were there to take her order and wash the dishes. 'Cape Town, the last outpost', she'd said in a mocking tone.

The whole thing had stayed with Marion. The girl's earnest account of a problem Marion had been unaware of. What struck her the most was that the complaint seemed inaccurate. For Marion there were black people everywhere – too many even.

'Do you like it here, Frikkie?'

He looked startled. 'You mean?'

'In Cape Town.'

He frowned. 'I'm from here.'

'Oh.'

'Well, the Eastern Cape originally but, yes, I grew up in Langa.'

'I see.'

'It's difficult to say "like". But Cape Town's my home.' He had a smile like lightning, all sparkle and flash.

Marion nodded. She didn't feel she could say much. With a look of bemusement, Frikkie continued the inspection. He invited Marion to study the stringer for the grand wooden staircase that had collapsed. And, considering she'd gone on about it, asked that she give a nod to the winders too.

'I like Frikkie.'

Hortensia frowned. They were sitting in the lounge on the extra-length couch. The TV was on but silent, a female chef was preparing one meal after another for a television audience. Neither woman was watching. Marion was trying to read the *Mail & Guardian*, Hortensia was knitting, explaining how knitting helped her relax. How she hadn't done it in years and was unable to remember why she'd stopped.

'Thought you said he was a cretin?'

'I said that?'

'That he didn't know his business and was trying to steal from you.'

'Frikkie?'

Hortensia pursed her lips. 'Yes, you like Frikkie the way you like Mama!' She giggled.

'You're laughing at me.'

Hortensia continued giggling, shook her head.

'Well, if you must know, I do like Mama. Upstanding man – so few about.'

Dr Mama had visited recently. He'd mentioned that soon Hortensia would be sufficiently recovered, Marion free to return to No. 12. The house next door was almost ready, but even once complete, it would be back to the settling of accounts, putting the house up for sale. For a few seconds all the harassments came back. Although Marion hadn't thought about it in a while, she now remembered the Pierneef, disappeared, not even a trace. Her time at No. 10 had been an excuse not to think about all this, but soon enough she would have to.

'You should call him.' A cheeky glance up from her knitting was the only show that Hortensia was being mischievous.

'Who?' Marion pulled herself from her troublesome

thoughts, relieved that, at least for the next short while, she didn't have to deal with them. 'Call who?'

'Mama.'

'What? Really?'

'Go on.'

'Well . . . he's a bit young for me . . . don't you think?'

'I thought you'd say he was a bit black for you.' Hortensia snorted loudly, her joke exposed.

Marion looked hurt.

'Oh, come on, Marion. I mean you're almost a hundred years old – what the devil would you do with Dr Mama, if you called him?'

'Hortensia, you obviously, in breaking your leg, broke your ability to count. I'm nowhere near a hundred years old.'

Hortensia grunted.

'And just because I'm slightly old doesn't mean I don't appreciate some male company every now and again.'

'I suppose so, yes.' Hortensia darted her eyes again. 'You ever think of, you know, seeing somebody? After Max.'

'Well, who, quite frankly?'

'Slim pickings?'

'Very much so. Mostly it's just big bores out there. Old and mean.'

'And what are we? Sweet as pie?'

'Well, we're not that bad, Hortensia. At least we're better than some of those other wenches. Some of the old women you see today.' Marion shook her head. 'I was at the mall the other day and saw one that had clearly been under the knife a few times. It looked like she would find it painful to blink.'

'Painful enough to just breathe at our age – why complicate things further? Bring the lines, I say. Bring the damned wrinkles. I mean, how much of a coward do you have to be, to be afraid of a few crow's feet?'

'Well, there are all the pressures. It seems unfair, you know. We women get the raw deal.'

'Hmm.'

'Although, now that I think of it,' Marion leaned forward, 'Sarah Clarke troubled me once with a story. Apparently there was a man, I don't think he lived in Katterijn, can't recall now. Anyway, Sarah claimed she found out through a friend whose son was a doctor who had a friend whose boyfriend was a plastic surgeon.'

Hortensia snorted.

'So, the story goes that this man – he was in his seventies, I think – married someone considerably younger. Not terribly young, as in twenty, but in her fifties, perhaps. And he, the man, went to have his . . . strut sorted out.'

'Marion, is there something wrong with the word "penis"?'

'I prefer "strut". It's a cleaner word.'

'A strut is a piece of building. This is biology, not architecture.'

Marion shrugged.

'Tell me what Gordon Mama says when he realises his date can't properly identify his anatomy.'

'Oh, Hortensia. Who said anything about a date?'

Hortensia rolled her eyes. 'Anyway.' She went back to knitting. 'I didn't mention he's taken a cruise.'

'What?'

'He's taken a cruise . . . with a lady friend.'

'How do you know?'

'He, being a gentleman, called to let me know that I could switch to a cane soon. He mentioned Trudy would be attending while he was away. Me being . . . interested, I asked where he was going.'

'Ah.'

'You sound disappointed.' Hortensia was smiling.

'Well. His loss!'

'That's what the young people say.'

'And they're right.' Marion rubbed her wrist. 'I'm too old anyway. I can't date. I've got aches and pains. Too many.'

'That's it, though.'

'What?'

'This. Getting old. More and more aches.'

Marion scowled. 'And trying to fix everything.'

'Does it work?'

'What?'

'The trying to fix?'

'Not really. I have four children, Hortensia. Three I haven't spoken to in almost a year. I never see them. Marelena, my oldest daughter, she calls, but I always get the sense, when we speak, that she's holding a gun to my head. And that I'm holding one to hers.'

Hortensia set her needles aside.

'No, the fixing doesn't work. I'm a terrible mother. There's no fixing that.'

'Why is it like that? Like a death sentence?'

Marion tried to find a way to explain. She had teeth in her heart. Marion knew they shouldn't be there, but there they were: teeth in her heart.

'I wasn't happy as a child. I know that sounds so pat but . . . I think I was angry with my parents.'

'Why?'

'I wanted them to be different. Be stronger. Which is crazy, because I wasn't any of those things. When the time came with my own children, I wasn't those things.'

Hortensia picked up her needles again. Marion played with her fingernails, she felt exposed.

'You think I'm ridiculous.'

'No, it's not that. It's just: what are you so scared of? Face your children. Face them!'

Marion shook her head.

'What?'

'You wouldn't understand.'

'What?'

'Nothing. Just that . . . you're lecturing me on family. You?'

'I'm not sure what you're getting at.'

'Come on, Hortensia. You're hardly the person to tell anyone anything about *family*.'

Hortensia had never slapped anyone and now, over eighty, she had discovered how adept she was at it. After the whack, Marion's two hands – one atop the other – stayed against the cheek. As if she was holding the pain of it in, or maybe keeping it at bay, Hortensia couldn't figure out which.

Marion left the lounge and, under half an hour later,

she dragged her small suitcase down and let herself out the front door. Hortensia marvelled at herself, at her sense of offence that Marion had not even bothered to say thank you and goodbye.

EIGHTEEN

No matter how much rage Hortensia had felt in her life, she did not know herself as someone who wrought violence. Whatever it was, Hortensia – a woman who had frightened many many people in her life – had finally succeeded in scaring herself. It was enough, she thought. It was done.

'Hello?'

'Hello, is that Esme Weathers? Ms Esme Weathers?'

'Yes, this is she.'

'Good evening, Ms Weathers. My name is Hortensia James. I am the widow of Peter James.'

'Oh.'

'Perhaps you know who that is. I don't know, and I'm sorry to call you like this. The circumstances require it.'

'Okay.'

'Peter died almost two months ago and he wanted me to contact you. He left a will and . . . I didn't know you existed, he wanted us to . . . know about each other.'

Hortensia gave the girl some seconds to comprehend everything.

'I'm sorry to pressure you, but his estate is being concluded. It's rather,' she wanted to say 'vindictive' but understood that was inappropriate, '. . . particular, but he's included a return ticket. His last wishes were that we meet.'

Having made the call, Hortensia now fussed: how would it be to meet Peter's child? Trudy came by and brought a cane. Mama was back from his trip, he phoned and it was nice to hear his voice. Marion was living next door, she supposed, far away, somehow, and unreachable.

'Ma'am,' Bassey came to stand in the hallway as Hortensia tested out the stick. It was made from a strong but indeterminate wood, varnished dark and gleaming.

'What do you think, Bassey?'

'Agnes is sick.'

'Oh dear. Is it bad?'

'Cancer.'

Hortensia walked beneath the Silver. A slight wind at her cheeks. She touched the trunk and traced the place a person (so long ago some thought it ought to be forgotten) had carved. Scars, long and deep, one two three – people were dying and someone was counting. Hortensia experienced a swell of sadness as she thought of her sister. She missed Zippy, but realised phoning her would not assuage the feeling. She missed their childhood, the lost opportunities they'd had for real friendship. And then Hortensia tried to imagine Beulah's grandmother, Annamarie, but her mind veered from that too. Then she thought of Peter. She thought of the already dead.

It was unpleasant to be back in a hospital, but Hortensia was glad to be on her own two feet and not flat on her back on a stretcher, at the mercy of others. Bassey had mentioned he would be visiting Agnes and Hortensia asked if she could go along. A young man picked them up from the house; Toussaint his name was, dark with bright eyes and a French turn to his accent. They drove to Red Cross Hospital. Cape Town looked strange to Hortensia from the back seat of the Renault. There were men at the robots with window-wipers and white bottles squirting soapy water. Hortensia asked Toussaint to roll down her window.

'It's stuck.'

'Apologies. Child-lock.' He drove on when the light changed.

'I'd wanted to give them money,' Hortensia said, rueful.

Toussaint and Bassey spoke in French. Hortensia felt left out, which made her listen closer, lean in. Toussaint's voice, the intonations, the way he pronounced 'Bassey', almost leaving off the last syllable; he had a familiarity with the name, the shorthand of intimacy. Bassey in the passenger seat stretched his hand and placed it on the back of the driver's headrest. All this was a small window into something Hortensia had never wanted to see. She didn't want to make friends with her house-help – that could too easily turn her into Jessica Tandy's Miss Daisy, a do-gooder, and all the complications of that. She wanted a clipped relationship, professional, a respectable exchange, good money for good service.

The man at reception said there was someone there already, so when they peeped through the door and saw Marion sitting on a chair, her back to them, Hortensia felt prepared. Agnes was sitting up, propped by a family of pillows.

'Mrs James.'

'I'm so sorry, Agnes.'

Marion turned around. Bassey and Toussaint went towards Agnes and the way they greeted each other brought again that sensation, like she Hortensia had missed out on something. She placed the flowers she had picked from her garden amongst the other vases and teddy bears that cluttered a small table. Agnes looked groggy from the operation.

'I'm so sorry,' Hortensia said again. 'I don't know what else to say.'

Agnes smiled. She was clearly weak, but also had that look of peace Hortensia had taught herself not to envy in others.

A woman appeared at the door. Hortensia would later learn she was Agnes's daughter, Niknaks.

Marion greeted her and then they all left, so the mother and daughter could be alone.

Toussaint offered Hortensia a lift home but she declined. 'I'll call a taxi when I'm ready.' She turned to Marion, 'Would you have tea with me?'

'Well.'

'I'd like to talk, Marion. Please.'

'Okay.'

They fell into step along the dreary hospital corridor. The pattern of their walking reminded Hortensia of the obstacle courses she'd navigated in her home with Marion looking on.

There was a small cafeteria. There was no Earl Grey, but something the waitress referred to as 'normal tea'.

Marion frowned. 'Tastes like wet paper.'

Hortensia cleared her throat. 'I'm sorry I hit you. I shouldn't have done that. It was wrong of me.'

Marion pursed her lips; it looked like she was thinking, and her lips seemed to be an instrumental part of that.

'What?'

'I was just thinking how . . . I hate it when you apologise. It doesn't last long enough and you never beg.'

Hortensia laughed. Marion smiled and shook her head in a certain way, as if to say she was tired of herself.

'I'm sorry I hit you, Marion.'

'I heard you.'

'The more I realised I'd never have children, the more I realised how much I'd really wanted to be a mother. Things weren't okay between my mummy and I, and I thought I could fix that . . . you know . . . with my own children.'

Marion sipped.

'I thought, if only I hadn't done it, lied to Peter. Ended it the first time. Like everything after was punishment. I shouldn't have hit you. But . . . no one had ever done that before. Thrown it, my failure, in my face like that. All these years. Not even Peter at his most nasty. I'd never felt that before. When you said what you said – that feeling. Never felt it . . . out loud.'

'I shouldn't have said it. It was cruel of me.'

Hortensia emptied another pack of sugar into the brown-coloured water.

'I called Esme.'

Marion nodded.

'She's coming.'

Hortensia brushed her head with the palm of her hand.

They drank bad tea as if it were gin, their teeth barred, the muscles in their necks tensed.

Frikkie and his crew completed their work. When she'd left Hortensia's, Marion had moved back into No. 12, enduring the dust and noise until finally the works were complete. Still, this was a temporary solution. The house was due to go on the market soon. Her children had mentioned two words that together gave her a fright – retirement and village.

Niknaks called. She said her mother, Agnes, was asking for Marion. Asking how? She was in bed back home and she'd asked for Marion.

Even with her scant grasp of religion, Marion knew what she was doing was a sin. What if this became the woman's dying wish? All the same, Marion manufactured busyness, suggested plans to Niknaks that she reneged on. Asked for the address of Agnes's home, then misplaced it.

'What are you playing at?'

'What do you mean: what am I playing at? And is there anything wrong with beginning a telephone conversation with salutations?'

'I don't have time for salutations, Marion. Niknaks just called me. I don't appreciate being dragged into your affairs.'

'What affairs?'

'I said Niknaks called me.'

'And I heard you.'

'So you have no idea why she would call me? And why I would be calling you? Without salutations?'

'Uhm—'

'For God's sake, Marion, go and see the woman.'

'Heavens!'

'Exactly. She called and had the temerity to be upset with *me*.'

'Who?'

'Niknaks. What a ridiculous name, by the way.'

'I thought the same. It's a nickname.' Marion heard Hortensia sigh. She was worried she would drop the phone. 'I'm hiding,' Marion said.

'I don't care. Go and see Agnes. She's not well. The suggestion seems to be that she is dying, but from my experience with Peter, that can take any number of years.'

After making arrangements with Niknaks, Marion called Hortensia and asked her to go with her to Khayelitsha, to the place where Agnes was living, a place she'd never been to. And Marion allowed herself the luxury of senti-ment, allowed herself to notice that Hortensia gave no hesitation. Yes, she'd sighed, but she'd also said okay and what time, and did Marion have the address?

They got into the car. Hortensia hung onto the strap. Marion gripped the steering wheel.

'You can't drive like this?'

'Like what?' She was sweating.

'Marion?'

'I'll be fine. I'm just a little nervous is all.'

'Of what?'

Marion gave a fake laugh. 'I don't even know,' she said. She caressed the wheel and put the car into gear.

Hortensia navigated, the map open in her lap.

'There must be an easier way. GPS or something.'

'Don't trust it. Turn here.'

Niknaks had also given directions. After they took Baden Powell Drive off the highway, Hortensia used only these notes. Still they got lost. Marion panicked at Hortensia's suggestion that she slow down and ask for help. They argued for several kilometres, Hortensia raising her voice, berating this woman sweating and working the foam of the steering wheel as if it were a length of dough.

'You are being stupid. Slow down. Stop the car. Marion Agostino, I will never speak to you again!'

The dramatic threat was effective. Marion pulled over. Her face was frozen. Hortensia had heard her draw in breath, but she hadn't heard her expel it. 'I think you're a ridiculous person,' Hortensia said as she buzzed down her window, stuck her head out.

A young man with an earring and, as far as Hortensia could distinguish, his trousers on backwards, told them in firm words where to drive. They were close by, in fact they had been circling the place. Hortensia thanked him, waved her hand for Marion to proceed.

As if death was taking roll call, there was a funeral next door to where Agnes lived. Marion struggled to get her car through the throng of people scattered on the short street.

'Drive,' Hortensia said.

'I'll run them over.'

'They'll move.'

Marion was rattled by the dancing, the shouting. The smell of meat, spiced and steaming, gave her a feeling of hunger although she'd already eaten. The front yard of the house was a bank of sand. There was a narrow stoep and a yellow door ajar. Niknaks, with a baby on her hip, greeted and led them through a parlour where others sat, down a dark corridor and into a small room. Agnes's eyes were open and her breathing laboured.

Marion went to her and touched the blanket she was wrapped in. Hortensia thought, not without envy, about that special kind of authority dying gives one.

'You can sit,' Niknaks said.

The baby started crying. Niknaks bounced her, but a man came into the room and took the child with him when he left. Marion sat beside the bed.

'I'll wait outside,' Hortensia said and she left the room. Niknaks followed.

Afterwards, Hortensia knew not to ask Marion what Agnes had said to her, or whether anything was spoken at all. They drove home quiet, both women subdued for reasons they couldn't pin down but that were crowding them.

'She said she'd wanted to be a teacher.' They were still sitting in the car, parked on the side of Katterijn Avenue, between their respective homes. 'That she wanted to teach the little ones. Numbers and letters, she said.'

Hortensia nodded. It was dark outside; there was not much to see in the quiet street – the people of Katterijn (forever impervious to Hortensia's common sense) had expressly asked of City Council that no street lights be erected – it's a conservation area, they insisted; street lights will only dampen our chances of seeing the stars.

'She said about me that I could have . . . Well, she spoke about her home. Childhood memories. About cows.'

'Cows?'

'Cows. She liked the way they grazed. And she said

about me that I am a hard woman, that when she was still young and new at my house she used to weep.'

'I see.'

'And then she said that she wanted to fly.'

'Fly?'

'I hadn't heard properly. It was a bit embarrassing; I thought she'd said "die". And I asked her. Can you imagine? But no, she'd said "fly".'

'Fly.'

Agnes had also given Marion something.

'Look there.' Agnes had pointed to a corner in the room. Marion rose.

'Inside the cupboard.'

Marion opened the door to a smell of mothballs, a stash of old newspapers, frocks on hangers. And a half-unwrapped painting she just then realised she really loved, a painting she would sell in order to live properly, but would be sad to trade. They'd picked the frame together: Stefano was four, Marelena was almost two and had marvelled at the gilt edges, Marion had agreed it was striking, Max paid for it.

'I don't understand how this got here.'

'By error. I didn't know until I started going through the boxes Niknaks had packed from the house. I didn't even know what it was. And then, once I knew what it was . . . how can I say? I'd heard you talking about "the painting, the painting". How much you needed it. So I thought . . . after the doctor said, "there's only small chance." I thought . . . maybe I should keep it. I was angry, somehow. With you. I can't explain.'

'No—'

'It doesn't matter what happens; a person should be true. Here is your painting. It's safe.'

'I'm sorry, Agnes. Agnes?'

'Yes.'

'I'm sorry.'

Grudgingly, Hortensia agreed to look after the painting. The works at No. 12 were completed, snags done, insurances sorted. All the money Marion and Max had ever had was apportioned out to the many debt collectors, some in suits, some in vests, some in T-shirts, their sweat-rings ponging up the hallway. The house was going to auction. Marion was to stay at Marelena's for the time it took to – as unsuspiciously as possible – find a buyer for the Pierneef. Marion fantasised about affording a modest flat; she'd attempted a spreadsheet to work out how many years she could go on living *and* keep getting her hair and toenails done. Marelena called with last arrangements about when Marion was moving in.

'Hello, Marelena, how are you? . . . Good, how are the girls? . . . Yes, I'm okay. I was just walking through the house . . . Yes, and guess where I'm standing right now? In your bedroom . . . Of course it's still your bedroom, don't be silly . . . No, I'm fine – just that, I'll miss it . . . Hmm? . . . Yes, midday tomorrow is fine, I'll be next door . . . Okay, bye.'

NINETEEN

Esme confirmed her flight times. It was like waiting for the sky to fall.

Marion came to visit. She let herself in. Hortensia hadn't asked for the key back.

'Your hair is growing,' Marion said, watching her standing in front of the mirror.

'As hair is wont to do.' Hortensia had her head turned; her tennis elbow was acting up and she strained to reach the back parts. She cringed. 'Knots,' she said.

'Do you . . .'

'What?'

'Can I help?'

Hortensia paused, her hand stayed afloat in the air for a few seconds, then she brought it down to her side. She wanted to say something but couldn't think what. She walked over to where Marion sat on the edge of the bed.

'You . . . you need to stand. I can't crouch. My leg.'

Marion stood up and took the comb from Hortensia, who settled on the bed.

'Comfortable? Your leg?'

Hortensia nodded. 'Be careful.'

'Okay. Like this?'

Hortensia's neck strained, then loosened. 'Alright,' she said.

'You know,' Marion said, once she felt she'd found a rhythm, bringing the comb through in slow, gentle motions, 'all these years and we never even . . . I wanted to invite you over once, to see my collection of Olivetti typewriters – I know you would have loved them so much. I had a 1950s "Lettera 22".'

'You just wanted to show off,' Hortensia said.

'Yes. You're probably right.'

They laughed.

'Do you think things would have been different? With someone different?' Marion asked.

Hortensia winced as her short Afro snagged in the teeth. The grey hair parts were more tender, which was unfair because they were more coarse than the hair on the rest of her head, more prone to knotting.

'Sorry.'

'Gently,' Hortensia whispered.

Marion laid the fingers of her free hand on Hortensia's forehead. Her fingertips were cool and damp.

'Sorry,' she repeated.

'I can take it from here. Thank you.'

Marion relinquished the comb and watched Hortensia. For several seconds neither spoke and there was only the noise of Hortensia's oldest clock, which sat in the hallway just outside the guest room. It was an eighteenth-century pendulum clock, wooden, with a tortoiseshell detail that Marion had teased Hortensia about. Not one for the rights of animals, are you? Marion had said. And Hortensia thought: not one for the rights of anything, really; but said nothing.

'Well, do you?'

'Different how? With you and me?'

'No, with Peter.'

'I don't know,' Hortensia said. 'Do I think things would have been different? They weren't. I've tried this so many times. Look where it got me. Things weren't different – that's all I have.'

'You picking her up?'

'I couldn't bear it. I've ordered a taxi, they'll come straight to the house.'

Marion nodded.

'I do try to remember one thing. About what you were saying before. I keep remembering how Peter and I stopped speaking – as in actually talking to each other about important things, not just the "hello, how are you, fine" things. That must be how you know it's finished.'

Before she arrived, Esme called Hortensia one last time.

'I thought I ought to mention this. It's not something I can imagine any differently, but sometimes it helps to manage reactions from people.'

'My dear, I have no idea what you are talking about.'

'I am legally blind, Mrs James. I travel with a guide dog, his name is Toby.'

This was a gift. She knew it was cheating, but Hortensia felt relieved at the prospect of not being seen. To be excused from scrutiny. She relaxed. She waited.

'Peter – your father – he . . .' Hortensia couldn't find any memories to share. There were some, tender, that she liked to keep for herself, and all the rest were linked to complaints, arguments. 'I forgot what I was trying to say,' Hortensia mumbled.

They walked side by side down a dirt lane, the vines stretching to their left and a grove of oaks to the right, between them and the rest of Katterijn. Hortensia looked to the girl on her left, studied her, assuming she could sneak as many looks as she needed.

'Do I look like him?'

'Well.' The truth was she didn't. She was her mother. She was all her mother. Except for the height maybe. 'Peter was tall like you. You do it a lot more gracefully, though.' Hortensia wondered why she wanted the girl to like her.

'Thank you.'

'So, what did you say his name was again?'

'Toby.' Esme slowed down and patted the neck of the brown collie as she said this, without losing hold of the specialised leash, without tripping, without missing anything. 'A lot of squirrels about.'

Hortensia didn't bother to ask how she knew, she preferred not to expose how inexperienced she felt, while walking with a tall beautiful forty-something-year-old who seemed, by some magic, to have retained all the really great qualities of being a toddler. As if it was the having of sight that made one grow old and jaded. She'd arrived, almost supernaturally, without bitterness, without recrimination – like an apparition taunting Hortensia, showing her up, embarrassing her and her foolish notion that sight required seeing. Esme didn't miss much.

A sorrow worked itself through Hortensia's body. A deep sorrow that, despite all the sadness she had already experienced, she had never encountered before. She slowed her walking, then stopped altogether and reached for Esme's hand. The girl, the child (Hortensia couldn't help referring to her as that, although she was evidently a very grown and mature woman), gave her hand willingly. And even though Hortensia thought she finally knew what to say, her tongue stuck in her mouth and it was the girl who said, simply: I can't tell you how surprising all this is. But still, I am happy to be here. After holding hands for a few seconds more, they walked on in silence, to where Peter's ashes had been spread. To the tombstone, which Hortensia described to Esme.

Esme let go of the leash and Toby stayed close to her as she put her knees to the soft ground, covered in leaves the size of a baby's hand, and felt the slab of stone. As she watched, Hortensia's mouth dropped open. Although she'd missed this until that very moment, the slab that Peter had commissioned was clearly a message to a child he knew he would never meet.

Esme's fingers moved over the rough surface, expert. Hortensia took only a second to realise that the girl was reading. 'My goodness,' she said.

Esme moved her hand back and forth over the message her father had left her.

The tombstone had remained a mystery to Hortensia. And now she realised that Gary's artwork was in fact some kind of letter. Had he known as he chinked away at the stone that he was writing in Braille? If so, he hadn't let on; in fact he'd given nothing away about the nature of his relationship with Peter. Hortensia now wondered whether they'd been friends. It felt sad to not know, it made Peter even more of a stranger.

'Milk?'

'Thank you.'

Toby sat by Esme's feet. Hortensia did not like dogs, but calling Toby a dog seemed inadequate. Or perhaps she had never understood the word, the creature it described.

'Are you not accustomed to dogs?' Esme asked, again surprising Hortensia with her observations.

'Well, I have a neighbour who has a . . . what do they call those? Always yapping.'

Esme smiled. 'Chihuahua?'

Hortensia set the tea down. 'No, a sausage dog, they call it.'

'Dachshund. Nice.'

'Can I ask you some questions?'

'Please.'

'I'm embarrassed. You should be the one with the questions. About Peter, your father. If you have any, I would do my best to answer.'

'What did you want to ask?'

'Were you born this way?'

'You mean blind?'

'Sorry. Yes, I meant blind.'

'Yes, I was. Makes it easier, I think. I've never known any different.'

'And your . . . your mother.'

'Did you know her, Mrs James?'

'Hortensia.'

'Thank you, Hortensia.'

'No, I didn't know her. I never met her.'

'I understand this might be hard, but . . . she was a wonderful person, Hortensia. I miss her so much.'

'I'm sorry. I didn't know she'd passed away. I mean she – they . . . I noticed that they no longer interacted, but I had no way of knowing what had happened.'

'I'm afraid I don't know, either. I'm sorry if you thought I could provide you with answers.'

'Not at all. I've had no answers all my life – why would that suddenly be important?'

Esme finished her tea.

'She never mentioned Peter?'

'She married when I was a few months old. It was many years before she told me who my real father was.'

'And? What did she say?'

Esme shrugged. 'That she had been young and careless.'

'She used that word? Careless.'

'Yes. She said she had written to Peter, not when she was pregnant, but much later; perhaps when I was ten or so. She wrote to the only address she had for him, in Nigeria. She wrote three times. She told him my name and she sent him our whereabouts, our address, and so on. By then she had divorced my father. My mother said she wrote to Peter and told him that she still loved him and that if there was any chance of being together, he should come and find us. She never heard back.'

'I—'

'We didn't suffer, Hortensia. There is no need to apologise.'

'He found you in the end, though.'

'Hmm.'

'In a way. He was much, much too late, but I suppose this was his way of finally writing back.'

It became a thing that Hortensia and Marion met daily at the bench underneath the Silver. It was cool beneath the tree. A car rolled past, she heard only the purr of the engine.

No one comes to see us, Hortensia thought. 'How's Agnes?' she asked.

'Sick.'

'I mean, you said you'd go visit her again.'

'Yes, I called Niknaks. She sounded diplomatic, but my guess is Agnes doesn't want to see me.'

'Fair enough.'

'I tried to say sorry.'

Hortensia snorted.

'What? I told her I was sorry.'

'Okay, Marion.'

'You should have seen her eyes, though, when she . . . "I was angry with you," she said. And her eyes, Hortensia.'

'She's sick, and her life – the majority of which she spent cleaning after you and your children, polishing your home – feels finished. I understand it. She blames you.'

'No! It's worse than that – she *doesn't* blame me. She doesn't have to blame me . . . She's just . . . watching.'

Hortensia looked thoughtful.

'She's going to die.'

'We all do eventually, Marion.'

'I'm worried she'll die and come to haunt me, you know?'

'Ah, I see. Trust you to find a way to be the star of someone else's death-scene. She's the one dying, but you're who we ought to be concerned for.'

'You know what I mean, though.'

'Well, yes, that is a possibility. She might die and she might come and haunt you. It'll serve you right.'

'Thank you.'

'What? Were you not despicable? Someone will write a book about it. *The Haunting of Marion.*'

'Stop.'

'But I'm serious, Marion. And we all know Agnes would make a terrific Haunter.'

Marion shook her head. 'She'd have been a good teacher, wouldn't she? She would have, wouldn't she?'

'Maybe. Please, stop shaking your head.'

'I'm in so much trouble. She knows all my peeves. Dripping taps. Tablecloths spread, but not ironed. Oh,' Marion gripped Hortensia's forearm, 'she could strangle me with the laundry – that was always our biggest quarrel.'

'You're ridiculous. I give up.'

'Let's change the subject. How's the girl?'

'Who, Esme?' Well adjusted was the term that came to mind. 'She's okay. I guess I expected her to be angry or something. Instead she's . . . lovely. Oh, guess what?'

'What?'

'She teaches piano. No small wonder her hearing is superhuman. She kept catching me out.'

'How?'

'Just . . . as in knowing things, noticing things I truly

– 269 –

felt – scuse my ignorance – a blind person ought not to notice.'

Marion scowled, a quiet form of scolding. A hadida called out, loped and took flight from Hortensia's garden onto Marion's roof.

'You glad you met her?'

Another hadida appeared, this one with coloured plumage, a pluck of blue feathers tucked in its wing like a handbag. It called out, flew onto the roof, its head bobbing.

'I suppose that was the point. Peter's point.'

'Do you think she needs you? With the . . .' Marion pointed to her eyes. 'Think that's what Peter was getting at?'

'Oh no, Esme certainly does not need me. Maybe the other way around,' Hortensia laughed. 'And when she left, I wondered if I'd ever see her again. Worried. She phoned when she arrived home, can you imagine?'

'Precious.'

'Being around someone like that. I kept thinking: I'm just a bad person, Marion. I'll die soon and I'll go to hell.'

'For what?'

'For being nasty. I know it's simplistic, but look at her, a person with every reason not to be and yet she's so . . . kind.'

'It's okay.'

'What do you mean, it's okay. Who made you that? The O-kay-Sayer.'

Marion bristled. 'I was thinking, that's all. That we're old. That it's okay. What else is there to say at this late moment?'

Hortensia shrugged. The two women looked and saw that the birds had taken off, two specks in an empty sky.

'So it's hell for the both of us.'

'You, Hortensia, scared of a little hell?'

'Who said I'm scared? You're the one whining about a ghost called Agnes. She's not dead yet, by the way. If only she'll outlive us both – I pray.'

'Ever notice how it's the good ones that die?' Marion asked.

'Hmph. I don't know about that, Marion. More like no nincompoop ever dies – notice that? The second you die, you become a kind of saint. You're absolved, your good deeds are dredged up and your evil pardoned, forgotten. When I die—'

'You have a will?'

'Yes. Yes, I do. Burn me in secret, throw my ashes in the gutter. Not a soul is to pronounce over my dead body . . . Not. A. Soul. No gatherings, no songs.'

'Gosh! So austere. When I die, I want my children to be forced to say nice things. I want Stefano to sweat as he recounts just one lousy memory, just one thought of kindness towards his poor mother.'

Hortensia sucked her teeth.

'I want Verdi playing. *Nabucco*.'

'Goodness me!'

'Candles. Incense. I want my face done up.'

'What?'

'Open casket. I want my face done up and . . .' she whispered, 'my toenails painted.'

'Foolishness.'

'Why not? Why not do what makes me happy?'

'But you'll be dead.'

Marion shrugged. She leaned back against the bench,

put her hands on her stomach, which was folds of over-stretched skin beneath a beige cardigan.

'Life's been pretty long,' Marion said. She was feeling up the buttons on the cuffs.

'That I can't argue with.'

'With not enough sex,' she said.

'Well.'

It turned into a still evening; a fine scent from the lady-of-the-night next door caught them. Hortensia pressed her cane into the warm earth and rose with a soft grunt.

'Hortensia,' Marion called after her.

Hortensia stopped but didn't turn, too much physical effort.

'I . . . uhm, I'm not sure what I wanted to say, now. It seemed right in my head. I guess I just . . . What I thought was . . .'

Hortensia shifted her weight. 'Yes, Marion. I agree completely.'

'No, but I really, I'm being serious now, I wanted to . . . try and—'

'Yes, yes. I feel the same.'

TWENTY

Hortensia had noticed that some people delighted in designing the events that would take place upon their death. Now she had to admit to herself that she was one of them. People who'd felt they had little control over their lives so took solace in the form of wills and instructions, large sums of money, maps and secrets. Peter seemed to be one such, too. After all that had happened, Marx called and asked if he could visit, asked if he could give Hortensia something.

'Your husband left this for you.'

Hortensia arched her eyebrow. However weak and frail her limbs were, her facial muscles were functioning fine.

'Now? He asked that you give this to me now?'

'Precisely,' Marx said and he left.

It was a brown envelope, ordinary, with the flap unstuck. The paper was thick, creamy. He'd written the date in a shaky hand. The '6' barely announced itself as a '6'. It was more of a 'o' that had lost its way. One page folded twice, evenly. A crooked date. And some scratches.

Hortensia tried to imagine it. He'd had a stretch of strength earlier in the year. Not strong enough to do much, but she'd seen one of the nurses scanning the bookshelf in Peter's study.

'May I help?' Hortensia had asked.

'He wants . . . "the staple", he called it. The stable?'

The nurse had fair hair and wrinkles.

'Or the steeple?' She had rings on her fingers.

Well enough to call for a book, but not well enough to pronounce its title clearly. Well enough to request pudding, but not well enough to keep it down. Well enough to ask for Hortensia, but not well enough to go and find her when she refused to come. And when the nurse had begged and said 'He's asking for you again', Hortensia had told her to leave her alone.

Was that when he'd called for paper? Having already arranged his will, was that when he sought to unburden himself? The date. That's as far as he'd managed.

She ran her fingers over the page. He'd made attempts at words, at the shape of words. His hands would have been shaking.

At first it had felt to Hortensia that Peter was just being vindictive. The tombstone covered in Braille had shocked her. The delicateness of that. And now an empty letter. He would have scratched at it with his over-expensive fountain pen. Struggled to form the shapes. And yet, he'd gone all the way, folded the letter and enveloped it.

Hortensia called Marx.

'Was there not some other letter?'

'Pardon?'

'The letter, the letter. Is there another one? A proper one.'

'I'm sorry, Mrs James, I don't understand.'

'Because this one is a dud. Empty. Did he not leave something else? Something clearer?'

'I'm sorry.'

'Does that mean "no", Marx? What, for God's sake, are you sorry about?'

Marx didn't respond.

'I didn't mean to snap. You met with my husband, several times, yes? I just wanted to know what was going on.'

'Mrs James—'

'Please understand, Marx, that I am humbling myself. I am asking you something. I've been through a lot. I just want to know what he said.'

'You mean?'

'You said he spoke of me. When we met, you said that. What did he say?'

There was a long pause.

'Mr Marx?'

'Yes. He, uhm, he didn't talk a lot, but—'

'I thought you said he spoke of me?'

'Yes.'

'Well, what did he say?'

'On one occasion he mentioned that you were a talented designer.'

'Oh?'

'Another time he mentioned that you gardened and were particularly fond of—'

'So just small talk then? Junk?'

'There was once he spoke. He was very sad, Mrs James. It was our last meeting. He insisted on buying me a drink afterwards. It was all quite awkward, but I got the impression he was lonely. Towards the end of his second Scotch, he told me this, and I couldn't forget it, although I feel bad to repeat it. He told me: My wife, I love her very much, but that's the easy part.'

'What's the hard part?'

'I don't know, Mrs James. He didn't say. The rest?'

The estate was wrapped up. The president of the hunting club called to thank Hortensia for the generous donation.

Perhaps Marx was right. All the rest had been the hard part. Staying, choosing the marriage over his child. You fool, Hortensia said softly (not unkindly) to Peter, even though he was dead and, unlike Marion, she did not believe in hauntings. You foolish man, she whispered. And she wished she could slap him on the wrist, embrace him.

There was talk that the Samsodien land claim had been finalised. A portion of the Koppie had been cordoned off but, to Hortensia's relief, a sizeable chunk still remained as public open ground.

Many of the trees had been cut down, though. With all the publicity, the National Parks Board had got involved and was implementing a plan to replace the alien vegetation with fynbos. Sap from the trunks bled out. And when Hortensia walked up to the Koppie she counted the stumps, occasionally squatting down to sit on one. Except there was a day she struggled to get up and, for several minutes, wondered if she would ever rise. She stretched her leg out, her broken leg (it had mended, yet she couldn't help but think of it as that) and massaged it for several seconds. And then she stretched the other leg out and massaged that one. Rubbing. The flow returned, Hortensia stood up.

When Marion visited, they came here. Everything is so dead, Marion said.

But the seasons continued regardless. Lime-green shoots appeared, then swathes of tiny sparaxis, bright pops of colour among the black and grey. The following spring, shocking-pink pelargoniums with their strong peppery scent carpeted the land. Gradually proteas and fragrant buchus appeared.

For Hortensia walking here became an exercise in Zen-like observation as more and more species came up; more flower species on that spread of earth than in most whole towns. Dragonflies, butterflies, sunbirds, frogs and lizards. Flowers bloomed in profusion, from microscopic bulbs to blossoming pea trees.

'Where did they all come from?' Marion asked, fussing a brush of fynbos with a stick.

'Careful! You'll damage it.'

'I didn't know you cared.'

Hortensia shrugged, not liking the amusement in Marion's eyes.

'I don't,' she said, eyeing a discarded Fanta Grape can; too old, too tired to pick it up. But she kicked it. Maybe she'd bring a rubbish bag next time, like the Save-the-Earth types.

'Gosh, the time!'

'What about it?' Hortensia asked.

'I'm making us a dinner.'

'Where?'

'Don't look like that,' Marion put out her hand. 'Give me your house keys, I'll walk ahead and start up. You can *count.*' She chuckled. On a previous walk Hortensia had been unable to hold the numbers back from her lips and Marion had caught on.

'Now you're making fun of me.'

'Just a small joke, Hortensia. Your keys. Come on.'

Hortensia relinquished her keys but didn't smile. She watched Marion walk off, grudgingly jealous for the smooth movement where hers, with all attempts at grace, was still a hobble.

'What are you making?'

Marion, without turning, waved her hand in the air in response.

Hortensia counted the stumps, the dead trees. She chided them the way a mother would a child who is in more trouble than it can be rescued from. The path narrowed and she paused, took a moment to stand and breathe in the sharp Rutaceae, stinging and succulent.

Only once Hortensia had descended the hill, passed the vlei and was walking up Katterijn Avenue towards No. 10 did she realise she'd done a ridiculous thing. The thought came and made her walk faster, made her not care about the occasional stab of protest from her healed but aching limb. Cook a dinner, my foot! Watch now. This stupid woman burns my house to the ground . . . or gives me indigestion.

Hortensia walked even faster.

ACKNOWLEDGEMENTS

Thank you to my family, always there, providing what is needed when, from food and shelter to love and encouragement. Jacqui L'Ange, Zukiswa Wanner, Paige Nick and Anya Mendel, thank you for reading this in its various stages of undress and for your partnership, insight and generosity. Elise Dillsworth, super-agent, you were with this story from very early on, helping, with expert searchlights, move it onwards. Thank you for your belief, patience and tenacity. Becky Hardie, thank you for your close reading and careful editing. I have learnt an immense amount as a result. I acknowledge Michele Rowe and her article 'My Place: Silvermine's true gold' published in Times Live, 6 November 2013, portions of which have been used, with permission from the author, on page 277. Several people provided me with information and anecdotes that were crucial to the writing – Lyle Cupido, Moegsien Hendricks, Lanice Holloway, Eve Mendel, Nomzamo Mji, Mrs Helen Richfield, Rosalie and Julian Richfield, Mrs Dvora Schweitzer, Marcel Tamlin, and Issy Wolman, thank you for giving your time and engaging with me. To the organisers and staff of the Ebedi International Writers Residency and Norman Mailer Fellowship, thank you for providing timely solace and invaluable opportunities for connecting with writers, readers and teachers.

Thank you to my friends, I feel lucky to love and be loved, writing wouldn't be writing without that.